THE LAST
DANCE

LONNA ENOX

Lonna Enox Publications
910 Pearson Dr
Roswell, NM 88201

The Last Dance
by Lonna Enox

First Printing – December 2012
ISBN: 978-0-9977424-0-4

Printed in the U.S.A.

0   1   2   3

To Mama
Who taught me to dream big dreams
And
To Brooke and Drake
Who inspired me to follow them

PROLOGUE

"Better pay my tab," she said. "Have to work in the morning." She carefully counted out the exact amount, added a couple of coins for a tip, and climbed off the barstool. Several patrons down the bar called "bye." She answered them as she walked unsteadily out the side door.

Whew! She hadn't realized she'd had so many beers. Still, good music and good dancing made your throat dry. Good thing she could walk the short distance to her apartment.

She shivered. It had been a warm day, but the night was chilly. She wrapped her coat closer as she walked along the well-lit parking lot. Maybe she should take the shortcut. The moonlight peeping through the trees would provide a shadowy stream of light to point her way down the dark alley. Besides, she knew every step of it, having taken it so many times coming home from work.

She crossed the back parking lot and turned right. Only a few steps from the alley's entrance, she hesitated, thinking she heard a voice. Glancing over her shoulder, she saw two silhouettes, one sitting in a car and the other standing at the car window. "Evening," she called, then squinted. "I didn't recognize you at first!" She smiled. "Enjoyed dancing with you tonight. It's been a long time." She waited for a response.

The one in the car touched the brim of his Stetson. "Oh, I didn't see you at first! Loved dancing with you, too."

With a self-conscious wave, she turned and stepped carefully off the paved parking lot into the alley. Her shoes felt wobbly. She stepped into one of the tire ruts, and her heels sank into the soft dirt. She giggled. She really shouldn't have had that last beer, but it had tasted so good!

Several dogs complained that she had invaded their alley. She smiled and waved to them, humming a country tune slightly off key.

Some nights she could sit all night and never get asked to dance. Tonight had been her lucky night. She remembered her mama saying that one Saturday night. Mama had let her watch as she dressed up and did her make-up that night and told her, "When you're big, you'll have lucky nights too." And then she'd danced off into the night with the current love of her life.

She had never been in love. Maybe some people just weren't meant to make men's hearts flutter. She smiled. But for those moments they whirled you around the dance floor, you were their princess.

She veered to the left a bit to avoid the large, rubber dumpster. Why were those dogs complaining so much? She glanced back—she didn't know why—and then she smiled shyly. "Well, hi . . . again!"

The blow to her temple came swiftly, and she collapsed with a soft grunt. She felt hands lifting her and smelled the sourness when she was dropped into the dumpster. Something warm oozed into her eyes. Her mouth opened and she reached wildly out with her hands, but they couldn't stop the blade that swooped down and sliced neatly across her throat.

CHAPTER ONE

I should never have bought the newspaper. It's a habit I'm trying to break. What world news I want to know I can get on the Internet or on television. When I give in to the occasional mood to show local interest, I end up clipping coupons that I eventually toss, reading the funnies, avoiding the obituaries, and skimming the want ads. But reading the newspaper seemed the best way to acquaint myself with this small town, something I considered prudent if I wanted to make it my home.

I walked to a small doughnut shop, ordered a cup of coffee and a jelly-filled, picked up a copy of the Sunday paper from the counter, and settled at a small table in the back. The waitress followed me, plunking down a cup and saucer and filling it from the coffee pot. "Cream? Sugar?"

"Black," I said and then bit into the gooey delight, my eyes closing to savor the sweet raspberry jam. When I opened them again, she had moved on, stopping all around the room to refill cups until her pot was empty. Apparently this was a popular place on Sunday mornings. The room was now full. Several people were obviously dressed for church; others wore jeans and sweats. Most everyone appeared to be regulars, chatting to the waitress and with others at tables next to them.

After living in a city of two million, this comfortable warmth reminded me of some of the small towns I'd lived in growing up as a military brat.

After I'd licked the last trace of jelly from my fingers and the waitress had refilled my coffee cup, I opened the paper. The bold headline caught my eye: LOCAL WOMAN DISCOVERS BODY IN DUMPSTER. Ordinarily, I would have scarcely noticed the headline—violence is a daily event in large cities—but the large two-column photo beneath the headline caught my eye. I had seen that woman. Last night.

"Terrible, ain't it?" The waitress had returned and was glancing over my shoulder. She moved toward my cup, but I shook my head.

"Did you know her?" I asked.

"No, but things like this don't happen here. Imagine that! Dumped in the trash! Who ever heard of such a thing?" She moved on to the next table before I could say anything else. I folded the paper, stuffed it into my fanny pack, and dropped a tip on the table.

"Come back," she called. I nodded casually. Right now I just wanted to release the tightness in my chest.

I scarcely noticed anything as I hurried back to the bed and breakfast, collected Flash, and turned my Jeep onto the highway.

CHAPTER TWO

The dead woman's face floated in front of me as I drove along the empty two-lane highway. When I arrived at the house my aunt had left to me, I stared at its shabby, weathered walls, no longer feeling the happy expectation I'd felt when I first arrived in Saddle Gap. It hadn't taken long to brush against something that could wreak havoc to my plans.

I'd arrived in southwestern New Mexico week before last. The three-day trip from Branson had become four because I'd had to become accustomed to driving my new Jeep, its back seat lying flat and loaded with the worldly goods I'd chosen to keep. It hadn't been as difficult as I first thought when I waved goodbye to my Mini Cooper. Of course, Flash hadn't agreed, yowling with displeasure from her hiding place under the seat. So I'd also taken more breaks to soothe her.

The front part of the old house had been converted into a gallery and gift shop. Aunt Rose had been an amateur artist and a member of the local craft guild. Besides her own paintings, my aunt had sold craft items from the area to locals and tourists. The house perched on a few acres of barren land and had been the only house for miles when I was a child. Now, manufactured homes dotted the area, though none were too close. Located at the western edge of Saddle Gap, a small town of around 30,000 residents, the house and property had been virtually abandoned for the eight years since Uncle Tom's death and Aunt Rose's move to a nursing home.

I had come here when I was about ten. Aunt Rose had actually been my mom's godmother, but Mom explained that when her own parents died in an accident, Aunt Rose had come and taken her to Saddle Gap where she'd lived until leaving for college. We had driven there at Aunt Rose's invitation.

Mom and I usually took trips in the summer when she, a teacher, and I were both out of school. Saddle Gap had captured my interest at first sight, and the two weeks were hardly long enough to satisfy my curiosity about the town and its historical legacy or to enjoy the fun of working in Aunt Rose and Uncle Tom's shop. So my mom had allowed me to stay for the rest of the summer.

I'd thought of the place often but had never returned after that summer. Mom hadn't either. She'd spoken of it, but a brain aneurism had stolen her life in an instant just before I graduated. In spite of the years, I still felt a connection to the place so when I received the attorney's notice of my inheritance, I'd been thrilled.

"Do you know what shape it's in?" Kevin had asked. "You'll put it on the market, of course, but they'll probably want you to clear it out first. Want me to handle it?"

"Like you really have time to do that." Kevin was my husband, an oil executive who had never understood why I didn't give up my career and become a socialite like the wives of his colleagues. But that's a whole other story. "I can handle it." But I'd not had a chance to do that until now—a whole year later—when I needed to start with a whole new slate for Flash and me. Just us. Alone.

Searching the Internet, I'd found a temporary spot for us to stay. La Paz Bed and Breakfast. When we arrived, I'd told the owner we would stay there about three weeks. That had been an ambitious estimate, but I'd welcomed the hard work. The weather had been sunny and warm for late March, and I'd felt sure I could be set up in business by the end of May.

I had spent all of the first week digging through the old house and hauling trash to the dump. It seemed as if my aunt and uncle had just walked away. Old bank receipts and letters filled the top drawer of the desk. Aunt Rose's clothes hung in the closet; his were neatly folded in the chest of drawers. Ancient cans of vegetables lined the pantry shelves. Dust covered the stack of outdated magazines and newspapers. Mouse droppings littered the floors.

The shop, if possible, had fared even worse. Aunt Rose had apparently not been able to sell the remaining merchandise or empty the shelves. Spider webs edged paintings on the walls, some connecting to those close by. Handmade objects lay under coats of dust on the shelves. A lower window had been broken, most likely in mischief, and layers of dust had covered everything.

It had soon covered me as well, as I filled trash bags. By the time I tumbled into bed the first night, I'd had at least a vague idea of the cleanup facing me.

Saturday morning I'd headed to the local home improvement store. After stocking up on equipment and cleaners, I'd wandered over to the library nearby to look at back issues of the newspaper. If I planned to make this my home—better yet, if I planned to reopen a business here—then I needed to tap into the personality of the area.

About ten, I'd dropped by the La Paz to collect Flash and the sandwiches I'd requested that morning. Flash had complained about being left in her carrier but bites from my tuna sandwich had pacified her. After our early lunch, I'd unloaded more cleaning supplies and other equipment I needed to start the renovation.

My first priority had been to fill more trash bags and then put padlocks on the doors. I'd nailed plywood over the broken windows and sucked cobwebs and dust from walls and floors with a shop vac.

We'd returned to our room exhausted but happy. But my photographer's eye hadn't missed the lizards and wild flowers and I longed to get this work finished so I could grab my camera.

Flash had listened to my chatter but she was a cat after all. So I'd decided after my shower to venture out for the evening.

"You should try Bart's," the cashier at convenience store where I'd stopped for gas on the way home had told me. "They have a live band. It's a bar—tavern they call it—but the food is great."

CHAPTER THREE

I'd arrived at Bart's shortly before eight o'clock, already feeling fresher after a quick shower and a change into a loose denim skirt and sleeveless top. At first glance, the bar had appeared drab, certainly not a place I would ordinarily choose. Several patrons had already been seated at tables. I'd found a spot in the corner, away from as much of the smoke possible. The door behind me led to a dining room where a few people lingered over dinner. Within minutes, a cute waitress had appeared.

"Name your poison, honey!" she'd said.

"Diet Coke."

"You sure?" Her eyes had told me she wasn't used to serving Diet Coke at Bart's.

My soda had arrived when the live music arrived—a singer who strummed the guitar but who actually depended on one of those machines that have a whole "band" in them. "Hi, New Mexico!" he'd called with practiced ease. "Hello, Joe!" A gray haired guy in a cowboy hat had nodded slightly from his place at the bar.

During the next few moments, the singer had greeted several others, all the time clicking switches and setting up for his evening. Finally, he'd drawn his guitar into a close embrace. The room had hushed expectantly and a second later he had begun singing the opening lines of a popular country western number.

As singers go, this guy—who had introduced himself simply as Dave—had been nothing extraordinary. But his choice of songs and his easy commentary had been appealing to the crowd. Within seconds, the small dance floor in the corner opposite mine had filled with couples, two stepping—or attempting to—as the watchers chuckled. I'd spent the next half hour just watching the dancers.

Then I'd noticed her. She must have been on the bar stool in the corner when I arrived. But I'd noticed her when the music started because she bobbed her head in a weird way, keeping time to the music. Occasionally, she'd taken a sip from the long-necked beer bottle in front of her, bobbing at the same time. But she'd never looked at the dancers, only straight ahead into the bar mirror.

Besides the bobbing, her outfit had caught my attention. Most of the customers in this bar had worn some form of denim. She'd worn a floral cotton dress and an old school jacket, the kind you might have seen in the sixties. Her hair was light brown and frizzy, either from natural curl or a perm. I might have pitied the sight she made had she not been so comfortable there, oblivious to the rest of us, nodding to the music.

Several times during the evening, she had danced with men who were obviously regulars there, but she hadn't seemed to be with anyone special. She hadn't been an outstanding dancer, but she had certainly kept up on a two-step or a waltz. Her expression, even as she danced, had been worth remembering. She'd had a sort of smile, not a smile of mirth but a sort of pasted smile. Whatever could have happened?

When I left about eleven thirty, she'd been on her stool, drinking a beer.

CHAPTER FOUR

I pulled into the driveway, noting that I had to get it resurfaced, and stopped close to the back door. "All I need is to get caught up in some murder investigation, Flash," I told her. She peered warily out of the pet carrier at her future home. Clearly, her look said, what I needed was to return to my senses and drive us back to Houston. "Better open a can of that cat food just as soon as I get you inside," I crooned.

Flash buried her face in the food dish, her dainty manners abandoned in her attempt to comfort herself. "It will be better," I told her. "Trust me." I hoped I wasn't lying.

I changed into faded shorts and tee shirt, trying to remember if I'd given my name to anyone last night. Had I used a credit card or made any other casual mistakes that could lead to me? I just wanted to be a casual stranger, catch my breath, start my own business, and live a quiet life.

The news article faded over the hours as I vacuumed cupboards and closets before scrubbing them with lemon-scented cleaner. Even though most places were open on Sundays, I didn't plan to shop today. Instead, I jotted down ideas, things that needed to be checked, and supplies for the things I could do. Flash insisted we leave at sundown.

After eating, feeding Flash, showering. and snuggling into the bed, I unfolded the newspaper and reread the story. Her name was Stephanie. She hadn't looked like a Stephanie, I mused. I tried to conjure how she might have appeared to a young mother. Her last name was Brown. Maybe her mother had wanted to liven up the last name. Stephanie Brown. Apartment C, Twenty-First Street. She had lived alone. Neighbors remembered her as quiet, unassuming, nodding a smiling greeting while never meeting your eye. She'd paid her rent on time, had had no visitors, and had worked as a housekeeper in the same motel that housed the bar where she'd danced a couple of nights a week. She had been thirty-two. Somehow I'd thought she was older than that. Still, I hadn't gotten a clear, close-up look at her, just the occasional neon snapshot as she'd danced along my side of the small floor and the long-distance view from across the bar. I really couldn't help the police. What could I possibly add to their investigation?

A weight landed on my feet. Flash padded up beside me and began her elaborate bath. The wind whistled outside and she stopped and stared intently toward the window, her pink tongue peeking out of her mouth. I reached out to stroke her fur. "It's okay, girl," I crooned. "It's much safer here than that huge city we just left."

Flash continued to stare, then gave me a disdainful look that said, "Yeah, according to whom?" She had a point.

CHAPTER FIVE

I woke early Monday morning, dressed in worn jeans and tee shirt, and hurried downstairs for a quick breakfast. When I returned to my room for a jacket, Flash looked at me mournfully. "None of that now," I said, as I loaded her into her cat carrier. "You need to get acquainted with our new home. I'll let you roam today since I've cleaned up the kitchen floor."

When I opened the back door to my aunt's—no—to my house a few minutes later, the lingering chill from the night before made me shiver. That wouldn't last long once I started working. In spite of the amount of work ahead of me, I felt excitement building as I glanced around the kitchen and into the rest of the house.

"Painting day today," I told Flash, as I opened her carrier, "thanks to that stop we made by the home improvement store." I put Flash, her food and water dishes, and the litter box in the kitchen and walked to the front of the house where my aunt and uncle had opened their shop.

The best I could figure, this room had started out as the whole house. Walls had been removed to leave a large, open area. The original hardwood floors had been covered in vinyl. The walls had been painted white. High, narrow windows flanked either side of the front door. The east and west walls also had a pair of matching windows over which Aunt Rose had hung heavy blue drapes to protect the shop from the sun. I set up a ladder and began taking them down, my head buzzing with redecorating ideas.

By mid-morning, I'd painted the ceiling a bright white and started covering dingy walls in a creamy pale yellow semi-gloss enamel. The room took on the spacious feeling I loved. By now, the temperature had risen, so I opened the windows. Flash ventured in, curled up on one of the sills, and slept while I hummed with the country songs playing on the local radio station and pushed the roller in a steady rhythm.

"Who are you?" a voice hollered.

I jumped, only just keeping myself from falling off the ladder, and looked toward where the sound had originated—the window behind my right shoulder. The face peering at me through the dirty glass was suspicious, although most of it was hidden beneath a Stetson. Then I saw the star pinned to his khaki uniform shirt.

"Who are you?" he yelled again, his voice rising as if the window was closed. "This is private property! Can't you read the no trespassing signs?" His arm waved to punctuate his statements, making his jacket lift to show the holster at his waist.

"I'll be right with you," I called and scrambled down the ladder. I set the paint roller into the pan and hurried to the door. I had locked it and the screen door, a habit left over from living in the city. When I opened it, I left the latch on the screen and looked out at him. He moved back until he realized I wasn't coming out. Stepping forward, he gave me a quick perusal, his eyes confirming the negative first impression he'd already drawn.

I resisted the urge to touch my haphazard ponytail or wipe at paint specks I could feel on my face. "Sorrel." I finally broke the silence. "Sorrel Janes. And I own this property."

"You got any ID?" he asked. I glanced over his shoulder and noticed the pickup truck with the sheriff's insignia on the side parked out beyond the gate.

I closed the door and went back to the kitchen for my driver's license and the papers that I'd been sent by the attorney. When I reopened the door, he squinted at them through the locked screen, glancing at me as if to confirm the information.

"I got the gate key from Price Brothers when I arrived," I finally said. "What's the problem, Officer?"

He didn't answer right away. Instead, he squinted and looked past me, over my shoulder. "We've had a series of burglaries out in this area," he finally explained, "so folks tend to report suspicious comings and goings."

I found the idea of my burglarizing homes ludicrous. It must have shown in my face because he hurriedly added, "This place has been vacant for a while, so folks were worried someone had kinda moved in— squatting, so to speak. We're just a few miles from the border so we keep a watch over vacant places."

"Well, now you know," I said, starting to close the door. "Thanks for checking it out."

"Ms. Janes? Are you planning on selling this place?"

"No." I knew I was being rude. Something about his whole attitude had made me

angry. He'd not smiled once, given his name, or even looked me straight in the eye.

When I didn't continue, he leaned forward and stuck a card into a loose door facing. "If you have a problem out this way, here's the number for the sheriff's office," he said and walked out to his truck without a backward glance.

"And thank you for the warm welcome," I muttered, wadding up the card as I watched the dust following his truck down the drive. "Time for food." At that word, Flash leaped off the windowsill and led me to the kitchen where I'd left the cooler filled with chicken sandwiches and a thermos of iced tea.

At sundown, Flash and I headed to the dump with the Jeep's back full of junk before returning to our room. I'd painted a second coat on the shop walls and cleaned those in the living quarters. It was a start.

"We're well on our way, girl," I told Flash. She merely squinted at the dying sunlight passing through the window.

CHAPTER SIX

The cell phone interrupted my shower. I grabbed it on the third ring, clutching the damp towel.

"Ms. Janes?" a strange voice asked.

"Speaking."

"Randall Byrd. *Daily News*. I received your letter requesting part-time employment . . . in photography?"

"Yes, well . . . I'd planned to come in to visit with you in a month or so. Right now I'm—"

"I need an extra camera today, Ms. Janes. We can postpone that official interview until later, but we have a real situation here. How soon can you meet me?"

"Mr. Byrd, I know I offered to do photographs for ads and social events, but—"

"This isn't an ad or church tea!" he growled. "We have another murder. I need a photojournalist out there right away."

"I'm a photographer, Mr. Byrd. I photograph wildlife—"

"How soon can you meet me?" he interrupted. "There's not anyone else, and I have a murder to cover."

I glanced down at the damp patch on the carpet. "Half an hour?"

"Make it fifteen minutes. You got a pen?" he asked without pausing. "You'll need to write down these directions."

"Wait!" I yanked my purse off the dresser, pulled out a pen, and scribbled the directions. "But—"

"I'll see you there. Hurry."

I quickly pulled on jeans, tee shirt, tennis shoes, and windbreaker and caught my hair into a wet ponytail. Lip gloss? I sure wasn't setting any fashion standards. I was out in thirteen minutes, after dumping a can of cat food into Flash's bowl and stuffing a granola bar and bag of peanuts in my bag. According to Byrd, it would take at least ten minutes to reach the location south of town.

I knew my directions were correct long before I reached the spot. Police cars, emergency vehicles, and an assortment of other cars and trucks blocked immediate view of the site. They were parked outside what appeared to be an abandoned ranch house. I swerved to miss a pothole in the dry, heat-baked road in back of the house and ended up parking next to an impatient balding man chewing on an unlit cigar. He opened my door before I could throw the gear into park.

"Sorrel?"

"Mostly," I smiled. He responded by pulling me out of my car. So much for my lame joke.

He stood first on one foot and then the other while I grabbed my equipment. My camera bag, complete with several rolls of film, extra batteries, and a couple of additional lenses, was heavy; but when he moved to carry it for me, I decided it was time to take charge. "I'm used to carrying these. Besides," I flashed another partial smile, "I need the exercise." Another attempt at humor that fell flat.

"We have a body here," he said. "Male. Not a pretty sight." The words were tossed over his shoulder as he strode toward a cluster of officers. Even my long legs had trouble keeping up with him.

"Do we know who he is?" Whether he didn't hear me or he ignored me, either way, my question hung in the air, reminding me of my newness.

The face that turned our direction clearly did not welcome us. "Randy! You know better than to bring people to a crime scene." He wasn't dressed in uniform, but he wasn't wearing the suits I'd become accustomed to seeing either. When he half turned, the sun glanced off a badge peeking out from his left shirt pocket. Must be a detective.

"Photographer," my taciturn companion muttered, staring at the scene before us. A gust of wind blew the foul odor into our faces, and the hum of flies and the distant complaints from ravens and vultures filled the silence. I breathed through my clenched teeth and concentrated on the sounds, including the occasional mutter or curse. I knelt down and busied myself with the equipment. When I rose again, the detective motioned me forward and reluctantly stuck out a hand.

"Reed," he said. His hand was calloused in spots, his grip firm. "Chris Reed." He was younger than I had first suspected, probably in his thirties in spite of his gray-flecked, tousled hair. His chin looked like he was trying to grow a beard, but the gray-blue eyes were definitely worth a second look. A small scar on his left cheek created a dimple. He had the slim waist of a teenager, but his shoulders belied any suggestion of anything other than strength. In spite of my five-foot eight-inch height, I had to look up into his preoccupied glance. Sweat stained the underarms of his western-cut shirt, and the red sand from the field smudged his jeans and coated his boots.

"Sorrel," I murmured.

"Nothing to apologize for—yet."

"No . . . my name . . . Sorrel." But Reed had already turned back toward Byrd.

"Randy, you know we can't have news photographers here."

"I'm a nature photograph—"

"We 'specially don't need one with a mouth and jeans so tight my officers can't concentrate on their job! You have to know we're running short-handed since that . . . other incident. My men need to keep their minds on the job." He glanced meaningfully over my shoulder.

Before I could protest again, a couple of red-faced young officers shuffled away and busied themselves.

Randall Byrd neither commented nor acknowledged anything. Instead, he leaned forward and continued to study the body sprawled face forward just off the back porch of the old house. "Do you have an ID?" he asked, ignoring the detective's implied criticism and posturing.

I swallowed my outrage. In all my years in Houston—no, Baltimore—I had to change my thinking—I'd certainly been met with similar attempts to snub my intelligence, looks, physique, or all three. I adjusted the lens and turned to Byrd.

"Do you want close-up photos?" I asked.

"No photos!" Reed answered emphatically. He put his hands on his hips and glared at me. I kept my eyes on Randall Byrd. Around us, people working the crime scene slowly grew still and listened to the conflict. Byrd straightened and turned to Reed.

"Who d'ya have taking shots today, Reed?"

"Tim there." Reed motioned to one of the young officers.

"Well, Sorrel here is new, but she's not green. She's an experienced photographer. She sent me notice that she was moving to our area and that she might be interested in doing some part-time work for the paper, that society garbage. But I figure she could take far better photos than these inexperienced guys here. How many dead bodies do you see in a year? Five years?"

"We've survived a long time without some experienced photographer." Reed squinted and scowled toward the nosy crowd beyond the crime tape. "All it takes is someone to snap the pieces of evidence." His cell phone suddenly buzzed. "Excuse me," he said, and walked a few steps away as he answered.

Randall Byrd turned to me. "Can you take some notes in case I need captions for the photos?"

"Sure, I guess so. But, Mr. Byrd, the detective's right. Most police departments don't even hire photographers any more. They use their own men."

"And you know yourself that a good photographer sees things that the average person often misses. Besides, Reed is shorthanded here. They had a woman killed and dumped in a dumpster a couple of days ago. I don't know if you saw the write up." I nodded noncommittally. "This area is also having a lot of petty crime related to the border . . . keeps the police busy. Added to that, the force just had one officer leave and another retire. This is not a metropolitan area. Finding experienced, qualified help isn't easy."

Detective Reed finished his phone call and started back toward us, stopping to speak to Tim, who yelped, grinning broadly, before hurrying off in the opposite direction. "You don't need a forensic photographer to take shots for the paper, Randy," Reed said, as he approached, just like the conversation had never been interrupted. "Did you check her references, by the way?"

Byrd grunted. "I know. But with that other homicide and Jose off on National Guard duty, I'm shorthanded. Thought you might use an extra hand yourself. Thought you'd appreciate the help. And yes—I checked her references...and her education. I'm too happy about our good luck to wonder why she'll even consider helping us."

Reed shrugged, then turned to me. "Tim's wife is on the way to the hospital. Their first baby. I would normally keep him here anyway since we're so shorthanded. But since you're here . . . I hope I won't regret this." He studied me closely, his eyes searching for something to reassure him. "I'm taking Randy's word that you understand how to conduct yourself. And I am officially putting you on the payroll for this morning. Those photographs will be police property. Randy knows which ones he can use, so you can take a few shots for him as well."

I nodded. I could tell from the quickly disguised grins among the officers that Reed seldom admitted defeat, and he'd get some friendly teasing—when he cooled down.

Frankly, I was surprised he'd allowed me to stay. I'd have to get used to small town ways.

CHAPTER SEVEN

As Reed joined the other policemen, Randall gave me his instructions. They were what I expected: a distant shot of the crime scene tape with the crowd, suitably vague. Behind him, I could see a television camera crew arriving. The lettering on the van identified a Tucson station. They'd come a long way. Odd.

"Ma'am?" My thoughts were interrupted by a policeman who appeared older than Tim, heavier, and self-important. "If you'll follow me, I'll explain where we are and what we need. You need to be especially carefully around a crime scene. It's especially important that you take great care with the film—or discs—you use. The rules for chain of custody require great care." He went through the steps, while I followed behind him with my equipment. Whether he considered me a frivolous society photographer or an empty-headed redhead, either way, his attitude suggested—no, screamed—that I had no place in his crime scene.

I didn't want to be at this crime scene any more than the detective wanted me there. I'd come to Saddle Gap to lose myself, start a new life, and put the nightmares from my past one behind. I needed a less serious job, one I could be nonchalant about. That was a good word. Nonchalant.

I had never become nonchalant about my job. I'd spent years with colleagues who joked either about the situation or about something else. One of the medical examiners I'd worked with most closely kept a running dialogue about her life. But I could never do that.

Maybe it was my childhood memories of how we behaved when people we knew died. My mom had followed an accepted protocol, and I had learned early on to follow it too. After all, we were Army. People who had passed deserved respect. Someone had loved them. They had mattered to someone.

I wondered who had loved this guy as I gazed at the decomposing flesh through the lens of my camera. His hair had been brown but was now flecked with gray and matted with blood and brain matter. It was difficult to guess his age because of the bloating. He had suffered horrible trauma, his face covered with dried blood from what appeared to be numerous blows from some heavy object. Vermin had already begun their scavenging, gnawing or pecking bits and pieces of exposed, rotting flesh. The sports shirt he wore bore numerous blood spatters, and a couple of buttons had been ripped off. The holes in his worn jeans shorts didn't look new. One of his worn flip-flops was missing; the other lay a few feet away. They were the cheap kind found in dollar stores or tourist shops, the piece between the toes possibly torn out during the violence.

I squatted a few feet away and photographed the soles of his feet. From their appearance, he had spent much of his time either barefoot or wearing the flip-flops. Was he a tourist? I didn't want to focus on the tragic picture that discarded flip-flop presented lying there amid the stench, flies, and impersonal strangers; but it tugged at my heart and threatened my own impersonal composure. Why hadn't I refused to come? This was the last place I needed to be.

Reed and the other officers spoke only to direct me to shoot something specific. Otherwise, I followed the markers that had been set at each of the details the police considered important, forcing myself to ignore the violence they suggested. I'd left without eating or drinking anything—and I certainly didn't want anything to eat—but when Reed brought me a bottle of cold water, I gulped it down. I mumbled, "Thanks," but he had already turned away. Obviously, I was still not welcome at his crime scene.

I could have been a ghost most of the day, and I was happy with that. Had they scrutinized me closer, they might have noted the evidence of my own ghosts fluttering across my face. I fished an old stick of gum out of my equipment bag and popped it in my mouth to keep my mind off my growling stomach and the horror before me.

By the time I snapped the shutter for the final time, the sun had already disappeared, leaving trails of orange and pink. For once, I didn't stop to admire it. My clothes stunk of death, my face burned from the hours in the sun without sunscreen, and my stomach growled in empty protest.

"Done?" Reed noted my jump and didn't try to hide the smirk. "You'll need to follow Pete here into town to the police station to fill out the necessary paperwork and turn over the film. You know the drill." His last words were tossed over his shoulder as he headed back.

"Aye, aye, sir!"

His shoulders stiffened momentarily, but his steps didn't falter. However, Pete, who earlier had given me instructions on photographing the crime scene, turned toward me with a face that was a study of horror, mirth, and appreciation for my audacity. "Ready?" was all he said.

During the short ride into town, I heard Dad's teasing voice echoing, "Sorrel, your smart mouth is going to get you in trouble someday." It would certainly make my relationship with the detective—if one could call it a relationship—dicier than it already was.

A twinge of regret flickered and then died. I had no place in my new life for sexy, difficult law enforcement officers.

CHAPTER EIGHT

The police station, looking more like a museum than a municipal building, would have been easy to miss. Pete smirked at my incredulity when he held the door for me. "This was an old train depot," he explained. "Saddle Gap was once a major railroad town, and the historical society wanted to retain as much of that era as it could. Sometimes we wish for more space or more modern facilities," he added, leading me past small offices and grimacing at the echo of our steps against the hardwood floors. But when he glanced at my face, he shrugged. Obviously, I wasn't a convert to his attitude.

It only took a few minutes to fill out the paperwork and turn over all of the film that I'd used. The desk officer counted the rolls, documented them, and presented me with yet another form to sign that included my promise that I had not kept or concealed any film. Pete waited for me during the procedure.

"You'll get a check when the rest of us do," he told me as he walked me to my Jeep. "Probably a couple weeks." He almost returned my smile. I wondered how old he was and if he'd ever been out of this small isolated town. "If you'll turn right as you pull out of the parking lot," he said, "the newspaper office is only a short distance. Do you need me to take you?"

"No, thanks. Mr. Byrd gave me directions."

The newspaper office filled a large building on a tired street someone had either humorously or hopefully named Majestic Lane. A plumbing shop next door and a resale clothing shop across the street seemed to be the only other occupied buildings on the block. Byrd had instructed me to park by the side entrance and ring the night buzzer. The door opened before I even removed my finger.

"Where's the camera?"

I'm not sure what I was expecting, but a tiny brunette wearing a tee shirt from her dad's wardrobe wasn't it. "I'm supposed to leave this with Terry," I said.

"That's me. Teri. If you'll give me the camera, I can get the photos downloaded and get out of here." Close up, I could tell she was more toward twenty-four than fourteen.

"Sorrel," I said and we smiled at each other.

"The camera?" I handed it to her. "Follow me."

For someone who scarcely reached my shoulder, Teri could really move quickly. I followed her through a maze of antique clutter, listening to her nonstop chatter. "I'm sorry to be in such a hurry, but I need to get the rest of the pages set up and then go rescue my sister. She's had the monsters all day, along with three of her own. When I called her an hour ago, I sensed hysteria in the air." She waved a hand toward an elderly man working on an elderly press. "Got the photos, Juan. Won't be long."

During the next half hour, I learned that Teri's husband, the missing Jose mentioned earlier in the day, usually worked this job. But she had trained to be his fill-in when he spent weekends—and last year three months—on Guard duty. When he was home, she filled her days chasing after the monsters—twin three-year-old boys whose brown eyes promised mischief in the photos on their dad's crowded desk.

"I also make soaps and lotions," she said. "*Touched by Teri* is my brand name. I'm experimenting with candles to finish the whole romantic bath concept. The difference in my stuff is I'm using natural plants to produce original scents."

"Do you sell them commercially?"

"Not as much as I'd like to. At the moment, I sell to friends, neighbors, and family."

"I'm reopening my aunt's shop and I'd be interested in talking to you about stocking some of them."

"That old abandoned shop out on the highway?"

"Yes," I said. "I know it looks really bad, but I'll get it in shape. Don't know yet if I'll keep the same name, though, Rosie's Oasis. Maybe."

Teri nodded, her hands and eyes on the keyboard in front of her. "Is that what brings you out here? I mean," gesturing toward the photos on the machine, "you really are talented here."

"Thanks. By the time I took these shots, I wasn't really happy with the light. But the sheriff has definite ideas about how he wants things done."

She grinned wryly over her shoulder. "Reed's like that. He's really a good guy, but you wouldn't know it when he's working. Now, on the dance floor…"

Dance floor. Had he been that cowboy that had danced with Stephanie? Maybe. It might have been her last dance. Poor thing. A picture of her smile—more a combination of smile and concentration—popped in my mind.

"Do you have any other stories on that woman they found in the dumpster day before yesterday?" I asked.

"A follow-up," Teri said, "but it's been cut a bit with this new body being found today. You'd never know it but things like this just don't happen around here. Well," she grimaced, "not until now."

I wondered if Stephanie and this unknown guy had thought this town was safe because of its smaller population and isolated location. Hmmm, no place was safe anymore. "Did you know her?"

"Not really. I saw her once when we went for dinner and dancing on our anniversary. She was sitting at the bar. From what I've read, she was a loner. Kept to herself. I don't think the police are finding many leads. Or, if they are, they're not giving us any information. That's not unusual."

I stopped myself from confessing that I'd also seen her. I really didn't want to get involved. I knew it seemed selfish, but I couldn't afford to start this new chapter of my life by rewriting the same old page.

"Wow!" Teri breathed. "These photos are really something special! Not what we usually print in our paper. What did you say you did before moving here?"

"I was a photojournalist for a city newspaper. I also trained in forensic photography." Some of it was true. Isn't that how it usually goes? Lying is easy when you add bits of the truth?

Teri was one of those people who needed to know everything but not in a bad way. She was just friendly and curious about people. In response to her queries, I told her about Aunt Rose leaving me the property and my decision to try something different, to take a break from the hectic life of city living—the stock answers I'd practiced for these kinds of questions until they flowed from my mouth without having to think about it.

When she finished, Teri sprang up from the chair and handed me the camera. "Well, you're done here. I know you're anxious to get home and clean up. Jose always is. Besides," another grin lit up her dark eyes, "I really have to rescue my sister—or the kids—whoever is on the bottom right now."

Before following me out, she jotted something on a scrap of paper from the desk. " Call me when you start stocking that shop. I'd love to show you my collection."

Later that night, snuggling in bed with Flash's purring body pushing into my side, I opened my laptop. But my fingers just didn't want to work—or maybe it was my brain. Certainly today wasn't anything close to doing what John had said when he warned me to keep a low profile.

CHAPTER NINE

A strange feeling tickles at the back of my neck as I reach to flick on another light. I always keep the small lamp burning beside my front door. In fact, it's on an automatic timer. Strange that it's off.

Where's Flash? She always meets me at the door. In the same instant, I notice that the light switch isn't working either. I press the keying flashlight in my left hand. It emits a tiny stream of bright light. I sweep the room with the light, my right hand gripping the doorknob behind me, ready to back out of the room if need be. Every sound is magnified—traffic a few streets over, the ticking of the big clock in the hall, a dog yapping next door, my own breath.

Everything seems in place. The pillows on the couch are still rumpled from where Kevin and I sat the night before. Our coffee cups are still on the bar where we shared a cup early this morning and Kevin—as usual—has forgotten to put them in the dishwasher before leaving on his trip.

I release the doorknob and sigh. Something must have blown a fuse. I step to the small hall table to the right to retrieve the larger flashlight we keep in the drawer there. Maybe I can find the fuse box.

Wham! My knee slams into something hard and unyielding. "Damn!" I fall onto the small table, my hand grasping at something to steady myself. Instead, I knock the tiny lamp off. I cringe as it shatters against the tile floor. I've dropped the key ring light as well, but at least the light hasn't gone off. I lean to pick it up when my eyes light on what I'd run into. Kevin's suitcase. Had he forgotten to take it with him? No, he never would have done that.

Then I smell it—that awful smell that haunts me for hours after a shoot. That smell that I always thought could never touch me here in the haven of our own home. The smell of blood, of violence—of death. I feel for the cell phone in my pocket and punch in 911.

"911. What is your emergency?" I swallow hysteria and try to speak in my usual voice. She repeats her question.

27

"Something horrible has happened at my house. The lights are off and there's this awful smell and the cat's missing and my husband's suitcase . . . I need the police."

She asks all of the usual questions and tells me I must not hang up the phone.

Clutching it, I take a step forward. Something weighs my foot down and I can't budge it. I fight for breath, even as I pray silently. Please, God, let this be a joke, a nightmare, anything but true.

Finally, I lift a foot but—wham! The force of the blow to my chest thrusts me backward, then footsteps run to the back of the house. I fight for air even as I hear sirens and loud blows hitting the front door. A blood-curdling scream rises from deep within me, shrill and loud like a siren.

"Ms. Janes? Are you all right? Ms. Janes? I called the police."

I could scarcely hear the words above the pounding in my head and the screaming.

"Ms. Janes? Sorrel?"

The deep voice sounded familiar, soothing and safe. My screams subsided and I opened my eyes. It took a moment before I recognized my surroundings: the southwestern pattern on the curtains, the soothing peach walls.

"We're coming in now."

A familiar hissing on my foot brought reality closer. "I'm okay," I called and reached down to pull Flash close. Then I pulled the bed covers up over my chest and called again. "It's okay. Just a dream."

But the key was already turning in the lock. Mrs. Sanchez peered inside before being thrust aside by Reed. His eyes took in the situation quickly, turning from concern to amusement. Flash growled, her fur fluffed, and hissed. I tightened my hold on her squirming body, wincing as she dug her claws into my arm. "Some dream," he finally spoke.

Mrs. Sanchez stood off to one side, hands clasped. "I'm so sorry, Ms. Janes. I never would have called Detective Reed, but I was scared. Your screams—"

"I'm very sorry," I interrupted, prying Flash's claws from my arm. "It was—"

"A nightmare." Detective Reed leaned forward and took the indignant black cat out of my arms and tucked her under his. Flash prepared to launch a new attack on this imposter, only to surprise us all with a loud purr as Reed scratched her under the chin.

"It's okay, Mrs. Sanchez," he said. "You did the right thing. Obviously Ms. Janes is a woman on her own here, and you would not have known that she wasn't being viciously attacked by some crazed stranger." His eyes held a malicious sparkle. "I think we need to leave her now, so she and her panther," he said, as he handed me a now docile, adoring, traitorous Flash, "can calm down. We'll wait downstairs," he tossed over his shoulder, ushering Mrs. Sanchez out the door ahead of him.

My first reaction when the door closed was to throw the quilts over my head. So I did . . . for a few seconds until Flash began yowling. I sat up and hissed at her. "Traitor! I can't believe you snuggled up to that vile policeman, purring and rubbing yourself on him!"

A soft tap at the door and a deep voice reminding, "We're waiting," made me catch my breath and scramble out of bed.

"Coming," I yelled, less than politely, and I ground my teeth at the soft chuckle, followed by footsteps thankfully receding down the short hall. I dumped a scoop of cat food into Flash's bowl and rummaged through a drawer for clean undies. No time for a shower this morning. Just a moment to brush my teeth and clean the sleep—no! Reed could wait for me to shower!

As I slipped out of my cotton nightshirt, I noticed how it clung to my body. Nightmares usually made me sweat—at least, this one did. I soaped myself, scrubbing harder than usual as if that could wash away the dream. I needed to pull myself together, answer the questions that would invariably follow.

As I toweled dry, I rehearsed the story: The scene I'd photographed the day before had given me nightmares. Sure, I'd had some experience with forensic photography, but I'd never seen anything this graphic or violent. The sights, the smells, a new environment—what else? Even to my own ears, my story hardly sounded plausible.

Oh, God. It had seemed simple enough. Drop my professional name. Change vehicles, clothes—all the trappings from my former life. Invent a new past and move out here, far away from Houston.

I leaned against the bathroom sink and forced myself to calm down, drawing slow, even breaths. The scar on my temple stood out against my pale face, and I reached for concealer. "It will only leave a small scar," the emergency physician had told me. "But with your career, you'll want to follow up with a plastic surgeon."

I had never gone. Maybe I wanted that scar to remind me of how fleeting life—and those we love—can be. Kevin would never again look at me and whistle. He'd never again say, "I have the most beautiful wife in the world . . . the universe. I am so lucky!"

Lucky. The word echoed through my brain as I stared in the mirror, fighting the urge to vomit. The hit to my chest that night had knocked me down and I'd hit my head against the table. I'd blacked out for a short time, rousing to paramedics. They'd set me on the sofa when they'd bandaged my head. "I need the bathroom," I'd said and staggered toward the master bedroom before they could stop me. Even though I knew what I'd find, nothing had prepared me for it—or for the smell. I knew that smell.

A loud hammering at the door caused me to jump back to the present. "I really do have other things to do, Ms. Janes."

I stepped into jeans, pulled on a sweatshirt, and slid my feet into tennis shoes. By the time I stepped out on the landing, Reed had apparently already retreated downstairs. "Jerk!" I muttered, reaching behind me to put my wet hair into a ponytail.

"Tsk, tsk."

I jumped, nearly stumbling down the stairs except for the hand that grabbed my arm. "Are you okay? I didn't mean to scare you . . . I was just teasing you a bit."

"I'm fine, Detective!" I pulled my arm and he released it, but it still tingled from the pressure of his fingers.

I walked into the small parlor and sat on the floral rocker facing the stairs. Reed followed, perching on the edge of the ruffled loveseat. Any other time, I would have giggled at the comical picture he presented.

"Reed," he said, his eyes searching my face. "I've seen you in your bed. Detective is too formal after that experience."

I swallowed a smile—with difficulty.

"Your photographs were quality work," he continued. "But we usually do our own photography. I doubt you'll be finding much here in the way of that sort of employment."

"I hadn't planned on that sort of photography," I answered. "In fact, I'm opening my own business. I just thought I'd do some light photography for the paper to help with expenses until the business really gets going. I never expected to do crime photos."

"You obviously have experience." He waited but I refused to elaborate. "Do you have them often?"

"What?"

"Whatever nightmare caused you to terrify Señora Sanchez . . . and whoever else happens to be staying here."

I blushed. "Not so often. I'm really embarrassed. And for you to make a needless trip—"

"Actually, I planned to look you up anyway." I hadn't noticed before that he had taken a small pad out of his pocket. "I need to ask you about Saturday night." When I remained silent, he prodded, "Bart's Tavern?"

"Oh."

"Vicki, one of the waitresses, described you. We're talking to everyone who was there that night to see if they noticed anything."

"Is this in reference to the man I was photographing?" I asked innocently.

Reed saw through my ploy. "No, this is in reference to Stephanie, the lady who was murdered and thrown in a dumpster."

I had begun rocking again without noticing it. So much for my attempt to remain low profile. "Yes," I stalled, quickly deciding I had to acknowledge facts he already knew. "I don't know anybody here yet. So I wasn't acquainted with her."

"She sat at the bar," Reed prompted. "The waitress said that you seemed to be watching people in the bar. Stephanie was a regular there. Liked to dance. You may have noticed how she liked to bob her head to the music." So Reed had visited the bar as well.

"Oh, that lady. Sad. I remember her vaguely."

"Do you remember anyone she might have talked to or danced with?"

"Not really. Bart's isn't really well lit, you know." I relented a bit. After all, the woman deserved to have her killer caught and punished, if possible. "I did see her dance a couple of times."

"Can you describe who danced with her?"

"Well, one man was sitting at the bar also. Probably sixtyish, balding, had a big ring on his finger . . . and really couldn't dance very well."

"Jim. Jim Cochran. He's retired Navy. A regular."

"I know she danced with some others, but I don't think I remember . . ." I stared at the ruffle on the loveseat a moment, purposely evading his eyes. "There was this cowboy." Reed waited expectantly. "He came in and sat at a table near the door. I only noticed because I had to go to the ladies' room and almost tripped on his foot."

"Description?"

"Young. Thirtyish. Didn't seem to greet anyone. Only stayed a short time. In fact, the only time he danced was with her. A waltz."

"Stephanie loved to waltz," Reed said. Something in his voice made me look at him closer.

"You knew her," I said. "I'm sorry. This must be hard."

"Part of the job. I knew her only slightly . . . danced with her a time or two." He closed his book then changed his mind and flipped it open again. "Were you there when she left?"

"No. I wish I could tell you more, but I really am so new to   town . . ."

He stood now and I stood with him. "You never know. Sometimes what you see is something that helps. Besides, being new may give you an edge. You would see things without the prejudice that sometimes people who know someone have."

Mrs. Sanchez reappeared almost as if she had been listening at the door. She offered Reed coffee and asked if I was ready for breakfast. I felt trapped and invited Reed to join me but he declined. Putting his hat back on, he smiled at Mrs. Sanchez until she left the room.

"If there's anything else that you remember, here's my card." He continued to stand there, as if not sure how to leave . . . or how to continue. "Whatever it is—the stuff of the nightmares—"

"Not to worry," I interrupted quickly. "Just a nightmare."

He stared into my eyes. Both of us knew I was lying.

CHAPTER TEN

Breakfast had been scrambled eggs and a strip of bacon wrapped in a flour tortilla. I grabbed an apple and a banana from the fruit bowl before I hurried upstairs to collect Flash. "We have work to do," I crooned as I stuffed her into the cat carrier. She gave token resistance as if she knew that her reaction to Reed had already earned her some recriminations.

It felt good to resume my renovation at the store. I'd decided to refinish the wooden floors, so on the way home the night before I'd rented a machine from a self-improvement store to sand the planks clean. Then I'd add a coat of stain. Surely, I could do this—even though I wasn't naïve enough to imagine that everything would go as easily as the man at the store had promised.

The first obstacle was removing the vinyl. I'd rented—at the salesman's insistence—an instrument that looked like a short-handled shovel, only it was flat and had a wide edge instead of a scoop, to slide under the edge of the vinyl and break it loose. By noon, I'd cleared the floor in my showroom and hauled the vinyl to the big dumpster I'd had delivered yesterday. Sweat made my shirt stick under my arms, which felt so heavy I didn't think I'd use them again.

Flash regarded me carefully, leaped down, and led me to her bowl in the kitchen. I scrubbed my hands at the kitchen sink and splashed water on my face before opening a package of soft food for her. Then I pulled a bottle of water from the cooler and settled on a stool by the counter.

The physical exertion had kept my mind from the unsettling events of the early morning, but they flooded back as I peeled the banana. No matter how much I wanted to, I knew that I couldn't avoid more questions. Call me unlucky but since I'd been in that bar Saturday evening, I knew from experience that Reed wouldn't back away. His job was to probe until he found answers. In fact, he'd been gentler than I would have been.

I reached for the apple. Had I really leaped right into people's faces, grilling them mercilessly for details, ignoring their trauma? Crime reporter for a television station, then news anchor. How had I waded into people's misery without it touching me?

A car door slammed, jerking me out of the past. Flash had already jumped up and begun meowing before Reed poked his head through the open back door. "Hard at work?"

Why did everything about this man irritate me? Well, that wasn't totally true. His looks didn't.

"No, I'm enjoying a vacation day here instead of on the beaches of Hawaii!"

"You ought to be careful working out here on your own, with the doors all open. Anyone could sneak up on you. We're having an increase in violent crime around here."

I pulled the pepper spray out of my breast pocket in one swift motion and aimed it at him. He jumped back and held his hands up in surrender. "Okay, okay."

I tucked it back into the neck of my shirt. "How can I help you, Officer?" I asked.

"Reed. Remember?" He casually scooped Flash up and tucked her under his arm, scratching her chin. I glared as my contented cat's purr filled the tense silence. "Your cat likes me."

"I'd always thought she had good taste."

Reed's slow grin didn't help my grumpiness. Then he sobered. "I wanted to follow up with you after you had the opportunity to think about our conversation this morning. About Stephanie."

"I really don't know what I can add."

"Can you tell me again about when you first noticed her there?"

"I arrived a little before eight and chose a table in the bar to listen to the music and watch the dancers while I ate. I don't remember if she was there when I arrived, but I'd noticed her by the time the waitress brought my Diet Coke."

"You said that you noticed her dancing with a couple of guys, right?"

"Yes, the older guy that had been sitting at the other end of the bar and a young cowboy type."

"Are you sure those were the only ones?"

"Well, no. I mean, I wasn't just staring at her every move that night."

Reed sat down in a creaky wooden chair by the table and positioned Flash on his knee. I munched my apple, watching the thoughts chasing across his face. "Do you remember any other people who were there just watching, like you were?"

"Reed, surely you have a list of every patron in that bar!"

"Yeah, but most of them were there for . . . refreshments . . . and their memories or their attention to detail aren't as good as yours."

"What are you looking for? I mean, from what I read in the paper, she was walking in a dark alley. Couldn't the person who killed her have been someone who wasn't even in that bar?"

"Sure." Still he sat, absently stroking Flash's chin. "I guess I need to recreate those last hours of her life."

I closed my eyes for a moment. "There was a rowdy birthday party group across the dance floor to my right. People kept coming and going from that table the whole time I was there. The three small tables in front of me had couples who seemed to be regulars because they knew each other and even circulated, greeting everyone. A table of four women— fiftyish looking—was on my left. They danced all night with everybody." I opened my eyes. "It's a popular place, you know. I enjoyed just watching. In fact, I'd have probably stayed even longer if I hadn't had that guy blowing smoke behind me."

"What guy? Did you notice what he looked like?"

"He wasn't at a table. Just stood against the wall smoking. I can't stand cigars."

Reed had pulled a small pad from his pocket and was jotting notes. "Can you describe him?" he repeated. "Things you would have noticed without looking. Like the cigar smoking you just mentioned."

"Not really. He must have come in right before I left. It was the waltz, you know, when Stephanie was dancing with the young cowboy. I started coughing and knew I'd have to leave. I glanced over my shoulder quickly as I got up. Surely someone else got a better view of him—like the waitress."

"No one mentioned anyone smoking a cigar."

I squinted thoughtfully but just couldn't come up with a clear image. "Sorry. I just remember a cowboy style hat. Not much help when every male, including you, is wearing one."

"How was it creased?"

"What?"

"You know, the brim. Did it have the taco look? Was the crown taller?"

I looked at him a minute. "The brim wasn't as wide as yours . . . I don't think. No taco look for sure. Businesslike. I'd say it looked more like a hat you'd wear with a western business suit. But he wasn't wearing a suit, I don't think."

"Was he alone? Did you hear him talking to anyone?"

"Maybe on a cell phone, now that you mention it. I didn't hear anyone answering, but I do remember him talking in low tones. Funny. I hadn't given it a thought till now."

"Facial hair? Glasses? Heavy set or slim?"

"I only glanced at him!" I shrugged. "I've told you all I know. Sorry I can't be more help."

Reed nodded. He put the notebook away, shifted a sleepy Flash to her rug, and stood up. I thought he meant to leave, but he stood as if in deep thought and then looked through the doorway.

I stood up, tossed the apple core into the trash can, and motioned toward the door behind me. "Is that all? I need to get back to that floor."

"Do you have those dreams often?" His question caught me off guard, and I wondered if that was his purpose. Probably.

"Not so much now."

"I used to come around here. When I was a kid." My head was beginning to spin at his quick conversational shifts. He must be one terrific interrogator.

"This place belonged to my aunt and uncle," I said. "I've decided to open it up again, with a few changes of course."

He walked toward the door without commenting then stood for a moment. "I meant what I said. Use caution. I have all of the murders I need right now."

"Have you found out what happened to the guy?"

"Random violence. Disagreement with the wrong people. We'll find who did it. Nice photos, by the way. Did I already tell you that?"

"And I've already been warned off about this place," I muttered, walking over to the sander.

"What?" His voice was suddenly right behind me. How could he walk so softly? I grabbed the sander I'd just knocked over as it headed toward the floor.

I relayed my visit from the sheriff's deputy and his attempts to scare me, even wanting to know if I was going to sell the property. "It's a wonder anyone moves to this friendly place—bodies strewn all over town and scare tactics from the welcoming committee."

Reed didn't react to my sarcasm. In fact, he was too quiet. I looked over my shoulder and caught an odd expression on his face. Finally, he said, "You're not easily scared," acting as if he knew me!

"Not usually but over six feet of brawn and a menacing attitude might do it!"

"Did he give you his name?"

When I told him he hadn't and I'd thrown away the card he gave me, Reed became even more serious, looking intently into my eyes as he enunciated each word: "Our sheriff's deputies are all Hispanic, all under six feet, and all but one needs to go on a diet. Do any of those fit your guy?"

CHAPTER ELEVEN

The house seemed strangely empty after Reed left that afternoon. I concentrated on the floor. My arms and shoulders felt numb, but the floor looked wonderful. Just stain tomorrow—and possibly a sealant—and I'd be moving in.

I left before sunset, muttering that I wasn't doing so just because Reed suggested it. Suggested? Ordered was more like it. But I knew deep inside that his comment about the sheriff's deputy had left me jittery.

Who had that guy been? Obviously he had gone to great lengths to fool me. What did he want?

A hot soak and an early night—that's what I needed.

My cell phone rang as I pulled into the B&B. "Sorrel? Teri. Remember me? The paper?"

"Sure, Teri! Hi! How are you?"

"I've been thinking about your new shop. I meant what I said about putting some items in it if you'll let me. Could we get together? Say tomorrow morning?"

"Well—"

"You sound tired. Bet you've been slaving out there all day. I'll tell you what, why don't you come on over to my place tonight and eat with us? I'd like to show you my pieces and introduce you to the wild creatures in my house."

"I—"

"No arguments. You'll feel better after a good meal." A giggle. "My sister just told me that I haven't let you get a word in. Did I mention that I'm the family chatterbox? Anyway, my house is on Adobe Circle. Number 5. It's just off Mission, that busy street that you cross just before turning onto your street. We're not far. See you about six!"

"I—" but a dial tone greeted my reply. I looked down at Flash. "I guess I'm taking a shower instead of a soak," I told her. "And then out to dinner. Lucky you! You get dinner in bed."

CHAPTER TWELVE

The monsters effortlessly won my heart within minutes. From the moment they opened the door and ushered me into their house, Javier and Josef talked and moved constantly. Their mother also chattered nonstop, not bothered at all that her sons competed with her. "Good! You found us!" she exclaimed. "I'll let the boys entertain you while I finish dinner. I won't be long!"

They hadn't needed an invitation, pulling me down the hall into their bedroom. Soon Javier and I were engrossed in building a Lego tower, while Josef—which he pronounced Hosef—routinely ran trucks into it and sent blocks flying all over the room. On one such demolition attempt, several blew under the bunk beds in the corner. I crawled half under them, collecting the blocks for another attempt, when a low whistle, followed by childish giggles, interrupted.

"Quite a view."

I knew that voice. It seemed to be following me around lately. I scuttled back as quickly as I could, thankful I'd worn slacks. When I finally sat up, my hands filled with Legos, the boys had already headed down the hall. "Dinner's ready," Reed said matter-of-factly and offered me a hand up.

I scrambled up on my own, dusting off my pants to give myself a moment to collect my composure.

"I've been meaning to ask," he continued. "Sorrel? Like the—"

"—horse." I finished for him as I headed toward the door.

"The mane."

"What?"

"That mane of yours. Sorrel."

I resisted the urge to touch my hair and walked down the hall, feeling his eyes on my tight jeans as I walked. Kevin had always said that my legs must inspire jeans designers.

Dinner, an informal, raucous affair of delicious spicy foods and laughter, eased my earlier discomfort. Reed showed a different side, keeping up a steady flow of teasing chatter with the boys. Teri had seated me opposite him, to her left, so she and I could chat. But both of us soon decided that would have to wait.

I selected small portions of the spicy food and took small bites. "Mmm. These tamales are so good! I may need a bottle of antacid, but I love them," I told Teri and gulped yet another glass of water.

"My mama and Tia Luisa make them. I keep telling myself I'll have to learn, but I guess I'm just too busy."

"Don't believe it! My wife is busy, yeah, but she is a wonderful cook. It's just that making tamales makes her squeamish."

"What's squeamish, Uncle Reed?"

"This wiggly, smelly creature."

Two pairs of eyes swung to their mama.

"Reed! Just because you were our best man and are the monsters' godfather doesn't give you complete safety." Teri pointed a butter knife toward him with mock threat, pretending it was a rifle.

Reed threw up his hands. "I give up, señora! Don't shoot!" He ducked behind Josef on his right amid childish squeals of laughter. I couldn't believe this was the same guy who had barked at me only a couple of days ago. He glanced unexpectedly toward me and grinned as if he'd just read my thoughts.

I quickly looked down at my plate and concentrated on eating the scorching but tasty contents.

Teri led me to her "laboratory" while the men hustled the boys through their nightly ritual. She had confiscated the upper part of the garage and turned it into a comfortable but functional workshop. Metal shelving filled with baskets of soaps and stacks of jars filled with lotions lined the longer wall at the end. One end held a computer desk, phone, and filing cabinet. On the opposite wall stood a counter, complete with a sink and a hotplate, numerous large aluminum containers, and another narrow shelving unit filled with supplies.

"I'm impressed. This is quite a set-up."

For the first time since we'd met, Teri seemed almost timid. "I designed and made the labels on my computer," she said, handing me one of the jars for closer inspection.

I opened it and sniffed. It tickled my nose—a delicate floral and a touch of spice. Teri had given her products Spanish names. This one was *Corazon*, "Heart."

"These will be a wonderful asset to the shop," I said and began describing the displays I was already envisioning in my store.

Teri eagerly piggybacked her ideas, creating a synergy neither of us had expected. As I moved along the row of samples, sniffing, touching, and falling more and more in love with her creations, Teri grabbed a notebook and started jotting everything down. "A habit of mine," she grinned.

Both of us jumped when we heard a throat being cleared in the doorway. Reed stood there, Jose just behind him. "Sorry to interrupt." What a lie! "But I need to leave and just wanted to say thanks for another delicious meal."

I glanced up at the clock above the desk. It couldn't be ten o'clock already! "Oh, my! I didn't realize we'd been out here this long!"

"Neither did I," Teri grinned. "But once I get started on my creations, time just flies."

"Thankfully your other creations are safely snoring away," Jose teased, looking around Reed. He waved a soda can at us. "Do you want something to drink, Sorrel?"

"No, thanks. In fact, I need to get home too. Getting the store in shape has turned out to be a lot harder than I thought it would be. I've got sore muscles I never knew even existed."

"You're doing it by yourself?" Teri asked, accepting the Coke and popping the tab. "You should have these guys help. Jose and Reed are good helpers. That's how I got this place."

I moved toward the door. "I'm sure Reed has more than enough to do with the cases he's handling."

Teri smiled and shrugged, but I knew I'd be hearing about it again.

Outside, Reed lost his playful attitude and insisted on walking me to my car.

"You might as well say it," I told him as I climbed in. "Something is on your mind."

"Who are you?"

"What do you mean?"

"These people are my friends. They think they're cautious, but they've grown up in this isolated area. And they haven't been outside of it much."

"And your point is?"

Reed leaned against my door, seemingly unaware of the blinds that twitched at the front window except that he adopted an air of intimacy. "You show up here, obviously with city attitude and sketchy, if not downright untruthful, stories of your past. As soon as you arrive, people start dying. Do you know how many homicides we have here in a year?"

"Whoa! What do my move here and your homicide count have to do with each other?"

"That's what I'm wondering."

"Coincidence."

"Right! You just happen to be in a bar the night a simple soul who has gone to that bar for years turns up dead in a dumpster. Hours later some unknown tourist is found dead in an abandoned house and you appear behind a camera! Next you're grubbing around an old store and working your way into the confidence of my friends. None of it fits. And I don't have time to think about why."

"There is no why, Reed, because that's what it is—just coincidence!" I started the motor. "It's late and I think you must need sleep. Besides, your friends are likely to get the wrong idea, if the movement around the blinds is any indication, that you and I are discussing something more pleasant than the dead bodies you're accumulating."

Reed stepped back but didn't smile. "Just don't add to the count, okay?"

"What do you mean by that?"

"There's no record that a Sorrel Janes ever lived in Baltimore, Maryland, and the only person who seems to know you is Randall Byrd's friend who recommended you for part-time work on his paper. You have terrifying nightmares, switch the subject away from anything personal, had a bogus sheriff's deputy already scouting out your new place, and seem to be nervous most of the time."

I stared at the steering wheel. "So are a lot of people. We live in a stressful world." I sighed. "Look, have I broken the law? Do I act like some murderer?"

Reed stared at me as if he could make me reveal the secrets he sensed.

"I'll follow you home." He hesitated briefly. "I'll figure it out—if I ever get any sleep."

"Not if I can help it," I muttered to his retreating back.

CHAPTER THIRTEEN

"Okay. Everyone look at me and smile." I prayed silently that this would be the last shot.

"Whoops! I lost my teeth!" I closed my eyes briefly, fighting the urge to snicker with the onlookers even though this had been the most frustrating half hour in my recent existence. Silently counting to ten, I smiled encouragingly while a caregiver rushed off to find more glue to squirt onto the rebellious dentures.

This was just the sort of assignment I'd asked Randall Byrd to give me, I reminded myself, as I waited for the Senior Center dance champions to get set for their photograph—again! During the past couple of days, I'd received assignments to photograph Girl Scout cookie sales winners, a ribbon-cutting ceremony for a new car dealership, and the Good Citizenship award winners for one of the local schools. This shot of the dance champions would finish my list, and I was impatient to return to the store. But I needed this added income until I could get the store operating on a profit and my other photography selling regularly.

One more time I arranged the seniors into partners and mentally crossed my fingers. "Beautiful!" The wayward dentures plopped out again. Thankfully, I'd snapped the photo just before they fell out. I slipped my camera into my shoulder bag and started down the line thanking my models. "You can look for these photos in the paper this week," I promised each of them.

As I left, the dancer with the denture problem asked me come back. I hadn't had a chance to see them dance, she reminded me. Almost on cue, her partner grabbed her hand and twirled her, making her short skirt and countless petticoats lift and sway side to side.

"I've got a copy of your newsletter," I reassured her and the rest of the group. "I'll try to attend the next performance." I could see the light of hope fading from their eyes. They'd heard this promise too many times before.

The activities director, Nina, wasn't pleased either. "We try not to make promises to them," she said, as she walked with me toward the exit.

"I'm sorry. That was thoughtless of me. It's just that I'm so new to your area I don't want to do the wrong thing. Guess I did it anyway."

Her face softened. "I tend to get overprotective of them," she admitted. "They are so excited about getting their picture in the paper."

I remembered Nina's comment as I wrote the captions for the photos at the newspaper office. The most important thing was to get the names correct as my dancers, Girl Scouts, and other proud faces would be clipped from the paper and put on display—probably on refrigerators or bulletin boards. I should have remembered that earlier when I was growing tired and impatient.

"Hi, Sorrel!"

I jumped. "Teri! I hadn't noticed you were working today!"

"I'm not actually. I just stopped by to bring a birthday cake for Mr. Byrd. His wife is away and he shouldn't go without a cake!" She winked. "Not sure if I'm buttering him up or it's just the mama thing kicking in."

"A lot of that going around today." I told her about Nina's reaction at the Senior Center. "I guess I'm not accustomed to the small town caring attitude."

"Yeah, I imagine Baltimore is a really different atmosphere with so many people. But, you know, my *tia* always says that people are the same. It's just that when you get a big collection of them, the bad ones show up more often and the good ones get more cautious."

I handed my copy and photos to the receptionist, Maria, and started out. Teri walked along with me, wanting to know how things were going at the store.

"Good but slower than I need it to be. I cleared out the living area yesterday. I've been so busy working on the store I'd forgotten about fixing up my own quarters. Living at the B&B is okay, but it's eating up my reserve cash—and it's not home."

"You're going to live there?" I could see the gleam in her eyes as we reached her SUV. "I don't want to be too pushy, but if you need furniture, I have a cousin that has a used furniture and appliance place. Would you like to go with me tomorrow to look at what he has to offer?"

"Sure." I'd planned on shopping for appliances and a bed tomorrow anyway. It would be more fun to have someone else along while I shopped for bits and pieces.

As I drove back to the store, I realized that despite how hard I'd been working the past three weeks, I couldn't stamp out the loneliness. Starting over had its limitations. I missed the energy of the city, the confidence of the job I'd trained for and had risen to the top doing. I missed the easy comfort of the life Kevin and I had created.

But even as I thought about what I missed, my mind turned to the unbidden thoughts of my discontent with that life. I had certainly enjoyed parts of it, but I had become increasingly lonely. With a public face and lifestyle, I no longer enjoyed much anonymity or privacy. People interrupting simple dinners or evenings at a ballgame had triggered stress. And Kevin, while proud of my career, resented those intrusions. He'd complained increasingly about how hard it was to take a daily jog, go to the mall, or just enjoy an afternoon together at the beach in Galveston. And more and more, he'd done those things on his own. Worse, I'd begun to feel he wasn't doing them alone.

My head jerked upward slightly. Why had that thought surfaced? Traffic noise refocused me on the business at hand, even as I struggled inwardly with guilt at my disloyalty. My eyes filling with tears, I quickly pulled into a parking lot.

It's my fault! I couldn't stop them, those thoughts and tears. I bent over toward the floorboard, pretending to search for something in my purse.

Someone tapped on my window. I quickly wiped my eyes and arranged a smile on my face before looking up. It was my favorite cop, motioning me to roll down my window. Was he following me?

"I need a favor," he said through my half-opened window. "Could you meet me at the bar?"

"Now?"

"Yep."

"Aren't you working?"

"Yep." The brim of his hat shaded his eyes, but I was sure they were filled with satisfaction at my discomfort.

"Look, I'm on my way to the store—"

"Really?" He glanced over his shoulder. I followed his gaze and realized we were in the parking lot of the library.

"I need to make some copies—"

"I'll wait."

"—but I forgot to bring the material I need to copy."

He just kept leaning on my window.

I shrugged. "All right, but I don't see what in the world I can help you with. Seems like from the moment I got here, I've been surrounded by police. Am I your only suspect?"

No answer. He just touched the brim of his hat and walked toward his car. I sighed and watched him drive away. Then I glanced in the mirror before pulling out of the lot behind him. My eyes didn't look too bad. Just tired, not teary.

CHAPTER FOURTEEN

Reed leaned against his car door outside Bart's, straightening up as I pulled into the parking space, his only acknowledgement of my arrival. I reached for my purse just as the door opened, making me jump.

"You sure are jumpy!"

I bristled. "How do you move so quickly?"

"Part cat."

"Alley cat!"

"Yep!"

"And where did this 'yep' come from?"

To control my irritation, I purposely avoided his eyes or any closeness as we walked toward the building. He opened the door to the bar for me, and I blinked as I adjusted from the sunlight to the dim interior.

"Been watching too many old western movies—in my spare time," he finally answered.

A snort to the left startled both of us. "That's a good one, Reed!" The voice belonged to a wiry gray-haired woman of indeterminate age, the owner, who smiled at me from a table near the window. "You want to watch him, honey. These handsome guys who've lived awhile without being caught are wily critters."

Reed walked over and pulled her into a hug. "Don't believe a word she says, Sorrel. This is Lena. She's the one who used to bring me cookies."

"I had to do something to make you behave!" She turned toward me conspiratorially. "Sweetens him up every time!"

"Lena was our whole office staff when I started at the police department. She worked hard to train me into a decent lawman."

"Does she know it didn't work?" I retorted

Lena laughed, heartily and deeply. "I like this one, Reed! Spunky! Better watch your back!"

Reed shrugged good naturedly. "Looks like the after work crowd hasn't arrived yet."

"Been a little slower since . . . well, you know." Lena picked up her glass. "I come in for my usual—Diet Coke—to catch a little gossip. Join me?"

"Next time, Lena. I'm still on the job. And looks like your buddies have arrived anyway." A couple of older ladies had entered and were walking toward Lena's table, curiosity sparkling. "You ladies be careful now. Don't over drink on that Diet Coke!" Reed admonished, his eyes twinkling with mischief, as he motioned me toward the bar.

We walked across the room amid their giggles. "Reed, you're a real flirt when you set your mind to it." But he ignored me. So that was how it was going to be. I felt a twinge of disappointment.

He asked me to sit right where I had been sitting the night of Stephanie's murder, so I slid into the back seat at the table for two, facing the dance floor. Across the floor, Lena and her friends watched, openly curious. Then he asked me to tell him again who had been sitting on my right and left.

I repeated what I'd told him a few days ago, and he jotted it down again on his notepad. Then, at his request, I listed the other occupants I could remember and where they had been. As I finished, he turned his attention to the hovering waitress. "Nothing just now. Sorry," he said. Then he turned to me. "Now, Sorrel, I want you to turn the way you did that night when you smelled the smoke."

My patience was nearly gone. "Reed, I've told you everything I can remember. I don't see how this can possibly help—"

"Just play along with me for a minute or two longer, okay? I need to visualize this place the way it was that night."

"Have you still not followed up on the idea that she might have been the random victim of violence that night? That maybe someone was just trying to rob her?"

"Can't rule that out, but it just doesn't fit—either this town or her. She wasn't the sort of person you'd approach to rob."

I sighed. "Okay. The guy was standing just behind there." I motioned over my right shoulder. "Why is he so important?"

"He may not be. I'm just trying to get a full picture of the bar that night. Something might have happened here that led to her death . . . or not." He shut his notepad. "Okay, I'm done. You can go." He started toward the door as I just sat at the table. "Thanks," he called over his shoulder, not bothering to even make eye contact.

Yeah, thanks, I thought, staring after him, keenly aware of the curious looks I was getting from Lena's crowd and a couple at the bar. He'd practically drug me down here, asked me a couple of inane questions, and then just walked off! I stood up, waved to Lena as I walked to the door, and stepped outside.

Reed leaned against his squad car, a phone to his ear. I marched past, clicked my key fob to unlock my door, and headed toward my vehicle. Then I stopped in the middle of the street, took a deep breath, and turned back. He was still speaking on the phone when I tapped him on the shoulder.

"Wha-a—?" he stuttered when he saw me standing behind him and lowered the phone just a bit from his ear.

"Reed, it's been fun, but you really need to work on making it last a little longer next time!" I purred. Then I planted a loud, smacking kiss on his cheek. How dare he treat me with such rude arrogance! I'd tried to be professional from the first moment I'd met him, but he'd consistently acted rude and terse when he spoke to me—unless his friends were nearby. Then he was funny, flirty, and likeable.

"Sir? Uh, no—" he muttered into the phone, trying to answer his boss and watch me as I strode back to my car. I could see him staring at me in the rearview mirror as I gunned the motor a little and sped out of the parking lot. Explain that to your boss, Reed, I thought and chuckled at the thought of his discomfort.

I'd only driven a block or two when I noticed the downtrodden apartment buildings ahead of me on my right. As I slowed down and stopped at the corner, a frayed remnant of yellow crime scene tape flapping in the breeze on one of the trees in the yard caught my attention. Could this have been where she lived? The images of her bobbing head and tapping foot, the dreamy smile as she danced, that worn school jacket returned as clearly as if I'd snapped them with my camera.

I shivered. How quickly life can be over! I knew then that I wasn't returning to the store this afternoon. I needed time with my camera, snapping the beauty around me to blot out the ugly.

I started to pull away from the stop sign and stopped myself. Wait a minute! Yes, it was sad that this woman had been murdered, but I hadn't known her. This whole situation was just a coincidence, a chance encounter. I hadn't even talked with the woman, so why had the police focused on me? Simply because I was a stranger to the area and admitted seeing her? I shook my head, trying to clear the thoughts from my mind. They were probably focusing on every stranger in the bar that night.

As I started to pull away again, another question shattered the second of peace I'd just found: How much of a background check had Reed run on me because I'd been a stranger in that bar? I could explain a cursory check that gave him no information, but a deep background work up?

I shook my head to clear it. I was getting paranoid, letting Reed get under my skin. And I had just played into his mind games with my silly little retaliation to his needling. Now he'd be angrier than ever.

A horn honked behind me. I glanced in the rearview mirror and saw a truck was waiting. I gestured apologetically and eased away from the stop sign.

Heading out of town, I tried to push Reed and his murder from my mind, but something kept niggling at my brain. Was he right? Had I seen something that I was just not remembering? Or was I really becoming paranoid?

CHAPTER FIFTEEN

"I love this bed! And the chest of drawers and nightstand are perfect!" Teri clapped her hands in delight, while her cousin and I stood back and looked at her doubtfully.

"I have some other pieces that are more modern," he said.

"But look at the character!"

"Look at the nicks and scars."

"Crackle paint will jazz it up and hide those."

"Look at the work involved."

"A few hours. Look at the money saved."

Berto and I exchanged shrugs. "It is a good price," I finally admitted.

"Good?" Teri gave me an exasperated look. "It can be better!"

In less than three hours, I had everything I needed—and some I hadn't known I needed—for about half what I had budgeted. Teri had even convinced her cousin and his friends to deliver everything that evening after the business closed.

From there, we visited another store where I bought a new mattress, which would arrive tomorrow, as well as an inexpensive computer desk and chair. Next, we visited the home improvement store for all of the paints, brushes, and other necessities for making my "almost new" furniture "vintage" as well as paint for the family parts of the house. I felt like I'd been sucked into a whirlwind, but I also felt exhilarated.

Flash complained when I returned to the room. I changed into paint gear after gobbling—and sharing—the fish sandwich I'd picked up for lunch. But she still hadn't forgiven me when I picked up my bag and started out the door again.

"It won't be long," I crooned, stopping to pet her shining fur. "We'll soon have our own place and you will have the run of it. No more living in one room. No more temporary quarters. We won't have to be afraid."

Afraid? That thought was so unexpected that I looked over my shoulder to see if someone had heard. Had that come from me? I glanced down at Flash, petted her again, and started toward my car. But all I could hear was Kevin's voice as I walked down the stairs and out the front door.

"You need to be more careful!" Kevin's voice had been edgy as he stood in the entry hall, his brow furrowed, his eyes darting to the clock as I'd walked into our home. "It isn't safe for you to be out in that neighborhood in the daytime. And at this time of night, it's downright foolish!"

"I wasn't alone. You know I had Steve with me. Besides, who in his right mind would take on a whole news van? There's some sort of code out there not to attack us." I'd grinned and made my zany face, trying to lighten the moment.

Kevin hadn't bought my act. "That blonde hair is a magnet," he had countered. "People are drawn to you wherever you are. And wherever you are is around murderers, rapists, serial killers—"

"It's what I do, Kevin," I'd said, as I slipped into his arms. Kevin hugged me so tightly I could hardly keep talking. I'd reminded him we'd have plenty of time of boring society stuff when we had a family and that he'd probably be as bored with me as I would be with it.

He'd let me go. I'd seen a hopelessness in his eyes. "Why must danger be exciting? Why isn't love, home, family, happiness exciting? Why isn't it enough?" He had asked that question often in the few months since our marriage. No matter how often I'd reassured him and reminded him it was all part of my job, he couldn't let it go. It was his job to worry, he'd say, and he'd done that all too well.

I'd felt stifled. I'd loved my job. It had been a tough climb from that small liberal arts college through the local weekly newspaper and countless other jobs to get the experience necessary for that "break." And finally I'd become a crime journalist for the local television station.

I'd met Kevin after I'd been on my dream job only a few months. He'd been guest lecturer on growing oil exploration at a class at the University of Houston, and I'd been taking some photography classes. Kevin had liked to say we "ran into each other" because that's what we'd done. I'd been heading into the elevator, looking down, and he'd been heading out, talking on his cell phone. Amid multiple apologies and scrambling to collect fallen papers and books, Kevin had glanced at me— and then he'd studied me. "You're that blonde," he'd said. "The one I saw on television the other night. How could you stand to be in that prison interviewing that horrible man? A gorgeous gal like you could have been a model."

Maybe that should have caused me to go more slowly, but it hadn't. Within three short months, we'd wed on the beach at Galveston with only a handful of friends witnessing us pledge our love before a gorgeous sunset. Flash and I had moved into Kevin's renovated house in Houston Heights. Then his parents had insisted we fly to Florida a few weeks later for a family wedding party.

From the first, I had sensed that Kevin blamed my job for our erratic lifestyle. He'd worked late nights, attended countless social events, and traveled constantly. But that was before he'd been promoted into a more stable position. When we married, he had expected his life to follow a more settled pattern.

My late night schedule worried him. My habit of running in the neighborhood before sun-up worried him. My careful watch on my diet worried him. "You don't have to starve yourself," he'd complained. "I didn't marry you because you're so thin."

"But my other love—the camera—demands that I stay thin," I'd laughed.

As I drove toward the store, I couldn't remember when he had stopped laughing with me and worried constantly instead.

He'd increasingly complained about my work, especially about whether I should be out late at night. When I'd reminded him that he visited areas for oil exploration that weren't exactly safe either, he'd said, "But I'm a guy." We'd slept apart that night for the first time since we'd married.

I'd known Kevin had grown up in a much different home than mine had been. His dad had been an attorney; his mom had served on countless charitable committees while maintaining an active social life. After we married, Kevin had expected me to delegate the night work and less pleasant parts of my job to someone else.

"Aren't you afraid?" he'd often asked.

Oddly enough, I wasn't. Fear was something I hadn't had time for. Life could not be lived in the shadow of fear. I'd followed my mom's adage: "There's nothing to fear but fear itself."

How naïve I'd been! I thought longingly of life without fear. That was what I missed—not the stress of the job, not the attention of being on television news, not the excitement of chasing the story—*and not being married!*

I suddenly found myself at the store, not realizing how I'd arrived there. I'd been totally engrossed in the past. The past. Remember that, Sorrel, I told myself. It is the past!

Stopping in the driveway, I looked at the house, focusing on the missing shingles on the roof, the peeling paint on the trim, and the overgrown weeds in the front yard. I'd been so busy working inside that I'd forgotten the outside. I sighed and pulled around to the back to park.

Inside, the store had been transformed. My refinished floors, paint, and new windows had brightened the whole room. Track lighting highlighted the outside edges of the large room, with the original antique light fixture—cleaned of years of dust and grime—hanging low in the center.

Aunt Rose had converted a closet into an office alcove with a low, short counter in front of it. She had always kept a quart jar of jellybeans on that counter, as well as a pitcher filled with flowers. Maybe that had inspired the simple daisy-sprigged wallpaper I'd hung in the alcove and the soft green I'd painted the counter.

The family living area looked far worse by comparison. On the western side were two bedrooms, the larger one in front of the smaller bedroom, connected by a bathroom. A small hall divided the living room from the bedrooms. Behind the living room was a tiny kitchen that led to a screened porch.

I glanced at the clock. Teri's crew would be here in just a few hours, and I still had to pull the faded wallpaper off the walls in the large bedroom.

CHAPTER SIXTEEN

When the alarm I'd set on my cell rang a few hours later, I staggered out of the bedroom, damp wallpaper scraps stuck to the bottoms of my feet, and plopped onto the bench built onto the wall beside the pantry. Before I could dial, the phone rang.

"Have you ordered the pizza?"

I groaned inwardly. Did this guy have to show up everywhere?

"Just about to do that," I said.

"I'll do it."

"No, this is my treat. I insist."

"Then you can pay me when I get there."

"Reed, I have to pick up an order at Dulces De Mi Corazon."

"Anything else?"

I was too tired to argue. "No. I have a couple of cases of sodas and water bottles iced down in a cooler here."

"Okay. Got it. I'm on my way."

Somehow I staggered back into the bedroom. The paper had peeled right off three of the walls. The fourth had required several coats of remover spray, a flat scraper, and a sponge. All I needed to do now was to cram the wallpaper into trash bags and sponge the walls one last time to remove any residue.

When I finished, I plopped back onto the bench and gulped a bottle of icy water. I didn't know if I could—or would—ever move again. I leaned back, closed my eyes, and counted the dozens of throbbing aches all over my body.

"Sleeping on the job?"

I jumped, blinking before focusing on the man standing in front of me. "Sneaking up on me again?"

"Not hard to do. You snored through several trips." He pointed to the card table set up in the center of the room, now laden with pizza boxes, bread sticks, and a couple of boxes of cookies.

I avoided staring at his lips, pursed to contain the grin twitching at the corners of his mouth. He leaned forward and I jerked away. "Hold still." He touched my ponytail and drew out a piece of wallpaper. "Interesting hair ornament."

I was saved from answering by the sounds of several vehicles approaching.

Teri had recruited—bulldozed more likely—several family members to help and supervised the unloading of Bert's truck with all my furniture before allowing anyone to eat. When finally permitted to do so, the group consumed the food like locusts amid introductions, laughter, and children's squeals. The tired old kitchen seemed to take on a new life.

When no scraps of pizza remained, Teri climbed up on the bench and clapped for attention. "Okay, now it's time to earn your food!" With that she doled out assignments. Some were sent to paint the bedrooms, some to paint the living room, and some to work on refinishing the furniture. I set the supplies for each project into the appropriate rooms. The furniture had been relegated to the back porch for refinishing.

A couple of hours later, we were clearing up. The pale peach and white living room was now warm and inviting. My bedroom walls glowed with coats of soft rose paint, the ceiling and baseboards bright white. The old mismatched bedroom furniture had taken on designer appeal, its original dark brown finish transformed to cream crackled antique. A couple of Teri's cousins and Reed had installed tan carpet squares in both rooms as well as the spare bedroom.

"Wow!" I looked around the suddenly quiet crowd. "I don't know how to thank you. It would have taken me forever to do all this, and I could never have done it so well."

"You can say that again." Reed's tone had just the right effect. Everyone started moving and chattering again. Then, as quickly as they'd arrived, they left. Almost everyone left, that is.

"This is a nice little place here," Reed said. "You can feel the happiness."

I never expected to hear anything so whimsical from him! But I knew what he meant. "There was a lot of happiness here," I began and, almost without being able to stop, I told him about my aunt and uncle and the wonderful summer I'd spent with them as a kid.

"Must've been your mom's aunt. You have a different last name."

That had not been said casually and I immediately grew cautious. Reed was too good a detective not to probe. "Have you made any progress on Stephanie's murder?" I countered.

"Ongoing investigation." His face closed.

"Well, I am an employee—sort of."

"I haven't cleared you as a suspect."

"What? You have to be kidding!" My voice was getting louder and my speech faster. "You've been considering me a suspect? That's the craziest thing—" The grin stopped me.

"Sure doesn't take much to set you off. That model figure and designer jeans didn't fool me. I figured you for a school yard brawler."

"Not me. I was playing baseball. And you're trying to change the subject."

"Ready to lock up?" he said, walking toward the front of the store. I followed behind as we went room to room silently, checking windows, lights, and locks. Back in the kitchen, he picked up the full trash bag. "I'll drop this in my dumpster for you."

"Seriously, Reed, I can't help thinking about her. Stephanie. She was a stranger, but I feel so bad about her death," I said, as I picked up my gear and followed him out. "I keep wishing I could remember something—anything—that could help you find the murderer."

Reed threw the trash in the back of his truck and guided me toward mine. "I liked her. She was an odd one," he said. "Sort of alone but content with it. Always smiled at me. Loved to dance." He sighed as we reached my car. "I don't know how much longer I can keep this case open without putting it in the cold files—and I didn't tell you that!"

I climbed into the Jeep and started the engine. "I drove by her place," I confessed to him. "I didn't really know where she lived, but after I left you at Bart's, I saw a piece of the crime scene tape and some young guys hauling things out to a truck. I hadn't realized she'd lived so close to the bar." I shivered. "What's that expression about a ghost walking across your grave? I had this spooky feeling, like someone was watching me. Silly, isn't it?"

Reed grabbed my arm and looked at me intently. "No, it isn't silly. This is an open, unsolved murder. You need to be careful. Don't drive by there again. Be aware of your surroundings, Sorrel. And, like it or not, I'm following you home tonight."

It was useless to argue. Stubborn, irritating, interfering man! Maybe something about me is a magnet for overprotective men, I fumed. I knew Reed was only doing his job—maybe—but I was glad to wave goodbye when we reached the B&B.

Yes, I thought as I got ready for bed, Kevin's nurturing had flattered me at first and I'd married the man of my dreams. But after the initial grief, I acknowledged that not having to feel guilty about my life was a relief of sorts. I was bright and I'd been very good at a demanding though sometimes dangerous job.

As I cuddled up to my furry friend, my last conscious thoughts before sleep were about the fun and excitement I'd found here in this quiet town. No one was going to drive me off. No one!

CHAPTER SEVENTEEN

"Did the señor find his way to your store?" Mrs. Sanchez poured a second cup of coffee and removed my empty plate.

"Reed?"

"No, your friend from back home."

My stomach lurched. "No," I said calmly as I replaced the full coffee cup on the saucer. "Did he tell you his name?"

Mrs. Sanchez shook her head. "He said he wanted to surprise you," she said, her voice beginning to rise in pitch, "so he didn't want to leave a note. I asked his name, but I think he didn't hear." She was speaking even faster than usual, her brow furrowed above worried eyes.

"It's okay." I raised the cup, trying to be casual. "What did he look like?"

"Not so tall," she said. "Oh, I'm so sorry, ma'am. I hope I   didn't . . . didn't do wrong in giving him the directions?"

"Don't worry about it. He'll likely find the store today. When did he come by?"

"Shortly after you left." The worry lines creasing her forehead deepened. "I am so very sorry. He just seemed to know . . . he said he'd talked to you recently."

I patted her arm as I stood, needing to get to my room to think. "You did nothing wrong. It's probably just someone I worked with before I came here." I smiled. "If he comes again, call my cell. And thank you for not giving out that number."

I walked up the stairs to my room, closed the door, and sat on the edge of the bed.

Who was he? What did he want? How had he found me?

I certainly hadn't left any trace of my new life behind. The police—and my good friend—had made sure of that in spite of my protests that it was unnecessary. I'd complained endlessly about the precautions, but maybe they'd had a point. Still, it didn't look like their plan was foolproof.

My reflection in the mirror stared back at me. I liked the woman I saw. "I'm not doing it again! I'm finished with running," I said and pounded my fists into the bed. "The life I'm building here has been my dream all along." What? When had I realized that?

My phone rang, making me jump. I looked at the ID and moaned softly. I'd forgotten about the deliveries scheduled for this morning. I answered and told the delivery person when I could meet him.

Mrs. Sanchez gave me a close look from her customary spot behind the registration desk, but I smiled casually and called a cheery goodbye on my way out the door. A couple of newlyweds who had checked in yesterday walked out of their room right behind me, so she didn't ask the questions I still saw in her face.

All the way out to the store, I made myself notice the cars around me. I even checked to see if the same car stayed behind me. Okay, so I'd not been following all of the directions the police detective had given me. Maybe because, as I started to do so now, I felt that familiar feeling of . . . fear? No, not fear. Anger. I'd been angry all along. How dare someone murder my husband? How dare someone push me into resigning the job I'd grown . . . tired of doing? Where had that come from?

By the time I pulled into the driveway, I'd lectured myself into a semi-state of calmness. The furniture van pulled in right behind me, erasing the last wisps of fear.

The delivery guys were kind enough to put the bed together and move the furniture from the back porch into position—for a tip. The desk and chair were a close fit in the small alcove. But I liked them. And, by the time the men left, I had regained my composure. This guy was only as important as I allowed him to be.

I slipped off my shoes, feeling the new carpet squish between my toes, and started making the bedroom mine. Atop the bed I placed my mother's quilt, its squares in shades of pale yellows, blues, and rose. Flash immediately made a furry circle in the middle of it. I hung sheers over the blinds at the window and several of my favorite photographic prints around the room. I was especially proud of the pieces I'd found left over in Aunt Rose's store—a big blue porcelain pitcher and bowl set for the dresser and a dainty lamp for the nightstand. A couple of hours after I'd started, I admired the cozy room I'd created, all traces of the morning upset successfully pushed aside.

But they resurfaced when I sat down at my new desk to eat the sack lunch Mrs. Sanchez had packed for me. Who knew I was here? My photography mentor and dear friend John Daniels knew, of course. He had recommended me to Randall Byrd. But he'd never give that information to anyone. He knew the danger.

What little family I had left was scattered and we didn't keep in touch. Kevin's parents blamed me for his death and certainly didn't care where I'd gone. My friend Sandy thought I was on a trip to Mexico and didn't expect to hear from me for another few weeks. Even then, I'd send my letters to John to send to her until we knew it was safe to let her know.

Could the man be John? If so, why wouldn't he just let me know? I took out my cell phone and dialed. After several rings, it went to voice mail. I was tempted to leave a message, but some inner caution told me that might not be wise. The cell number, one of those disposable types, would alert him without registering my name.

The only other person who knew my location was the detective in charge of investigating Kevin's murder. It had been his idea for me to disappear for a while. Fortunately, I hadn't told anyone about inheriting this place, so Saddle Gap was a safer alternative that some of the others. Still, the detective had cautioned me to be constantly alert to anything unusual. Someone "from home" asking for me did just that.

No one had yet determined whether Kevin had been murdered randomly or been killed because of me. He was certainly not the sort to inspire the violence his murderer had displayed. No, I'd murdered him as surely as the one who'd held the knife, stabbing him over and over and finally slicing his throat. His mother had screamed that at me again and again at the funeral home while half of Houston listened. "Your ambition and ego destroyed our only child!" she'd ranted. "Why couldn't you do as he asked? Why couldn't you quit that job and become a real wife? Instead, your thirst for the spotlight, being in front of that camera, running around half the night in search of lowlife trash—!"

I'd mercifully fainted.

When Kevin died, I'd been following a particularly disturbing story about gangs and drugs in school. After the first story aired, I'd received the common threatening emails and anonymous letters that such stories often inspire. I'd learned to ignore them as the blustering that they usually were. This time, however, one note had been especially intimidating: "Mind your own business, bitch, or I'll take what's yours." I had forgotten about it until I that horrible day.

I'd been hustled out the back of the mortuary into a waiting van after I regained consciousness. The detective had explained that I must disappear until they could determine the motivation behind the murder. Undercover officers had picked up street chatter focused on me. My life might be in danger. I couldn't even go to my husband's funeral service.

The next few hours and days were still blurred in my memory. The police had taken me by my house to collect a couple of boxes of memorabilia and business papers, a few clothes, my cameras, and Flash. Then they'd driven me to a small town in Arkansas where someone else had taken my car. I'd driven alone to John's cabin near Branson in a Mini Cooper. No one else had known my destination.

Occasionally, I'd feel guilty about missing Kevin's funeral. But the huge, impersonal affair had been so alien to what he would have wanted— a simple sunset memorial service, maybe at the beach in Galveston where we'd married. He would have wanted to be cremated, too; but his mother and father had taken total control of the service.

Instead, in the small cabin with no company besides my cat and the occasional call from John, I grieved for my husband, my life, and my lost dreams.

The official word to the public was that I had taken a few months to recover from the shock. The unofficial word on the street was that I was in a substance rehab clinic. In a month, a new crime reporter had filled my spot. No one cared where I'd gone—at least, I'd hoped no one cared. I'd prayed they'd forgotten.

My blonde hair had grown out, returning to my natural red. John and the police had helped me change my official identity from Stacy Lee Jamison, my television and adopted persona, to my birth name, Sorrel Lyn Janes. By the time I'd arrived in Saddle Gap, any resemblance to the television news star had vanished. I'd grown thinner, if that were possible, and no longer wore the binders to make my breasts look smaller. I wore minimal make-up, letting the freckles that sprinkled my nose and cheekbones show. I adopted a basic look, with my hair in a simple ponytail and jeans my everyday apparel.

I'd known I couldn't stay in Branson with John indefinitely. And I certainly couldn't drift through the rest of my days waiting until the police decided I was safe. Instead, I'd searched for a quieter life on my own. Not being in the public eye freed me to choose a new home.

With my much older half-brother, a career soldier, stationed in Europe and no close relatives, my natural resources were nonexistent. Then I'd remembered the little place that my great aunt and uncle had left to me. I'd loved the area as a child, before those dreams of fame and the excitement of television had struck.

Photography had always been a passion with me. Somewhere in the back of my mind I'd figured that I'd pursue it once I retired from television journalism. My retirement had just arrived a little sooner than I'd expected and I'd started thinking about it in earnest. What better place to pursue my photography than my great aunt's house? I could even reopen the little store and sell my photos and crafts from the area.

I hadn't seen the house and store in years and had no idea how run down it might be. But it was mine and no one else—living—knew it even existed. My needs were small and I had a little money saved that could be accessed for me. Maybe it would work. And so, in the early hours of sleepless nights, I'd forged my plan.

Now, the horror of losing yet another dream filled me with anger and resolve. Someday—I hoped it would be soon—the person responsible for Kevin's death would be found. Until then, I had to be careful. But I refused to be a victim.

Mrs. Sanchez was waiting at the front desk when I walked in. She followed me into the dining room and then went into the kitchen. A few moments later, she returned with a hot plate of enchiladas. She assured me as she set the plate in front of me that my friend had not returned.

I nibbled at the food, trying to ignore the giggling lovers at the other table. Finally, after eating enough that Mrs. Sanchez would not be insulted, I went to my room.

Flash meowed nervously as I packed my things for a quick exit, if necessary, and snuggled into my lap any time I sat down.

"It'll be all right," I reassured her, scratching her behind her ears. "It'll be all right." It had become my mantra—but I still wasn't sure I was right.

CHAPTER EIGHTEEN

Flash watched me quietly from her carrier, sensing my tenseness, as we stood in the front door of the B&B. I'd carried my luggage to the Jeep this morning before anyone was stirring, left an envelope in the room with money for my bill, and then brought Flash down as if I planned to take her for a daily outing. I'd forced myself to drink coffee and had accepted a breakfast burrito to take with me so that Mrs. Sanchez wouldn't be upset. She had been so kind during my stay here. I'd even given her a framed photo of Flash I'd taken. She and the cat had developed a friendship during our stay, as unlikely as that had seemed when we first arrived.

I knew it was cowardly not to tell her in person. Cowardly. That was a term I never thought would describe me and I hoped it would never do so again.

I scanned the street quickly but thoroughly, my heightened sense of caution kicking in, before stepping outside. All was quiet. My hand tightened on Flash's carrier and I started toward the Jeep.

"Planning to run away?"

I whirled around so fast that Flash screamed in complaint. Reed took her carrier before I could protest and began walking toward my Jeep. I followed.

"You are the spookiest woman I've ever seen," he said, as he stuck his fingers inside the wire door of the carrier to stroke Flash's nose, "or do cops just scare you?"

"Do you have to sneak up on people to get them to talk to you?"

His laugh broke the silence of the early morning hour, so genuine I felt my lips twitching into a grin. "It helps."

"I don't have time for a long chat."

We stopped beside my Jeep. Reed leaned against it, still stroking Flash's nose through the wire door. I heard a car engine and glanced over his shoulder. A small green car had parked at the house on the corner.

"What I don't get is why you're so jumpy."

I sighed, feigning a casualness I didn't feel. "And why are we having this conversation?" I said. "I thought you were a busy detective."

He opened the door and set Flash's carrier on the front seat. Then he turned and pulled a small notepad from his shirt pocket and flipped it open. "I find no record of a Sorrel Janes in Baltimore—or anywhere except here. Social security card is legit. But no employment records, no credit cards—smacks of a new identity."

The small car, now filled with high school students, passed, vibrating all of us with its stereos. I shrugged. "Are you finished?"

Reed's eyes bored into me. "Mrs. Sanchez called. She was worried about you. Said something about some guy pretending to know you and asking questions. I told her I'd talk with you to make sure everything's all right, but I notice you've packed more than lunch in your car today." He glanced toward the back of the car at my luggage. "Were you planning to leave without telling anyone?"

"I left her a note, Reed, and paid for my room. I wasn't cheating her, if that's what you think. But I've got the store now and—"

"About half finished. Your bedroom is okay, but you haven't started the kitchen."

"Ever hear of a microwave? Besides, redoing the kitchen is expensive and it will serve my needs just fine for a while the way it is. Look, I need to cut my expenses and it will certainly be easier to work on the place if I'm on the site. And—why am I even explaining myself to you? Am I still a suspect or something?"

"A person of interest."

"What? You're joking!"

"No, I'm not. I've been interested from the start. Beautiful, classy redhead appears just when we have the first murder of the year. Skittish. Avoids people even though she says she's setting up a business. Knows her way around a crime scene but hires on to snap photos of geriatrics. More nervous than her cat. Secretive."

A car engine started behind me. "How about joining me at the store for a cup of coffee?" I kept my eyes on his face in spite of the overwhelming urge to look over my shoulder.

"It's just a city water truck," he said softly, "and that coffee sounds good. I'll follow you out." He grinned. "This is getting to be a habit, you know—following you."

All the way to the store I ranted to Flash about my stupidity. Why had I offered the invitation when all I wanted to do was get rid of him? Maybe he'd get some call and have to leave, I reasoned. Not if he's investigating me, I countered. I could get some free labor, I reasoned. All I had to do was just start working while the coffee perks. Or I could slip up and say too much, I reminded myself. Dizzy from this point-counterpoint, Flash curled up in her carrier and went to sleep.

Before I could get out of the Jeep, Reed walked over to the passenger side to retrieve Flash's carrier. His mood seemed to have changed on the drive to the store though. He now seemed preoccupied.

I managed to get in front of him so I could unlock the door. Once inside, I then busied myself grinding fresh beans for the coffee, the aroma soothing.

"I don't have any cream, but there's the powdered stuff." Silence. I looked over my shoulder into Reed's eyes. "If you don't mind, would you open Flash's door and let her out?" I turned back to fill the coffeemaker while he silently freed the cat. She meowed at him then began to purr. When I glanced around again, she was on his lap.

I placed mugs on the counter. No more stalling tactics left, I sat opposite Reed and my traitorous cat at the small table.

"I like this kitchen," he said, stroking Flash's neck. "I'm glad you haven't modernized it."

I glanced up at the tall cabinets, the cheery double windows over the sink, and the vinyl floor. "I figured a coat of yellow paint and curtains—plus a good cleaning—would do it. In fact, that's today's chore. The paint." I wasn't lying. That had been the plan, substantiated by the paint supplies in the corner.

"Must be something really bad to make you abandon this place."

"What? Why would you say I'm abandoning anywhere?"

"You packed up your stuff. You left a note for Mrs. Sanchez and slipped out during her busy time. Your vehicle is packed for a trip. And you've put off setting a time for Teri to set up her display here in the store."

"Our schedules don't meet, Detective."

The coffee pot beeped, the brewing process finished. I busied myself filling the mugs.

"Black," he said, as I offered the nondairy creamer.

I sat down opposite him again. We sipped quietly, the tension easing a bit. Flash hopped into my lap, kneaded her paws, and settled down.

Reed decided not to increase the tension between us and turned the conversation back to the store. "What sort of things are you going to sell here besides Teri's soaps and lotions?"

I explained my concept and detailed the note cards I'd made and the photos I had prepared. I told him about my Young at Heart section where I was going to promote the crafts and products some of the members of the Senior Center made. He smiled at that and asked about whether I was buying the items from them for resale or simply taking their goods on consignment.

I felt myself relaxing. He seemed really interested, and I found myself drawn into telling him my dreams for the store. As I talked, Reed refilled our cups, listening and offering resources for other products. I hadn't even realized how much time had passed until he glanced at the clock and said he needed to leave.

"Do you know this is the longest we've talked without arguing?" He took a last gulp. "Good coffee." He rose, put the cup in the sink, and turned. "By the way, I'm to tell you that Teri will be here this morning—about now, in fact."

Just as he spoke, I heard the crunch of tires as a car pulled in back of the house. I gasped, looked out the window, and saw her. Reed had purposefully kept me chattering until she came. He'd known I was planning to leave!

CHAPTER NINETEEN

True to form, Teri descended like a whirlwind. In seconds, she'd recruited Reed to carry in boxes and poured herself a cup of coffee. Within a few minutes, Teri's boxes were stacked neatly in her corner of the store. She was just explaining to Reed that she needed him to stay to help when Jose arrived with the shelves he'd made for the display.

Reed had carefully ignored my glare as Teri talked. Now, passing by me to help Jose, he whispered, "I'm glad I was wrong and you weren't bolting." I resisted the childish urge to stick my tongue out at his back.

Jose and Reed left as soon as they'd positioned the shelves where Teri wanted them. She'd painted them southwestern colors—peach, fuchsia, green, turquoise, lilac. I couldn't leave now, so I followed the original plan and painted the kitchen while Teri worked on her display, filling the shelves with her lotions and natural soaps. It was almost noon before she emerged from the shop to inspect my yellow kitchen walls.

"That's perfect!" Then she eyed the counter with distaste. "What are you going to do with that?"

"As little as possible. This is an expensive project setting up a store."

She ran her hand over the worn countertop. "Maybe later."

So why was I painting this place and putting so much work in it if I had packed up to leave? I could hear Mom repeating her favorite adage: If you think you can or you think you can't—either way, you're right. Teri's voice interrupted my epiphany.

"I need to go pick up the heathens."

"Did you mark all of your items? And I need an inventory list."

"On your desk, Mom. The CD marked Teri's Inventory." The impish grin belied the sarcasm in the voice. "I'm so excited! How soon do you think we'll be open?"

71

"Well, the guys who're repaving the driveway haven't given me an exact date yet. I called them a week ago. And I still have to find a roofing company."

"Let me take care of that! Let me know what you want and your budget! I'll—"

"I know! You have a cousin who does that."

"Well, not exactly, but I bet I can find someone who'll give us a bargain." Teri pulled out her pad and pen and handed it to me.

"Why do I feel like I'm being railroaded?" I grinned in case she didn't know I was teasing, took the pad, and wrote down some numbers that would keep me on my budget. Kevin and I hadn't needed to buy a house and hadn't been married long enough to spend much of our savings. We'd each held a good paying job, and I still had half of the nest egg Aunt Rose had left me. I would have Kevin's life insurance later. Still, I wanted to be frugal until the store either thrived or bombed. With the economy, who could know?

"That's about what I'd planned," I told her, handing her the pad.

She looked at it, pursed her lips for a second, and then nodded as if agreeing with herself. "Yep, I can get it done cheaper than that," she said and returned the pad to her purse. "So what are you doing for lunch? I don't see your usual picnic lunch anywhere."

"I forgot it today, but that's—"

"Meet the brats and me at McDonalds. A little grease and carbs will restore your energy!" She slipped out the door then peeked back in for a moment. "Besides, I get tired of having to crawl up those tunnels to break up their wars. You're thinner."

"I have paint on me!"

"Wash off what you can," she called. "You redheads look good in yellow!"

It felt lonely listening to the crunching of her tires as she drove off. I changed out of my paint shirt, scrubbed my arms and face, and pulled on capris and a top. On my way out the door, I turned to pat Flash, who had found her place in the center of my bed. "You keep an eye on things. I'll be back soon."

She blinked and made herself into a tighter ball of fur on the bed. I glanced at the window I'd opened earlier and crossed the room to close it.

But when I tried to lock it, the catch looked odd. Bent just a bit—as if someone had pried it open.

My early morning wariness returned as I scanned the room looking for signs of an intruder. I noticed a drawer that hadn't been pushed in straight. Had I left it that way? Was the bed quilt rumpled a bit? Were—?

"Stop it!" I realized I'd spoken aloud when Flash raised her head and meowed inquiringly. I shook my head, hoping to slow my imagination. Then I turned back to the window, pushed the lock in place, then grabbed my purse. My heartbeat drummed in my ears and my chest hurt as I moved through the store and house, checking each window and door. Finished, I swallowed and stepped outside, walking quickly to the Jeep.

Don't be afraid, a gentle voice whispered from the past. *A little fear isn't a bad thing because it makes you cautious. But it shouldn't steal your life. Life's an adventure.*

On the way into town, I called John again and listened as the call went to voice mail again. Maybe he'd gone on a photo shoot. Spring is the time he chases the loons, I remembered. I'd spoken to him just after I'd shot the crime scene for Randall Byrd, and he'd reassured me then that my trail was growing colder by the moment. I just prayed he was right.

CHAPTER TWENTY

I'd not slept much last night. After lunching with Teri and the twins, I'd returned to the store and unloaded and unpacked my things. Flash and I couldn't camp out in the B&B forever! Then I'd called Mrs. Sanchez to reassure her that Flash and I were fine, promised to visit her soon, and invited her out to the store.

My cell phone had awakened me. As I answered, I glanced at the time. Surely, it wasn't eight o'clock!

"Ms. Janes?"

I cleared my throat. "Speaking." My head ached from lack of sleep, surpassed only by my aching arms.

"I hope you're free today. This is Randall Byrd and I need a photographer."

"As a matter of fact—"

"We're running a feature Sunday on the recent crime here. Sort of a 'here's where we are now' piece. It will likely take a couple of days. You'll be working with Jason." I vaguely remembered a thin kid with a scraggly beard and glasses who was a decent writer.

"What other stories are you running?"

"Well, there's some school news and a couple of those sorts."

"Those would be more my style."

I realized after a second or two that Mr. Byrd hadn't answered me. "Sir?"

"Call me Randy. And we both know where your talent lies. I need someone who can pull the reader into this article, speak to us through the photos. You can do that." He paused briefly before continuing. "I'll see that you get a small feature when your store opens—so people will relate the photography they've seen in the paper to your store."

It was a persuasive argument. Free advertisement would help my budget. "When do you need me?" I finally asked. "I have someone coming this morning to start on my roof and another crew starting on the parking area."

"Jason wants to start around noon. The hotel where Stephanie worked doesn't want their maids disturbed until the rooms are cleaned. I'll give him your number and let the two of you set up the schedule. And use your digital camera." He hung up before I could answer.

By the time Jason arrived, the roofers had already torn off the old shingles and were pounding overhead. In the background, a hydraulic hammer pummeled the small asphalt patch that had been the parking area, breaking it into pieces that could be picked up with a front loader and dropped into the dumpster. As Jason parked out of the way, I headed outside to cancel.

"You can see that I can't leave. I tried to tell Mr. Byrd—"

"No problem," Jason interrupted. "Teri is on her way to watch over things for you.'"

And, as if his speaking the words were magic, Teri's van pulled in. In typical Teri style, she was chattering long before she reached us. "I've found the most wonderful potter, Sorrel! She lives about 50 miles away, out on a ranch, and she came by the paper to pay her bill. We got to talking—"

"Why am I not surprised?" Jason muttered.

Teri glared at him. "Anyway, I mentioned your store—"

Jason gave a loud sigh. "She'll love hearing it all when we get back. I don't need to take her on a shoot with her eardrums on overload."

Teri made a face. "Why do I get the feeling that people think I talk too much? I'll remember that the next time I'm making chili rellenos."

"I'm the one who talks too much," Jason exclaimed. "Remember that when you're cooking—anything!"

Before I could say anything, Teri herded me and my cameras into Jason's car.

"I'll make sure these guys don't slack off," she said. "Besides, I'll have help carrying my boxes of products into the store."

Jason was quiet and unimposing and hardly looked old enough to be out of high school. He had an inviting smile, though, and I watched the housekeeping supervisor where Stephanie had worked warm up to him before he could even ask a question. He'd outlined the photos he wanted shot during our ride over, encouraging me to take any others I thought might be better.

I snapped the supervisor's cautious look as she answered his first question.

"Stephanie worked here longer than me," she said, "and I've been here eleven years. I heard somewhere that this was the only job she'd ever had. And she only missed a couple of days in the whole time she was working. Sweet but sorta odd."

"Do you know whether or not she was dating anyone? Did she seem worried about anything?"

"No, she never mentioned a boyfriend, and she didn't seem different from how she always was. She had always been private. I mean, she would speak to everyone and sometimes smile at what they said, but she didn't offer much conversation." I thought of the smile as she waltzed.

According to the supervisor, Stephanie hadn't gone out with any of the other housekeepers. The only thing she'd ever done was go dancing over at Bart's. She had always hummed some dance tune as she worked.

Jason waited a moment while the supervisor answered a call from the front desk. Then he asked about Stephanie's family.

"I don't even know if she had a family. She usually worked the holidays—never wanted off except for New Year's so she could go to Bart's big celebration dance every year. She just came to work and went about her life. She was just a very private person." She clearly had told all she knew and wanted to finish up. "I'm sorry. I wish I could help you, but I can't. I've told the other housekeepers that if they want to talk to you to drop by the break room. They should be there soon."

Jason thanked her and turned to his left. I tagged along, wondering if the supervisor's careful make-up had been for our benefit.

"Wait!"

We turned around. The supervisor smiled prettily at Jason. "I do remember someone saying that she had talked about maybe falling in love and getting married someday. That seemed odd since she really didn't talk about a boyfriend or anything. She was a hard worker but just sort of stayed in her own world." She shrugged. "I'd think she'd be the least likely to be murdered."

The women who had worked with Stephanie had little to add. One girl, Carla, remembered a necklace that she'd worn once—a small heart with a stone in it. She had blushed when asked about it but didn't give any details. "I just mentioned it because she didn't wear jewelry—most of us don't here at work—but one day she had it and then she wore it every day. I noticed because she touched it sometimes when she was idle. Then one day she didn't have it."

Before we left, I took a few photos of the outside of the motel. I really couldn't see where this was going. The police had surely been over all of this.

Stephanie's apartment had been cleaned up, so there was little need to visit it; but Jason wanted to talk with her neighbors. "You don't need me there then," I said.

"Probably not. But would you mind just going along? I'd like to get these interviews done and detouring to take you home might make me miss someone."

When we walked up to the apartment complex, his real reason for wanting me there surfaced. An older, suspicious face peered through the safety-chained door at his first knock. "Who's there?"

"Jason and Sorrel from the newspaper. We're doing a feature on Stephanie, the girl who lived next door, and we'd like to visit with you about her."

"I didn't know her." We heard scraping as the latch opened and she peeked out. Her eyes lighted first on me and then on Jason. Then she opened the door a bit wider.

"She lived here a long time, according to the landlord." Jason smiled invitingly.

"You seem like a neighborly person. Didn't you ever talk with her in passing?"

"A little." The door opened further to reveal a small, skeletal woman I suspected had already seen her eightieth birthday. "I'm supposed to look at an ID," she announced.

"That's wise." He pulled out his newspaper photo ID, which she took and studied at length. Then she looked at me.

"I work part time," I said. "So I don't have a paper ID. But I have my driver's license." I dug into my bag and handed it to her.

"Pretty," she said. Then she turned and beckoned for us to follow her. "I can't see a thing without my glasses." I heard Jason smother a chuckle.

The tiny apartment smelled old, but it looked neat enough. Framed photos cluttered the small side tables and hung on the walls. Colorful afghans were draped on the sofa and the well-worn rocker-recliner. She clicked off a television blaring one of those court room dramas and motioned for us to sit on the sofa. And, being a good hostess, she offered us something to drink, which we declined as graciously as we could.

Jason quickly jumped into the article. "We want to let people know who Stephanie was," he began. "We want to try to understand how this horrible thing could have happened to her. Would you mind if I used a recorder, so I can quote you correctly?"

She straightened in her chair a bit. "Well, yes. I'm Frances. Spelled with an 'e,' you know. With an 'i' is the masculine version. But everyone calls me Frannie. Last name is Birton." She spelled that out as well, her eyes on the recorder Jason had set on his knee.

"Did Stephanie know you by name?"

"Yes. She always spoke to me when she saw me. One time she came into my apartment. I had dropped a bag of books and she carried them in for me."

"Did she ever mention where she was from or anything about her family?"

"Well, no. We didn't know each other that way, don't you know? We were just neighbors. She went to work almost every day, and I go to the Senior Center, to church, and sometimes to my daughter's house. You just caught me here today because my daughter has an appointment and rescheduled our visit. So we were only home at night at the same time. She liked to go dancing of a night on the weekends. She talked about that."

"Did she have friends over often?"

"I'm sure I don't know about her social life. I never heard anything. I mind my own business. And she minded hers."

While he'd been asking questions, I'd snapped a couple of shots. I wanted to catch the play of emotions, but she seemed more aware of the camera than I would have liked. Jason clearly was not eliciting anything new from her.

He'd come to the same conclusion. "Well, thank you for the time, Ms. Birton." He rose, turned, and then halted when she reached out and caught his hand.

"It's Birton with an 'i,' remember."

An hour after we'd arrived, we left the apartment complex and headed out the highway to the store. "Not much there," Jason said. "Nothing to make you even look at this person twice. Obviously, her murder was just an act of random violence. I don't know why Mr. Byrd wants a feature on her. Human interest, I guess."

"I know how I'd do it."

"How?"

"I'd play up the mystery."

"What mystery?"

"Here's some woman, working in a low-end job, living in a low-rent apartment complex, seemingly living her life without harming anyone, kind to the elderly neighbor and then she's murdered and dumped in the trash. What did she ever do to attract that sort of violence? How sad that the only time we noticed her was after she was dead."

Turning into the driveway, Jason pulled off to the side to avoid the barricaded parking area and stared at me. "You need to be on this side of the story," he said. "That's a brilliant angle."

"Not really," I said. "Unfortunately, it happens all the time. Some people live on the edge, while others burrow comfortably into their lives. It's always a mystery when they're the ones who are murdered." I gathered my equipment. "Are we done?"

"No. I want to visit Bart's this evening. About seven?"

"Sure. What's your deadline for this thing?"

"As soon as possible. Byrd wants it for the weekend paper, including your photos. I'll be by about six-thirty."

CHAPTER TWENTY-ONE

The roofers hadn't quite finished, but they were gone. So was Teri. I walked around to the back of the house with my camera equipment, making note of my surroundings as I'd learned to do.

A note taped to the back door from Teri assured me that the roofers would finish in the morning and the parking crew would come to stripe the parking spaces. She hoped I liked what she'd done in the store.

As soon as I relocked the door behind me, I walked through every room, checking locks, angry that I felt compelled to do so. When would this end? Would I ever regain my old self-assurance?

I punched redial on my cellphone. Still no answer. It didn't mean anything was wrong, I reminded myself. John wasn't the sort to stay at home. Still . . . maybe it was time for step two in our cautionary communications plan.

I sat on the bed, opened my laptop, then turned to Facebook. I'd joined the online group under the name Walden Pond. Possibly people would think I was male or an English teacher with the oblique reference to Thoreau. John had signed up as Dwight D. Eisenhower. A less likely political creature than any I'd ever met, John also hoped for anonymity.

"I fish daily and lift my face to the clouds," I wrote on my update. Then I scanned the ongoing chat and updates.

"Poetic there, Walden!" Suzy Q commented under my message. Nothing from Eisenhower. Maybe he wasn't on just yet, but he would get a notice that a message had been sent. When he saw it, he'd know that I was waiting for a message.

Flash leaped into my lap and started kneading. "Ouch!" I lifted her down and stood. She headed toward the kitchen. "You little pig! We've hardly moved here and you already know the route to the kitchen."

I left Flash lapping at her dish and walked into the store.

"Wow!"

Teri had turned her area of the shop into a desert oasis, using pastels, miniature pots of cacti, and clever arrangements. On the top shelf, she'd placed a small electric fountain that resembled a waterfall. I pulled out my cell and called her.

"Hi!" She sounded breathless.

"I'm looking at your display. Wow!"

"You like it?"

"No, I love it! And I'm so glad you chose the back corner of the store for your display because it draws your eye from the moment you walk through the door. It lures you to browse through the whole store. And it makes me anxious to get even more artisans. I'm going back to the Senior Center tomorrow to recruit. Are you free to go along? I wouldn't mind a second eye."

"Let me check the schedule. Oh, don't forget that lady with the pots that I was telling you—boys!" Something crashed in the background, followed by an angry howl. "I'd better go referee!"

I joined Flash in the kitchen. She had plenty of food, but I had not had time to go to the grocery store for me. I munched on peanut butter and crackers, with an apple for dessert, all the time thinking about the steaks they served at Bart's. But I didn't expect Jason or, more accurately, Mr. Byrd to be buying me a meal tonight.

I took a quick shower and changed. Bart's had been fairly casual that Saturday night and during the week would likely be more so. Besides, I'd left anything more formal far behind. Dressed in jeans, flats, and a navy polo, I pulled my hair into a pony tail and smeared on lip gloss. There, I shouldn't attract too much attention, I thought, as I checked my appearance in the mirror. Carrying the camera would more than do that for me. By the time Jason arrived, I'd added a light-weight khaki jacket.

"I've been thinking about what you said," he said, as we pulled onto the main road. He'd dressed much as I—jeans, an open-necked sports shirt, and cowboy boots, of course. "We need photos that reflect her and that last night—where she liked to sit, the dance floor, that sort of thing."

"The barstool. I'll bet it was the same one every time."

"You knew her?"

"No. I just happened to visit Bart's for the first time on the night she was killed."

"Man! Guess the cops have had plenty to say to you."

"Yeah, but I really didn't see anything. And I do not want my name mentioned in the paper," I said more emphatically than I realized. At his surprised look, I softened my tone. "Look, I did notice her—I notice people—she was interesting, but that's all."

"So tell me about her as you saw her."

"Well, she was different." I told him about the school jacket and her sitting on the barstool and bobbing her head in time to the music. And I mentioned that she was asked to dance often.

"She must have been a good dancer then," Jason said

"That's the thing. She wasn't really. I mean, I watched her waltz with this young cowboy and it was sort of like she was a stuffed doll and he just hauled her around the floor. She wasn't smiling or anything. Just had this spaced out look on her face."

"That's weird," he said, as we pulled into Bart's driveway. "Why would anyone kill her?"

"Why does anyone kill anyone?" A shiver ran up my spine. "You know, Reed brought me here the other day just sure that I wasn't telling him everything—or maybe hoping I'd remember something."

"Did you?"

"No. Have you been in the bar on a Saturday night? It's dark and noisy and I didn't know anyone there. I did remember smelling a cigar behind me, but that was the only new bit of information. And that doesn't strike me as anything that could solve the murder."

Jason cut the ignition and I reached into the back for my camera bag. "You know," he said, "it's not dark yet. Why don't you snap a picture of the dumpster?"

We headed across the parking lot and down the alley. The dumpster where she had been found was about halfway down the alley, a big oval rubber thing with a flexible lid. You wouldn't know there had ever been a crime by looking at it. I shuddered at the picture my mind conjured up, even as I snapped the camera.

Jason stopped me after the one shot. It was all he needed, if he used it at all. He really just wanted to get a feel for the place. We looked around a bit longer before heading back to Bart's.

"Must be dark at night. I can't imagine why she would've walked this way."

"It's a shortcut," Jason said. "Maybe one she took all the time."

"So the killer may have been someone she knew?"

"Usually, they are, aren't they? What do they say on those crime shows? Murder is usually about money or passion?"

My chest tightened. What had been the motivation for Kevin's murder?

Several more vehicles were now parked on the lot. Jason held the door for me and looked quizzically as we stepped into the familiar smoky, country western atmosphere. "You okay?" I nodded and smiled.

We nabbed a small table near the dining room door where I had sat before. I busied myself with the camera, making the adjustments necessary to work in this lighting.

"What can I get you to drink?" It was the waitress.

"Dr. Pepper," Jason said and looked at me.

"Diet Coke." Most of the customers were in the dining room, and I wanted to get the photos taken before they drifted into the bar. "Her stool is over there. The fourth one from the door."

"Okay, now how could you remember that?"

"No hidden talent, actually." I smiled and squatted down to line up a shot. "I was sitting at this table and she was in my line of vision when I looked this direction, which I did often because there was this really loud-mouthed guy three stools this direction who was telling stories about when he was in the Navy." I snapped several shots and then scooted to get another angle.

"You have a reporter's brain." The drinks had arrived and Jason was sipping his.

"Me? Not at all. I'm just nosy. I notice trivial details." I turned toward him, grinning, and felt my face tighten. Standing beside him was Reed, his eyes admiring the curve of my tight jeans. I did my best to seem nonchalant. "Hi. Fancy seeing you here."

His eyes gleamed. "My pleasure," he replied, touching the brim of his hat in that courtly cowboy style.

"What else do you want, Jason? The dance floor?" There was no live music tonight, but two couples had already stepped out onto the floor and swayed to the country love song playing through the sound system.

"Sure. Reed, you want to join us?" The waitress bringing Jason another soda paused.

"Coffee," he said, nodding to her as he pulled a third chair to the table and sat down beside Jason.

"Glad you're here, Reed. I have a question or two."

I focused on my shooting and closed out the sounds. Thirty minutes later, I felt I'd gotten the shots we needed. The place had begun to fill up; and curious eyes had begun to penetrate my concentration, making it difficult to get clear shots. After returning my camera to its bag, I sat down at the table and picked up my glass. Most of the ice had melted, but it still tasted cool. I finished it in one long drink.

"Photography must be thirsty work," Reed commented, achieving his intended goal.

I nodded coolly. "Are we about finished, Jason?"

"How about a dance?" Reed continued as if I hadn't spoken.

"I don't—"

"It's a waltz."

"I'll settle up for our drinks and make a quick trip to the little room down the hall while you guys waltz." Surely Jason could read my expression.

Reed stood up and offered his hand.

He was a surprisingly good dance partner. Some men, while good dancers, were lousy dance partners, dragging their partners around like baggage—sort of like Stephanie!

"What's wrong? Step on your toe?" Reed questioned my hesitation.

"No." We swirled for the final measure of the waltz.

As we walked back, Reed kept his hand lightly on my back. I stopped short of our table, seeing Jason standing, my camera bag slung over his shoulder, and turned to Reed. "The cowboy she was dancing with? He was a good dancer, but he was a lousy partner. He slung her around as if she couldn't step on her own. It's so sad that her last dance was with that sort of guy."

He looked at me searchingly for just a moment. "Thank you."

That night, after I'd checked Facebook again and found nothing, I snuggled in bed with Flash. "I'm tired of being this victim," I told her. "I'm not going to be slung around on the dance floor of my life any longer. Starting tomorrow, you and I are taking charge of our lives! We were never cut out to be 'fraidy cats!"

Flash purred agreement and closed her eyes. But for quite a while I lay there, hearing Reed's "thank you" and thinking about what he meant.

CHAPTER TWENTY-TWO

I'd delivered Jason's photos and spent the last couple of hours at the Senior Center, recruiting new consignees for the store. Four of the seniors had agreed almost instantly to place their crafts with me, thrilled that I not only appreciated the quality of their work but also was willing to give them a chance to earn a little money. One of the women who everyone called Granny said I'd given her a "whole new reason to get up in the morning." I felt humble at that. Little did she know that she and the other consignees were giving me a chance at a new life.

When I drove into my driveway, I found I'd returned home just in time to write checks for the roofers and parking lot stripers. They'd done great work and Teri had found me great prices. Still, my heart fluttered as I looked at the new balance in my checking account. I needed to get my store open—and soon. Tourist season was approaching. And Teri had assured me that, although this area didn't have a huge draw, the neighboring towns and the state park close by brought a steady flow.

After the workers left, I checked my Facebook account. "Sunny skies here. Cool and clear." It was the message I'd been hoping to see each time I'd checked since my posting. Dwight D. Eisenhower, my photographer friend, was reassuring me that all was safe. My identity had not been discovered. No one had followed me here as far as the police knew.

I took a deep breath to relax and suddenly bolted upright in my chair. If all was safe, who was the friend who had dropped by the B&B? And who was that mysterious deputy sheriff who had visited me here? Were they the same person? What did they want? I so wanted to believe my friend's message but couldn't ignore all the unanswered questions, questions that went beyond my security in Saddle Gap.

Had Kevin's murder really been a random home invasion? Or had he been targeted? Or was I the target, as the authorities believed?

"Hello!" I jumped at the sound of a woman's voice. "Sorrel? Where are you?"

Teri. Thank goodness. I got up and poked my head around the door, hoping I didn't look as panicked as I was.

"Out here!"

As usual, she entered the room in a whirl of chatter. "I've got Uncle Ramon here with the shelving you ordered. He brought a couple of his boys to help unload. Can you unlock the front door?"

When I saw the display shelves Teri brought for her display, I'd known they were perfect for the rest of the shop. Never did I expect Uncle Ramon to finish them so quickly! Then, again, it was Teri's family. Once they had their minds set, they jumped into a project and it was finished! The men unloaded the units, placed them, and were on their way out of the store before Teri could tell me all the news.

"Don't forget about Sunday," Uncle Ramon reminded Teri as he left. I looked at her quizzically.

"Just another one of our get-togethers. Uncle Ramon is hosting this time," Teri said, as she admired her uncle's work.

The idea of that kind of family life appealed to me. I'd been much younger than my brother—half-brother, actually—and after my dad died he had moved to his mother's. I had been seven and I'd never seen him since. He'd contacted Mama a time or two after he joined the military then drifted away. Mama said his mother resented the fact that my dad had gotten primary custody. I didn't even know where he lived. Except for my mama's godparents out here, I knew almost nothing about my family.

"Do you like them?" Teri fidgeted. For the first time since I'd known her, she sounded anxious.

"I love them!" I scanned the room. Even with the five new shelving units, I had room for a comfortably wide aisle down the middle and on each side. And I could still put in a table or two so that everything wouldn't look too uniform.

"By putting them at a slant, you can also watch for shoplifters," Teri continued.

I grimaced.

"I know, but I think you need one of those cameras. They're not expensive and even if you never save the film, you have a deterrent."

"I'm actually ahead of you on this one, Teri. I've already ordered one. Security, you know."

But, of course, she didn't know. When the police suggested we install added security devices at home, Kevin had agreed. I'd thought it unnecessary. As an investigative reporter, I'd followed many stories that made people uncomfortable or turned them into enemies. But my job had never spilled over into my life.

Spilled. Kevin's battered body and blood. The blood was—

"Are you all right?" Teri's voice had become quieter yet more forceful. "You need to sit down, Sorrel. You look really pale." She put her arm around my shoulder and started guiding me toward the small area in back.

"Sorry." I reached around her shoulder and gave her a little hug. "I just get so excited about getting the shop going I sometimes forget to eat." I tried to smile. "Want to share lunch?" I let go of her shoulder and took a step toward the back of the store when I stopped myself and turned around to lock the front doors. After making sure they were secure, I again started toward the kitchen.

I smiled at Teri, but I could see in her eyes that she wasn't sure if I was okay or not.

While I made a sandwich—Teri had passed on the chicken salad— and filled two glasses with iced tea, Teri looked through my newest acquisitions, making suggestions about how they might best be displayed and about possible prices. As we sat as the table discussing various ideas, she even agreed that my decision to paint the shelves a soft cream color for displaying these wares was better than the vibrant colors she had suggested.

"Do you know when you'll be opening?" she asked, as I finished my last bit of sandwich.

"I'd originally planned on Memorial Day, but everything has gone so quickly. Who would have thought the rundown place I accepted title to a few weeks ago would look like this?" The living quarters were finished and the other structural changes to the store had been completed except for the sign outside and the security cameras. I had appointments to get those done right away. I just wasn't sure I had enough merchandise.

Teri agreed but thought that after I hung my own photos, I'd have enough to open. As I took another bite of my sandwich, Teri ran through the list of all the merchandise I already had and the consignees who still had to deliver their goods.

"What if I open next week while I'm finishing up some details?" I asked. "Sort of a practice run, you know, to get accustomed to the whole operation. Then I could advertise the Grand Opening for Memorial Day when I would have more merchandise and could put out some advertisement."

Teri took a sip of tea, as she mulled over the idea. "That's really clever. I like it, Sorrel. Maybe you could just open three or four days a week until the Grand Opening. I could come in a morning or two to help."

I could hardly believe how much I'd—we'd—done in such a short time! How could I have managed without Teri and her family?

Teri took a last sip of tea and took her glass over to the sink. "I've got to get going."

"Teri, I—"

"Don't tell me anything, Sorrel. Not yet." She placed her hand on mine. "I know I'm the world's biggest chatterbox. Sometimes things just fly out of my mouth, especially to Jose. I see the haunted sadness in your eyes, the caution in your speech, and the watchfulness in your every move. It's hard for me to wait, but I don't want to know until you are truly ready to tell me." Suddenly she giggled. "You can't know how hard that was to say. My natural nosy self is bubbling over inside to know absolutely everything." We both laughed. "You know, I hope, that if I can help—"

"I do." My cell phone rang and Teri, pointing to her watch, made a hasty exit. I carried my dishes to the sink before answering.

"John! I was getting worried about you."

"I've been down in Florida shooting flamingoes for a calendar job. Just got home. Your note on Facebook, problems?"

I tried to explain what was going on as quickly as I could: Stephanie's murder, my role both as photographer and suspect, the mysterious stranger, and the shop.

"Whew!" he said. "Staying out of sight seems to be almost impossible for you."

"I know. I've wished a dozen times I hadn't gone to Bart's that night."

John asked me the same questions I'd been asking myself: Who could the mysterious guy be? Whether he and the fake deputy sheriff were one in the same? My answers remained the same: I didn't know.

None of John's contacts had notified him of anyone who might be following me or who had been checking up on me. But he advised me to be cautious. "Are you installing security in that store? Is it too far out of town to be safe?"

"Yes to the first; no to the second."

He chuckled. "I guess I do sound like a mother hen. Ironic, as I have no chicks."

"I am trying to be safe," I insisted, "but I won't make any more changes to my life, John. Enough is enough!"

"I hear you. But let me check with our friend. Just to see if he's heard anything."

We chatted a few minutes more, catching up on his trip and the more mundane aspects of my life. I even promised I'd find someone to help in the store just to have an extra body there, even though I doubted I'd need it. But it would be nice to have someone to cover the store when I wanted to do a photo shoot—or maybe I just wasn't as gutsy as I'd like to think.

CHAPTER TWENTY-THREE

"Sorrel, I just wanted to call you personally to let you know how much I like those photos you shot for Jason's story. I wish you had let us give you a byline though. You know, it could have given you some good publicity for your little shop."

Even though Mr. Byrd's offer had been generous, the last thing I needed was something to draw more attention to me as a journalist. Besides, I didn't want my store connected with a crime spree. He eventually seemed to understand.

Before ending the call, he reminded me that I had promised to shoot photos at the upcoming Cinco de Mayo celebration and suggested I contact the school to submit my name for consideration when they selected their photographer. Yearbook photos, sporting events, prom? Not likely, I thought, but I thanked him and we ended the call cordially. I didn't mind his small newspaper jobs, but my new future was in nature photography.

I glanced at the box of ink drawings sitting on the seat next to me. Mr. Byrd had caught me halfway home from the national park on the Arizona border. I'd arrived just before sunrise and snapped glorious photos of the sky, the mountains silhouetted against it. Through the morning, I'd snapped a variety of birds, deer, and a wild goat or two. Then, during lunch at a rustic café in the back of a general store, I'd met a couple of retired teachers from Maryland who had rented a nearby cabin for the winter. They had captured hummingbirds and other desert critters in small ink drawings and watercolors. And now I had a box of them to add to my inventory.

It was as perfect a day as I could have wanted—until Mr. Byrd's call. I hadn't thought of anything more than the pleasure of the park's beautiful settings. Now, once again, my thoughts had turned to murder.

Back in Saddle Gap, I stopped at the Quick Stop and picked up some milk and a copy of the paper. At the bottom of the front page was a notation and small photo advertising Stephanie's story in the Life Times section. I was tempted to read it right there in the parking lot, but Flash was waiting for some company. Besides, I wanted to read it at leisure.

My cell rang just as I opened a can of food for Flash. I checked the ID before answering. "Just a minute, John. I can't hear you over this yowling, starving creature." I chuckled, expecting to hear him laugh as well, but he didn't. I dumped Flash's food in her dish as quickly as I could.

"What's wrong, John?"

"Maybe nothing."

"You wouldn't have called if it were nothing."

Still he waited. Then he cleared his throat. "Someone has been snooping around."

"About him?" Silence. "Me?"

"I think we should cancel the Facebook accounts."

"But nothing's showing up on it in either of our names."

"Yeah, maybe you're right." I could almost hear him thinking. "You're not online anywhere else, are you?"

"No. My business files are on computer, but I don't have a website or anything. Have you spoken to our friend?" Even though we were using disposable phones, John and I avoided using names whenever we could. "Friend" had become our name for law enforcement.

"Yes."

"I told you about the one here who checked up on me after the incident."

"Yes, but this occurred yesterday."

Yesterday. Images of the stranger who had shown up at my door flashed through my mind. "It couldn't have been the same one then."

"No, this inquiry doesn't seem to have come from a friend. It's time to take care again. "

"I will."

"I called because you asked me . . . ." He hesitated, choosing his words. "I don't want anything to happen to you, but . . ."

When the silence drew out too long, I finished for him. "Life is an adventure."

"Yeah. Take care."

Take care. Wasn't that what I had been doing? My pulse was racing and I felt this incredible urge to run—anywhere! Tucson. I could reach Tucson if I drove west through the night!

I raced into the bedroom, pulled a suitcase from the closet, threw it on the bed, and opened it.

"Meow?" Flash hopped up into the suitcase and blinked at me.

What a cute photo! If I put it on notecards, I bet they'd sell really well!

"Meow?"

What? I stopped and looked at Flash. Then I surveyed my pretty bedroom. Did I really want to run again and leave the people here, my new friends, my new dreams, my new home all behind? Why was I panicking? I picked Flash up and snuggled close. "We're not going anywhere," I whispered. "Your mama is just a little hysterical at times."

Later, as I buttered bread for a grilled cheese sandwich, I reasoned there was no need for panic. In spite of the caution I'd taken after Kevin's murder, nothing had ever surfaced connecting the creeps I'd been investigating to me.

And Kevin? An oil company executive? He got out in the field, but a large portion of his time was spent in the office, on the golf course, or conducting business over dinner. I smiled at the thought of him being involved in anything connected to intrigue or murder. Had I smiled? I added sliced tomatoes to the plate with my sandwich and poured a glass of milk. As I took my plate to the table, Flash gazed longingly at the glass of milk in my hand. I poured a tiny taste into her bowl and sat down to continue my self-pep talk.

Someone could have been checking up on me for any number of things. In fact, it was probably Reed. He was nosy by nature, so maybe he was just snooping and using unofficial sources to do so. Yes, that's all it was.

It was only after Flash and I had settled into bed that night that I remembered the newspaper article. I grabbed the paper from my night stand and turned to the Life Times section.

Jason had led with the photo of the dumpster. It had been overfilled when I photographed it, a couple of bags spilling their contents onto the ground in front. I glanced at the story.

LOCAL WOMAN'S MURDER STILL YESTERDAY'S GARBAGE

by Jason Halloway

Only last week, Stephanie Brown's lifeless body lay wedged behind bags of garbage in this dumpster in the alley behind Bart's Bar and Grill where she had spent the night before dancing. Witnesses think she left the bar about midnight. She likely walked into the alley as a short cut, something she had done many times. Sadly, this had been her last short cut.

Police detectives have few leads in Stephanie's murder. She lived a quiet life. A hotel maid by day, she was a nice, friendly neighbor to those in her apartment complex and a frequent visitor to Bart's on Live Music Nights. No motive for her death has been identified.

Jason had included quotes from her supervisor and a couple of neighbors, and he'd sprinkled smaller photos on either side of his article. But it was the opening dumpster shot and the final shot—the empty dance floor—that set the tone of his article.

As I looked at it, I remembered once more watching her dance. She really hadn't been a good dancer, but she didn't seem to care. Neither did her partners. Of course, some of them had been too drunk to notice. That last dance, she had seemed like a lifeless doll, flung around in the waltz by that young cowboy. Had she known him? What had she been thinking? Surely this woman was a hapless victim. Like Kevin? Like me?

I sucked in a quick breath. Victim? Me? Yes, I had been acting like a victim. I'd tossed everything in my—new vehicle—and run. True, I'd had plenty of encouragement to do so, but for the first time I wondered if I'd relied too heavily on well-meaning advice and warnings. And now that I had started a new life—one that I was fast realizing had touched back on dreams I'd had so many years ago—I was allowing myself to feel like a victim once more. Even if danger lurked, I had to face it or I'd be jumping every time I heard a noise for the rest of my life.

I patted Flash's warm body curled against my thigh. "Flash, you and I aren't hapless victims. We're not 'fraidy cats! We're women—strong and brave and full of dreams. We aren't going to have any more life stolen from us." She blinked up at me, yawned, and coiled tighter.

My early morning hours and all the drama in my life had left me exhausted. But as I drifted off to sleep, a plan had already begun to form in my mind. "The best defense is a good offense," I murmured.

CHAPTER TWENTY-FOUR

"What sort of sign do you want?" The young man had shown me a variety of choices and now waited with poised pen. Of course, my budget was dictating much of my choice.

"I won't be open late, so I really don't think I need a lighted sign."

"Okay." He flipped through his sample book. "But you're off the road a bit, so you need something taller that can be seen from a longer distance."

I nodded as I studied several samples. I had finally chosen a new name for my shop, Uniquely Yours, because everything in it would be handcrafted. No two items could be exactly alike. My new sign had to exemplify that as well.

As I turned another page in the sample book, the sign nearly jumped off the page at me. It was perfect! An old-fashioned needlework sampler, framed, sitting atop a tall pole. "That's it!" I beamed. The salesman was relieved.

I paid the deposit and he left just as the security company arrived to install the cameras. As they started indoors, I stepped out to look at the spot we'd just chosen for the sign. The salesman had promised installation the next day. Now I just needed to frame my own photos and place them around the store and everything would be ready to open.

By midafternoon I had matted a variety of prints and sorted them according to types: critters, landscapes, buildings, and random shots of objects. My favorite, a small bird perched atop an ancient fence post, would be a good shot to reduce and put on notecards. Looking at it made me happy. But before I did that, I had to finish framing the rest of the photos.

My cell rang, interrupting me just as I'd started cutting the next matt. I answered automatically, without checking the ID.

"Sorrel? It's Reed. I need you to meet me—"

"Can't. I've got guys here installing security cameras."

"Put the coffee on."

I stared at the phone, hearing only the dial tone. He'd hung up without letting me reply. Who did he think he was?

A few minutes later, I heard his truck drive up and him come in through the back door. I purposely kept measuring and cutting frames.

"You didn't make coffee," he said. Apparently, he expected me to obey his orders.

"I didn't want any."

When he didn't answer, I glanced over my shoulder. He stood with his arms crossed, his eyes focused on the seat of my worn, tight jeans. I straightened up as casually as I could, laid down my tools, and turned to face him. "I have iced tea in the refrigerator."

"It's too warm for coffee anyway." He dropped his arms to his side and followed me into the kitchen.

I'd placed the pitcher and glasses on the counter and had just begun to pick up one of the glasses when he came up behind me. "Let me do it," he said. "You look like you've had a busy day."

"All right. I need to check on the guys out in the shop. I'll just be a minute." And I left, walking as confidently as I could.

The workmen had already begun clearing up their tools and leftover materials. The older one smiled when he saw me. "We're done here. I've got a booklet for you to read about how this system operates. If it's confusing to you, just call and I'll come back out and demonstrate it for you."

"I've had one of these systems before."

"Shouldn't be a problem then, but if you do have one, just call." He stuck out his hand and smiled. "Appreciate the business."

I let the men out the front door of the store, locked it, and looked at the keypad beside it. I'd need to get the code down before I set it, but it looked straightforward enough.

Reed had made himself at home at the kitchen table, half of his tea glass already empty. "Sun tea," he said.

"The best kind," I agreed, sliding into the chair across from him. "So what's up?"

He looked around the kitchen. "You've done a lot to this old house in a short time. When do you think you'll be open for business?"

"Soon. I could use more merchandise, but the sign is going up tomorrow. And as you can see, I'm framing my own prints."

"Any more visits from your deputy sheriff?" He looked at me intently, his eyes probing.

"No."

"Odd that someone would warn you off like that. This place has been empty quite a while."

"Eight years." I drank thirstily from my glass, set it down, and held his eye. "Want to tell me what this is all about?"

"Want to tell me who you really are?" he countered.

"I'm exactly who I've always been, Reed. Do you make these sorts of accusations to all the new business owners in town?"

"For someone who is obviously a skilled forensic photographer, educated, and gorgeous, you've left almost no trail."

"Gorgeous?"

"And don't tell me no one has ever told you that." He stared at me for a long minute.

"You really did it! You checked me out!"

"You were one of the few people in that bar that no one knew," he said. "Of course, I ran your prints and made a quick check since you were working for the department that once. But since you've been so closed mouthed about yourself, and suspicious things keep occurring, I expanded the check a bit, more to get a feel for motives than anything else."

"Do you really think I killed that woman?" I asked.

"No, your timeline checks out. And although you're strong, I don't see you heaving her up into that dumpster on your own. She wasn't a lightweight." He rose, picked up the pitcher from the counter, and brought it over to the table. "More?" I nodded. He filled my glass, then his, and set the pitcher between us.

"She seemed like a nice person." I'd said that so often it was beginning to sound like a refrain.

He nodded. "I really came out here to ask you for a favor. Would you go dancing with me tomorrow night? Well, first we'd eat at Teri's—"

"Huh?" I sat up straight, my back against the back of the chair, my hands flat on the table. "No. No, I—"

"Just wait a minute and let me explain. Teri has this thing about trying to match me up. She's done it before. And she won't quit until we go out a few times and then tell her sorrowfully that we just aren't a match."

"And if we tell her right now?"

"She'll first keep trying to push us together, and then she'll stop inviting me over to eat those delicious enchiladas." He gazed mournfully. "And I'm awfully tired of my own poor cooking and restaurant food."

I couldn't help but giggle at this silly side of Reed that I'd not seen before. For the first time, I felt myself relax with him. "Why not just go over for dinner then? Why the dancing?" Before he could answer, my inner imp emerged. "Besides, you still aren't sure whether or not I'm an axe murderess."

He chuckled. "Because she and Jose want to double date—that's her story. Anyway, better to die full of her enchiladas than of my frozen pizzas."

CHAPTER TWENTY-FIVE

Dancing after eating Teri's enchiladas was a challenge. Thankfully, I'd worn a loose top over my tight jeans.

Reed and I line danced with Teri and Jose, chatted with some of the other patrons over drinks, and watched the other dancers. To anyone, even Teri, we appeared to be having a great time. "I don't know how you did it, Sorrel, but Reed's the most relaxed I've seen him in a long time," she told me when we went to the ladies' room.

I didn't have the heart to tell her that the whole evening was really a sham. Reed wasn't truly relaxed and the evening wasn't purely social. He'd been scanning the place regularly and watching me to see if I reacted to any of the voices I heard. I hadn't.

We'd returned to the table in time for a waltz—the last waltz, Teri told us. They needed to get home to the monsters!

Reed stood and slowly gathered me into his arms. As he guided me around the floor, I looked into his eyes and knew that we were both thinking of Stephanie and her last waltz. But not until we were driving home did either of us speak of Stephanie.

"I have to let the case go to the cold files," Reed said, staring straight ahead at the road. "But I'm not going to just let it drop."

"I'm glad."

"It just doesn't make any sense. She had to have seen something she shouldn't have seen or stumbled into something."

"What about that other man? The one I photographed for the newspaper?"

"What about him?"

"Do you think they're connected?"

"There's no evidence that they are."

We filled the rest of the drive with innocuous comments about the evening. The great food. The good music. The pleasant company.

When we arrived at the store, he drove to the back of the house. I said goodnight and opened the door to leave when he placed his hand on my shoulder. "Do you think we diverted Teri?"

I chuckled. "Sure." How naïve men could be!

Inside, I chattered to Flash as I slipped into my nightshirt, telling her about the fun and laughter that had filled the evening. Reed could be a great date when he wasn't being a cop. He was also a good dancer. It had been a long time since I'd spent so much time not feeling guilty about Kevin.

Kevin. Lying in bed, cuddling Flash, I revisited my favorite memories of Kevin. They weren't as sharp as they'd once been. As I remembered the short time we'd loved each other and shared our lives, I realized that we had already been drifting apart. Was anything forever?

I stroked Flash, her purring lulling me to sleep. My last thought was not of Kevin but of waltzing.

CHAPTER TWENTY-SIX

I stepped back and eyed the wall. Were the framed photos grouped appealingly? Should I group them by subject matter? On the walls on either side of the front doors, I'd hung landscape photos. Down the side walls, I'd hung critters and things: old barns, a tennis shoe lying beside a cactus, an abandoned car. At the back, I'd hung a few of my character shots.

I'd not framed too many of those. Not many people want to hang a stranger's photo in their homes or offices. Many of them I'd taken at the bridge where people cross from Mexico, others alongside the roadside or along walking trails. One I especially liked featured a weathered cowboy driving a renegade herd of horses. I liked the determined look on his face, the way he sat in the saddle as if he were glued there. I'd blown that photo into a long, narrow print to include the horses he was intent on steering into a waiting corral.

"I like that one too." Teri stood beside me. She smiled as she glanced around the store. "I like all of them."

As we started toward the kitchen, I glanced around the shop. It looked so much better than my dreams. The pottery display in the front corner Teri had been setting up all morning was so appealing. She had a real flair for creating beautiful visuals that drew the eye—and people tend to buy what they are attracted to. All I needed were some homemade jams and jellies, which were arriving in the next day or two, and everything would be just right.

"Sorrel?" Teri was already in the kitchen setting the table. The chicken had been cooking in the crockpot all morning and was ready to serve. I quickly rinsed and tore lettuce, sliced a red bell pepper, dumped sliced olives, and sprinkled spices over them. Then I sliced a loaf of bread and popped a few slices into the microwave as Teri began dishing up the chicken.

For a while, neither of us spoke, savoring not only the meal but the few minutes of relaxation. After Teri took the last bite of her second helping, I offered dessert, but neither of us had room. Still, we weren't ready to abandon our kitchen oasis just yet.

Between sips of tea, Teri eventually brought up our double date at Bart's. "How did you feel about our evening out?" she asked.

"It was fun even though I'm not very good at some of the country dances. Reed's a good dancer," I said before I could stop myself. I had promised myself not to mention him.

"You're probably curious about him. If I know Reed, he hasn't been very forthcoming about himself, has he?"

I shrugged.

Teri then began her brief biography of Chris Reed. He was a local boy, raised on one of the ranches in the area until his dad was killed when his horse stepped into a prairie dog hole and fell on him. Reed had been twelve at that time. He and his mother had tried to keep the ranch going, but when she was diagnosed with cancer, they had lost the ranch because of all the medical expenses. In high school, Reed had been a football hero. Everyone had expected him to attend Arizona State or one of the other big schools that offered him scholarships. Instead, he had joined the Marines and sent money home to his mama. After being discharged, he'd returned home and attended the local Arizona State branch. He'd earned his degree in criminal justice and psychology and then attended the state police academy. His mama had lived long enough to see him graduate.

"Every girl in town tried to land him," Teri continued, "but he was married by the time I was old enough to be dazzled by him."

"Really?" As I cleared the table, I tried to imagine Reed married; but the image just wouldn't form in my mind. Teri jumped up and began washing the dishes, keeping her mini biography of Reed rolling.

"Didn't last long though."

"Can't imagine why," I said, trying to feign less interest than I had.

"Oh, but he's so-o-o . . ." she said, as she brought her hand up to her forehead, feigning a swoon until neither of us could hold back the laughter any longer. "My *abuelita* had hopes for me, but it was never anyone but Jose for me. Since middle school."

"Reed would have been too old for you, wouldn't he?"

"He's in his late 30s. Not really much of a difference now, but maybe then . . ."

I picked up a dish towel and began drying dishes. "You do know he thinks I may have something to do with the murder."

Teri giggled. "No way." I didn't answer. "You can't be serious? He's just—"

"No, really! I'm new in town, I happened to be there where she last danced, and he thinks I'm mysterious."

Teri just shook her head. "He's just giving you a hard time. Reed has to know you couldn't murder someone. Maybe it just gives him a reason to come by to talk to you. You know how men are."

My cell phone chirped. I'd put it in my purse but kept the ring tone as loud as I could. I left Teri wiping down the table as I hurried to get the phone. When I checked it, I had a text message from an unfamiliar number. Thinking it might be from John, I clicked it on and read, THOSE WHO PLAY WITH FIRE, BURN. There was no signature.

I immediately pushed redial. "The number you are trying to reach has been disconnected," the nasal computerized voice said.

"Sorrel?" Teri had followed me down the hall.

I handed her the cell. She gasped. "This is some sick joke! Who would do such a thing? Do you recognize the number?"

I shook my head. I could think of any number of scenarios for the message, but the one that paralyzed my tongue surely could not be. They couldn't have found me here! We'd been so cautious! Besides, burning wasn't their typical threat. Their messages would involve knives or guns as weapons of choice. Or could it be the bogus deputy sheriff or the friend from home who had talked with Mrs. Sanchez? Were they connected? And why? How was I a threat to anyone anymore? I was no longer a journalist, just a shopkeeper wanting to live a normal, peaceful life away from the media spotlight.

Lost in my thoughts, I hadn't been aware that Teri had retrieved her phone and had made a call until she put her arm around my shoulder. Hugging me to her side, she told me Jose was coming right over and was calling Reed as well.

"Reed?" Just what I needed. "Teri, this is probably some school kid joke! Reed is a detective with things like murder to solve. He can't just come running every time I have some silly threat. Besides, if we needed to call someone, we would call the sheriff. And Jose?"

"Don't be silly. Jose was coming to pick me up anyway. Now sit down. You're pale as a ghost." As I sat, she busied herself filling the kettle and brewing a cup of tea. In a few minutes, she set a steaming cup in front of me and, for a few moments, we both forgot about the threatening text.

"Wherever did you get this?" I asked. "This is the most delicious tea I've ever tasted."

"Oh, I forgot to mention it earlier—I knew I was forgetting something. My cousin Julio's oldest daughter makes it. She wondered if you had a place in the store for it. I have several blends that she's created."

I took another sip. "This is her own blend?"

"Yes. She calls this one *Bonita*. I thought we could arrange a small tea display with the pottery, you know, around the teapot and the mugs."

"Perfect!" I drained the cup and reached over to grab her hand. "Thank you, Teri. You're a genius! And you can't know how much better I feel."

Flash suddenly sat up in her basket near the pantry and cocked her ears toward the back door. A second or two later, Jose called out, "Girls?" and entered, closely followed by Reed. Flash hopped out and sidled up to Reed. He leaned down to pick her up and cuddled her while watching me.

"Look. I'm sorry for calling you two over here. I overreacted and Teri felt she needed to call you. It was just a dumb text message. Probably kids."

"How would they get your number?" Jose asked, his arms still around Teri after she'd given him a hug and a quick whispered update.

"Random? Just dialing numbers? You know how kids do—dial strange numbers and tell people they're watching them." Even to my ears, it sounded farfetched. "Tea anyone?"

"I'll get it." Teri sprang into action before I could leave the chair. Reed and Jose sat down across from each other.

"Is there any reason someone would try to scare you, Sorrel?" Reed asked, settling Flash on his lap and stroking her fur.

"Not that I can think of."

"First you have this strange person pretending to be a deputy sheriff—"

"What deputy sheriff?" Jose asked.

105

Before I could explain, Reed gave a summary of what had happened earlier. "And now this," he mused. "Odd."

"It's the first I've heard about a deputy sheriff," Teri said, setting glasses of tea in front of the guys. Teri pursed her lips and looked at me for a second or two, her brow furrowed. "Sorrel, you're out here by yourself basically—no neighbors too close. I'm not sure you should be staying here just now. I wish we had an extra room—"

"Hey, I appreciate your wanting to protect me, but let's not panic. It's just a crank message. Certainly not reason enough for me to relocate and change my whole life."

Jose glanced around the room, craning his neck to see into the store. "I know you have fire alarms," he said, "but do you have security cameras?"

"Yes, I do. Both in the shop and on the parking lot. I figured I needed cameras in both locations since I'm basically out of town and on my own—"

"Exactly the problem, Sorrel."

CHAPTER TWENTY-SEVEN

Reed had been so quiet up to now, just stroking Flash and listening. I looked at him quizzically. "Security cameras and alarms are good, but they don't solve the problem. You're still here alone. Until we figure out what's going on and put an end to it, you should move back to the B&B for a while. I'm sure Mrs. Sanchez has room."

"No! This is my home. Flash and I are comfortable here. We're not letting some crank text scare us off."

"Well, then, hire somebody to work with you. You'd at least have another person around while you have the shop open."

"I'd love to do that, Reed. But I can't afford that. Besides the hourly salary, I'd have to pay all sorts of taxes and social security . . . I'm just not that big an operation. I've poured so much money into getting this place ready, matting and framing my prints—I'm bleeding money." I wasn't that desperate yet, but it wouldn't be long.

The few seconds we were silent seemed more like hours. Jose, Teri, and Reed seemed intent on finding a solution to a problem I wasn't sure really existed. I knew they were only trying to protect me, but I needed to take care of myself.

"I've got an idea!" Teri's bright voice interrupted the silence. Both men rolled their eyes. They'd experienced too many of Teri's ideas, but I was intrigued. She had come up with some interesting solutions to other problems. The least I could do was to listen, and I prompted her to share.

"The seniors! They have a lot of time on their hands. Maybe we could come up with some way for them to help out. Instead of paying them and all the paper work that entails, maybe you could donate to their activities fund." The men groaned, but I could see the possibilities. I knew from recruiting my consignees that they wanted to contribute in meaningful ways to their community and to live, not just pass their days at the Senior Center doing crafts and playing bingo.

That afternoon, after I'd finally shooed everyone away, I called John from yet another disposable phone so I wouldn't have to use our coded talk. His voice sounded warm and comfortable. I told him about the store and the progress I was making. Then I told him about the text message. "Am I just being paranoid?" I finally asked.

"Maybe. Do you think this cop might be trying to scare you? If he thinks you're a prime suspect, maybe he's trying to juice you a little."

I thought of Reed's worried eyes when he left. "I don't think so. In fact, I don't think I'm really a prime suspect. I think he just senses that I have untold stories."

"Untold stories. Now that's one way of putting it." John chuckled. "Someday you'll have to write a book and put him out of his misery."

We laughed but the mirth lasted only a moment. I breathed deeply. "John, I'm . . . I'm tired of this drama . . . this hide-and-seek game."

"It's never been a game, Sorrel," his voice quiet but serious once again.

"I know," I sighed, "but I want my life back, John. I want my life back . . . or at least my right to live my life as I choose. I'm loving setting up the store, living in this small place, making genuine friends, and snapping my pictures. If things hadn't happened as they did, would I think of this text as anything more than just a kid's prank?"

"But things have happened, Sorrel." I reluctantly agreed and asked him if he'd heard any more from his contacts. This time he took a deep breath.

"Not yet. They still haven't verified who the target was and they haven't given me any other indication that things have changed for the worse."

I nodded, forgetting for a moment that John couldn't see my reaction. "Then I'm not going to hide out in a closed room and worry. I'm going ahead with the store and my new life. You've got to promise you'll come see it. And you'll die when you see the country around here. It's a photographer's dream."

Before we ended the call, he promised to send me some of his photos after I'd gotten the store going. But we both knew that wouldn't happen until things had been resolved, until he could ship them to me safely.

Flash and I snuggled down that night after both Teri and Reed had called. It was weird but I felt more connected to these people and to this very different life than I'd ever felt as a celebrity in Houston. Would Kevin have been able to make this transition? But I already knew the answer was a resounding no before I even asked the question.

I stared up at the ceiling, barely lit from the sliver of moonlight peeking through the bedroom window. Kevin might have hated my job, but it was the job that had brought me to his attention. If I hadn't been a celebrity, we would never have been together. Not for the first time did the thought flicker in my mind that my job would have soon caused a real rift between us. Had he lived long enough, that is.

Suddenly, the blood flashed through my brain. My breath caught and I fought for the calm as the therapist had taught me. *Easy in, easy out.*

Flash purred, trying to calm me.

Let the calm flow through my toes, my fingers. Let it go. "Let it go. Let it go"—those words echoed in my memory from that first night at Bart's. Maybe Reed was right. At the oddest moments, memories from that night reappeared.

CHAPTER TWENTY-EIGHT

"And the winner is…ticket number 618!"

"Darn! I was sure I was going to win that vase! Just my luck!"

I swung around to focus my camera on the loser, a member of the dance team who would be performing next. Her short skirt stood almost straight out to the side, thanks to the numerous petticoats underneath, and swayed with her mood. Her partner, wearing a vest of matching fabric, nodded in mock sympathy. I suspected she had more vases than she needed.

"The lucky winner is this young lady here," the announcer continued. Another dancer stood beside him to pose for a photo, smiling mischievously at the loser and holding the vase triumphantly overhead.

"Grace, you didn't even want it! You know you don't have room for it!" my loser complained. "You knew I bought the ticket just because of that vase."

"And that ends our raffle today," the announcer interrupted. "Next, let's give a big welcome for our own southwestern dancers, the Toe Tapping Twirlers." Polite applause accompanied the dancers as they assembled in the center of the room, the disappointed ticket holder at the head of the group. Everyone stepped back to give them plenty of room as I edged close enough to take photos without framing the elbows or hands of bystanders in the shots.

As the Twirlers swung around the room amid occasional outbreaks of applause, I worked quickly to capture the dancers' expressions and movements. I marveled at their energy. All of them were seniors who had probably not seen seventy in some time. Just before the number ended, I swung around to take candid shots of the audience and saw the Mariachi band that would be playing for the street dance later that night. I needed to get some shots of them as well.

"I figured I'd find you here." I whirled around at the sound of his voice. Reed had sneaked up behind me again!

"Taking photos for the paper," I replied, scanning the room as if looking for other shots.

"You been here long?"

"Most of the afternoon. I worked at the store this morning while the other guy caught the speeches and the luncheon."

"You about ready to open?" Reed had stepped close enough that I could smell his aftershave. It had a sort of saddle soap smell to it that I liked.

"Tuesday, but Memorial Day is the Grand Opening. That way I'll have time to get my ad in the paper, arrange for more stock, and install the computer program I ordered to help me keep tabs on the different vendors."

"Any more strange calls?

"No. I still think it was just a one-time thing. Probably kids." I waved to one of the dancers, who took it as an invitation to come over. "I need to mingle," I said and started to move toward the approaching woman.

Reed caught my elbow. "Come with me tonight."

"Oh, I . . ."

"Teri and Jose will be there. Besides, since you've never seen a Saddle Gap Cinco de Mayo celebration," he said, grinning down at me, "you can't miss this one. I'll pick you up about five thirty."

"I can drive—"

"Wear something that swings when we dance." Then he nodded to the dancers who had clustered at my side and left.

"He's so handsome!" Elvia sighed.

I smiled. "You were wonderful out on that dance floor, Elvia. I don't know how you can remember all of those moves!"

"Many a young lady has had Reed in her sights, you know. You must be really special."

I chuckled. "While I have you all here," I said to the group, "I need some people to work in my shop occasionally." I started handing out business cards as I gave them more details. "I'm opening Memorial Day weekend, so I'll need someone then for sure. But I'll also need people to work at other times so I can do my photography. I can't pay you, but I will donate the money for your work to your activity fund." I could see approval on several faces.

"I might be able to do a morning a week," a tall, bald man offered. "Gets kinda boring sitting in front of the TV or going to those craft classes."

Several of the others nodded in agreement and, within moments, I had promises for five mornings or afternoons a week. "Thanks! You all are real gifts! Call me next week and I'll start fitting together a schedule." Then I excused myself to catch up with the Mariachi band before I headed home to shower and change.

I'd parked on the north side of the convention center, per Randall Byrd's advice. "You might get hemmed in otherwise," he'd said. "No one follows any rules for parking during fiesta weekend." He'd been right. I had to walk on the graveled flowerbed to get around the vehicles wedged into every possible crevice.

As I rounded the corner, a group of young boys, laughing and pointing at a vehicle similar to mine, caught my attention. When they saw me, they scattered.

"Hey," I shouted and stopped. What was that smell? I walked a few steps closer. It was my Jeep!

I ran to the car but stopped a foot or two from my front left fender, the smell overwhelming, and gasped. Someone had smeared excrement on the windows, hood, fenders, and doors. Toilet paper had been stuck into it for added measure. I edged around the side, being careful not to touch it, and saw that the back had been equally detailed. The two vehicles on either side of mine were pristine. I had been targeted. But who could have done it? And why?

As I pulled out my cell phone, I saw the small card wedged under the wiper blade on my back window. I gingerly reached for it with my index finger and thumb: SMELL THE STENCH. I heard feet running toward me and quickly stuck the card in my camera case.

"Oh, Sorrel!" Teri gasped. "One of my cousin's kids said a Jeep had been 'poohed' and when he told me what color it was, I hoped it wasn't yours."

She hugged me and began speaking in rapid-fire Spanish to no one in particular. Jose, who had followed closely behind, whistled softly as he surveyed the damage. He tapped Teri lightly on the back and kissed her on her mouth when she turned. He then looked over at me. "Sorry," he laughed, "but I had to shut her up. The boys were learning too many new words."

Teri gasped and glanced down at the boys. "Don't do everything I do—just what I say!" she admonished them. "No—!" The chuckling from the crowd that was gathering interrupted her thought. She just stared at them for a second or two, frowning at their lack of outrage at what had happened to my car.

Jose walked around the Jeep. "There's even some in the hubcaps on this side," he said. "Someone did a thorough job."

"I need to call a tow truck and get this thing to a car wash to be detailed."

"Don't tell 'em the true condition," one of the bystanders yelled and was rewarded with the laughter of several others.

Teri looked at my pale face. "I think we can save the jokes," she called. "Did anyone see someone fooling around back here?" She addressed her question to the group of young boys, pinching their noses, who had inched closer again. They shook their heads collectively. She eyed one of the boys and walked over him. "Hito," she said, "sure you don't know anything?"

"I'd like to talk to you guys." When had Reed gotten here? He turned to the bystanders. "I think we've all seen—and smelled—enough. Go on back to the fiesta. We need the space to get the tow truck in."

"Oh, I need to call—"

"Already done," he said. "You'd have had a hard time getting anyone this afternoon, so I called one. Are you okay?"

"Sure," I lied. "I've just had one prank too many and want to go home."

Jose and Teri offered to take me, but I finally convinced them that I was fine and that they needed to stay and enjoy the day with their family. Reed asked one of his younger officers to take me while he waited for the tow.

As he opened the door of the truck for me, he said, "See you at . . . better make it six." I just nodded.

All the way home, the young officer chatted easily about the fiesta. "It's about the biggest party of the whole year—except maybe Christmas," he said. "With us being right on the border, we have such a huge Mexican ancestry that we celebrate Cinco de Mayo even more than July 4."

"Are you from these parts?" I asked.

"All my life. So's my wife. She's an elementary teacher." That sent him off into stories about school, and I settled back into the seat and pretended to listen.

The phone call and now this. Someone must have followed me—in spite of all our efforts to keep my whereabouts secret. And whoever it was, was closing in. I clenched my jaw when I felt the chill creeping up my spine. I was not leaving my home. Not this time.

Home. I was using that word often. This was home. Maybe it had always been home, even though I'd only lived here that one summer. I would not run from here. I would fight, but I would not run again.

"Ma'am?"

I'd been so deep in thought I hadn't realized we'd reached my shop. The officer jumped out and opened my door. "Let me walk you to the door. The detective insisted," he added quickly. "And I'm to take a look around—outside and inside."

"That's ridiculous. One kid's prank doesn't mean I have to be coddled and protected." I forced myself to chuckle at the ridiculous notion, found my keys, gathered my camera bag from the floorboard in front of my feet, and stepped out. He walked slightly ahead, glancing casually in every direction.

"Ridiculous or not, I like my job and I have my orders," he replied firmly. He took the key from my hand when we reached the porch. "You ready to key in your security numbers when I get this unlocked?"

He was ready to leave a half hour later, after searching the house, the store, and the surrounding area. At the door, he reminded me to lock up.

"I don't want to seem unappreciative, but isn't this a bit dramatic for a schoolyard prank? After all, this is probably just fiesta fever. Right?"

He shrugged, started down the steps, halted, and then looked over his shoulder, his face solemn. "Ma'am, I've lived here all my life. This isn't anything that is normally done. It wasn't a prank. It was malicious. It feels almost like a warning. I don't know why, but you need to take care. Now please go in and lock up while I wait."

CHAPTER TWENTY-NINE

When Reed arrived that evening, he wore the same worried expression that I'd seen in the police officer's face, which softened as he looked at me. He exhaled, whistling softly. "You look fantastic!"

I'd taken a long bubble bath while I talked to John. He'd promised to report the latest incident, especially the note, to our detective friend. Then he'd tried to coax me into returning to Branson for a couple of weeks, telling everyone I was on a photo shoot.

But I was adamant. No more running. This was my home, my first real home of my own. That house in Houston had been Kevin's. He'd already bought it, decorated it—or his mother had—and he hadn't wanted me to change a thing, not even move a chair. I was so busy, I didn't argue—or maybe I didn't care. But this place was mine. And no one was going to run me off.

"And I think I see a blush," Reed continued and laughed.

"You wish!" I smiled, but his admiration had lifted my spirits. I'd found a white peasant blouse trimmed in eyelet lace and a slim ankle length denim skirt. "Sorry, I didn't have any swirly skirts." We both knew I'd lied, and I probably would have worn one had he not suggested it earlier.

He glanced at my feet. "Sandals. Guess I'll have to watch my step," he said, looking down at his boots. "Do you have your keys?" he asked, as I added a shawl. I patted a pocket in the skirt. "Then let's hustle. I don't want Tia's enchiladas to be sold out before we get there. And the *posole!*"

Reed had been an easy companion all evening, joking with people we met, introducing me to so many people that I knew I'd never remember them all, and teaching me several of the Mexican dances. Jose and Teri had sent the twins home with her mother and joined us for the dance. No one had mentioned my Jeep, and I'd soon relaxed and found myself laughing more than I had in a long time.

On the way home, Reed casually told me my Jeep would be delivered to the house in the morning. "Do you want to get some clothes and stay at the B&B?" he asked. "I mean, with no vehicle . . ."

"No, I'll be fine. Besides, Flash would hate being all on her own. I've already been gone all day and half the night."

He was quiet a moment. "Sorrel, it wasn't a prank."

"Reed—"

"Hito saw a man give two older teens money and a bag. He hid in the hedge and watched them do it."

My chest tightened.

"Hito said they put a note on the windshield," Reed continued. "Were you planning to let me see it?"

We pulled into the parking lot outside my store. Reed turned off the engine and turned toward me. "Don't you trust me yet?"

"It's in my camera bag." Neither of us spoke as we walked up to the door and I punched in my code. Reed waited quietly while I went into the bedroom and came back with the note. I watched his face as he read it.

"Not a dumb guy," he said finally. "*Stench* isn't a common word and it's spelled correctly." He paused a moment, holding the card between his thumb and forefinger and lightly shaking it toward me. "But this is definitely a threat, although I can't figure out to what." He looked at me for a long moment. "Mind if I take this with me?"

"No, that's okay."

"Sorrel?"

"Yes."

He leaned forward and kissed me gently, keeping his arms to his side. "Thanks for the evening. Call if you need anything." He took a card from his pocket. "My private cell."

After he left and I'd locked up, I undressed slowly. Funny that a simple kiss could excite and comfort at the same time. "This cowboy detective is deep," I told Flash. Then I gasped. "Flash? Where are you, girl? Hiding?"

I walked from room to room, calling for her. I even checked the whole store, thinking maybe she'd curled up on one of the crocheted pieces, which she'd tried to do a couple of times before. With each step, I felt the panic rising. This was so not like her!

"Meow! MEE-O-OW! "

The angry yell sounded muffled and was coming from the direction of my desk. I rushed over and heard her again, pinpointing the sound to the bottom desk drawer. Wiping tears from my eyes, I pulled at it but it was stuck. I could see fur peeking out. "I'm here, girl," I tried to soothe her. "Be patient. It serves you right for hiding out in this silly drawer."

After working several minutes, I had it open enough to let her out. She'd crushed my neatly arranged folders and shredded papers in her attempts to extricate herself. Once free, she glared at me balefully and dramatically limped toward the kitchen. I slammed the drawer shut and followed. "Mama has your special tuna cat food," I murmured. "Poor baby."

After a huge feast, a visit to the litter box, a long drink of water, and an elaborate bath, Flash finally made several circles on the quilt beside me and lay down. She looked up as I stroked her fur then purred. "I'm so sorry, baby," I crooned again, scratching along her jaw. "I got so busy I neglected you." I shut off the light and she snuggled closer.

I was almost asleep when I realized I hadn't opened that desk drawer in days.

CHAPTER THIRTY

"Don't touch anything! Just come back in here."

The young paramedics had led me out of my bedroom, shielding me as much as they could from the bloody scene I'd stumbled into. It returned to me tonight as I huddled in bed with Flash, having checked and rechecked the locked windows and doors once again.

How could someone get in with the new security? I'd had the installer set the system to accommodate Flash's movements so she wouldn't set it off. But he'd assured me that any person would be detected moving around in the house or shop. I'd had the windows wired, as well as the doors, in case someone tried to come in that way. And I'd put my own security code in right after the installer finished. There truly was no way someone could have come in without setting off the alarm.

"Flash," I murmured, snuggling her close again. "Your mama is losing her mind. She must have left that drawer open without realizing it! Crazy!"

I'd fallen into a fitful sleep just before dawn, only to awaken to pounding.

"Sorrel!"

My eyes burned. I sat up and squinted at the clock. Could it be nine o' clock? Flash stretched, yawned, and settled back onto the bed. "I wish I were a cat!" I muttered.

"Sorrel! Are you okay? I'm counting and then I'm coming in!"

Teri! I rolled out of bed and headed for the kitchen door, pushing my wild hair out of my face. "Give me a second!" I grumbled, punching in the code.

Teri rushed through the door in full mother hen mode, arms full of bags emitting wonderful smells, chattering nonstop. "You should have just come up and stayed with us! We could have found an extra bed, you know! I can't believe what those kids did to your Jeep! It may not be safe for you to stay out here, you know."

I just stood there in my oversized sleep shirt and watched this chattering whirlwind. Only after she had coffee brewing, burritos and salsa on plates, and a full review of the vandalism of the day did she notice me. "You overslept?"

"Watched a late movie." I didn't want to go into everything that had happened with Flash. I waved my hand at all of the food. "Let me hop in the shower—won't take five minutes." I trotted out at the same time her cell rang. That would keep her busy!

Seven minutes later, I stepped out of the bathroom in worn jean shorts and tee shirt, my wet hair up in a ponytail. I sniffed the freshly brewed coffee. "I'm on my way for a cup!" I called from the bedroom as I straightened my bed.

Silence. I walked through the bedroom door toward the kitchen and saw Reed. "Where's Teri?"

"Minor crisis. One of the twins took a tumble and may need stitches. I was in the parking lot, coming to see how you were doing, and she told me"—he grinned—"a whole lot of things I'll never remember. But I think she'll be back in a while and you're to eat."

"Hope he's okay. Do you want some coffee?"

"Yeah. He'll be fine. Typical for a rowdy little boy."

"Please get yourself a burrito. They smell wonderful and she probably brought enough for an army." I picked one up and took a bite, savoring the flavor. "But they're so delicious I never complain."

We ate in companionable silence for a bit. Reed refilled his cup and poured me another as well. "Your Jeep is here," he said. "The boy followed me in. I put your keys there on the counter."

"Thanks."

"You sleep okay?"

Keep it simple, I warned myself. A partial truth is easier to remember. "I sometimes get headaches and they keep me awake."

If he didn't accept my explanation, Reed decided not to probe further. "Still planning on opening Memorial Day?"

"Uh-huh. Teri is helping me organize a Grand Opening event. Her uncle is grilling hot dogs and one of her cousins is making tamales. Several of the people who have items on consignment will be here to celebrate our venture." I grinned. "I know, I know. You start me on this subject and I'll run away with you."

"So I'd better get going."

"Thanks for getting the Jeep to the carwash." He got up to put his cup in the sink. "And, Reed, I don't think I even told you that I had a good time last night."

"We got a little sidetracked . . ." His cell phone rang. He looked at the ID and took the call. As he concentrated on the voice in his ear, he gathered paper to toss in the trash. "Be right there." He looked around for the trashcan, tossed the paper, and headed out the door, calling over his shoulder, "Take care."

I sat there for a moment, wondering what could have happened that he left without his usual warnings. Then decided to get started on the tasks for the day. I was already running behind schedule.

Quickly, I changed into jeans, gathered my camera equipment, and left a message for Teri that I'd be away from home for a bit. First, I needed to make a call to the security company to have them check out my system. Next, I needed to stop by the newspaper to download photos for the Sunday edition. And finally, a stop at the library.

I settled into a quiet area toward the back of the reading room and spread the latest newspapers before me. The Saddle Gap Library subscribed to a number of out-of-town papers, including Houston. After a couple of hours, I'd satisfied myself that nothing new had surfaced on Kevin's murder or my disappearance. If it had, it hadn't been reported at least.

On the way back to the house, I called John.

"Things are quiet," he said. "In fact, the weather appears to be cooling down." Kevin's murder was headed to the cold files to await some break in the future and let the police working the case move on to more recent crimes.

"I guess it's that time." I wasn't surprised. But was no active investigation good or bad, given what had been happening here?

We talked photography for a bit and discussed the possibility of his coming out to do some shooting, finally agreeing he should wait because of the immigration issue heating up in the area. Warnings had already been issued about wandering in the national forests alone, although that might have had nothing to do with immigration.

"You be careful," he warned before hanging up. "When we get caught up in that next shot, we forget everything around us. Remember, that's isolated country out there."

I hung up just before pulling into the parking lot, where a small car was parked in front of the shop. A tall, thin man was leaning against the front fender. I pulled up next to him. He straightened up as I got out and walked toward him. "May I help you?"

"Yep." He handed me a business card from Security Plus. I also noticed an ID badge on his shirt. "What seems to be the problem? The paperwork says this system is newly installed."

"Maybe it's just my first time security customer paranoia or something but I think someone got in."

I started toward the front door of the shop, and he fell into step beside me. "What makes you think that?" I listened for something in his voice to show that he considered me a hysterical female, but it wasn't there. He sounded merely curious.

"My cat." I stopped on the porch and faced him. "When I got home last night, I couldn't find the cat. Then I heard her crying. She was in the bottom desk drawer in my office."

His look suggested that his conclusion of hysterical female wasn't far away. "Well, cats are notorious for hiding—"

"This desk drawer hadn't been opened. I hadn't been in the office for a couple of days. How could she have gotten in?"

He shrugged. He'd decided to soothe me. "I'll check the system," he said, "but if someone had broken in, the alarm would have rung and alerted authorities. Did that happen?"

"No."

"Is anything else disturbed?"

"No."

Now I began to feel foolish. Feeling myself begin to flush, I turned toward the door, unlocked it, and reached inside to punch in the code.

"I think I'll check things outside," he said kindly. "I'll be inside in a bit."

Except for the two displays that Teri and I had planned to set up today, the shop was finished enough to open right away. I had seen it in my mind, but the reality was so much better.

"Ma'am?"

I jumped and whirled around.

"Sorry. Didn't mean to scare you."

I gulped. "Startled, that's all. Sorry . . . I was deep in thought."

"Have you noticed that you haven't been getting phone calls?"

"Phone calls?"

He held up a piece of cord. "Your phone line has been cut. I'm surprised the phone company hasn't contacted you to let you know. How long since your phone worked?"

I glanced at the phone on my desk. "I don't really use this one yet. I only got it for the security system and the store, which isn't open yet. So I just use my cell."

He pulled out his own cell and dialed a number. "I'll get right on it."

Cut. It took a moment to sink in. Someone had intentionally cut my phone line.

"Ma'am?" The man was holding his cell out to me. "The phone company needs to speak with you." He handed me his cell.

I held the phone to my ear. "This is Sorrel Janes." I then answered the security questions the operator posed. I could hear her take a deep breath before continuing.

"Ms. Janes, are you married?"

"No."

She paused again. "Ms. Janes, I must apologize. The new girl noted here that your husband called and said he needed the line shut down so he could work on a security system."

"When?"

"The work order is dated the day before yesterday."

My mind was reeling but I willed myself to remain calm. "Did you send someone out?"

"No need. That is done remotely." Another pause. "I'm sorry, Ms. Janes. She's still in training, and he must have been persuasive. This matter will be taken under serious consideration here."

I should hope so, I thought. "What do I need to do to get the service restored?"

"Well, it can't happen today, as late as it is. I understand from the gentleman from your security system that the wires have been cut. I can send someone out first thing in the morning."

"If service was stopped, then why cut my wires?"

"I can't answer that one, ma'am. Maybe they were cut beforehand—maybe when you were mowing your lawn? But then the alarm company would have been alerted."

I disconnected and numbly handed the cell back to its owner. "Ma'am? I think you should call the police."

The same young officer came out to take the report. "You can pick up a copy of my report in the morning at the station if you want," he told me. "I'm sorry, ma'am, but it is likely vandalism."

"I'm not even in the city limits."

"Well, we have a lot of vandalism in the rural area. Lots of illegals sneak across the border and they often leave trash behind or destroy things en route. I wouldn't even be here, but the sheriff is tied up with a large group caught an hour ago and the Saddle Gap PD covers for the sheriff's department when needed."

"I hardly think they'd be cutting phone wires."

He shrugged. "You might want to spend the night in town," he offered.

"This is home," I told him. "Thank you for coming out."

He grinned for the first time. "Favor for a certain detective."

I'd known he'd not find anything. Whoever had done this wasn't an amateur. It had been carefully planned. Despite John's earlier statements, nothing was cooling down.

CHAPTER THIRTY-ONE

"Okay. Let's make a list, logically and factually, in chronological order." Flash yawned, stretched, and curled up on my feet. Clearly, she wasn't interested in my attempt to organize the events of the past days and weeks.

First was the investigation and report I'd done. Then Kevin's murder prompted my immediate drive to Branson. My identity change and move here followed. The evening out where I'd watched Stephanie before her murder—how I wished I'd just stayed home! My photo assignments covering the murder of that vagrant and the senior dancers weren't dangerous assignments. Oh, when was the mysterious cop? He was before the photo assignments. Then there was the friend who visited the B&B and asked after me. My photo assignment with the feature on Stephanie's murder. All of the redecorating on the shop. My photo shoot at Cinco de Mayo and the vandalism to my vehicle and the threatening message. Now, the sliced phone cord and the entering of my house.

I'd already searched through my office and couldn't find anything noticeably disturbed. Nothing seemed to be missing from the shop. Reading over the list, I searched for a connection and found—nothing.

Back to the list! Kevin's murder could have been random. After all, my whole life change had really been a secret dream of mine for a long time. Maybe I'd used Kevin's murder as a catalyst to chase the dream. I'd seen people, like Stephanie, who had died shortly after my arrival. Sad but no great mystery. And the fake sheriff? Maybe it was someone pulling some scam. The friend at the B&B? Hmm, that one I'd have to think about. The vandalism. Kids? The phone line. A prank? Illegals?

My cell phone rang and I stuck the list in the shredder before answering.

John's call couldn't have been more perfectly timed. I heard him take a deep breath and pause before exhaling. "Birds are chattering to the east." I wasn't surprised, given the list of events I'd just reviewed. Still, I tried to ignore the tightness in my chest. Either Kevin or I was back in the news.

"It's difficult to sleep at times with so much noise," he continued. "I'm hoping the bird hunters weed them out." The police were working the case again—still. It was no longer considered cold. We continued our coded dialogue, but I wondered if we were fooling anybody, assuming someone was listening. We agreed that until something more definitive surfaced, there wasn't much we could do but hope it was just noise without substance.

"And you?" he asked casually.

"Doing well but I'm thinking of setting a trap for a varmint that sneaked into the henhouse last night."

He paused. "Steal any chickens?"

"I don't think so."

"Pesky critters. You'll have to reinforce the fence around your hen house. Probably should get help." He knew the risk of involving the police, calling more attention to me.

"I'm taking care of that." I hoped I sounded more confident than I felt.

I changed into cutoffs, a tee shirt, and my running shoes then rubbed in some sunscreen and pulled on a cap. Although the news about the police working Kevin's case again was unsettling, the recent break in here disturbed me more. I knew I could either live in fear or enjoy life. The choice was mine. Running always helped me sort out the issues and gain a better perspective.

An hour later, refreshed from a shower, I decided to spend the day in the porch turned workroom matting and framing more of my photos. I cranked up the volume on a modern tango by Karl Jenkins. So beautiful! Soon my mind felt free, the terrors of the past weekend flying away. I began with several shots of Gambol's quail, matting and framing them so they could be purchased either as a grouping or as individual prints.

By the time my stomach would no longer be ignored, I had finished three of the quail pieces and a couple of the sunset landscapes. I glanced at the clock on the kitchen wall. Two o'clock already? I cleaned up and foraged in the kitchen. "Tuna salad okay with you?" I asked Flash, as she began weaving around my ankles, pausing once to meow.

While we ate, I listened to the phone messages that had accumulated. The security company had run a check on the land line. Randall Byrd needed a call back. Teri had a "terrific idea." A hang up.

Mr. Byrd answered right away. "Sorrel? Those photos you took at Cinco de Mayo are outstanding!"

"Thank you."

"I've got another project for you."

"I appreciate that, Mr. Byrd, but with the store's Grand Opening on Memorial Day, I don't think I'll have time for another project."

"This one could be spread out over a couple of weeks. I want to run it for Memorial Day, in fact."

"I don't—"

"Just hear me out." I knew I was in trouble; he was about to either capture my imagination or wear me down. "I'd like to do something regarding the border problems. And before you tell me that it's an inflammatory issue, let me explain. There are two sides to this issue, and I'd like for us to attempt to show that."

"I don't know, sir. I'm not sure how we would do that."

He outlined briefly what I already knew. The ranchers had a valid complaint. The illegal aliens crossed their land, cutting fences that allowed the cattle to get out. They left a trail of litter that was not only ugly but destructive if the cattle ate any of it. Some of them even stole vehicles or terrorized the ranchers' families trying to get what they needed to survive. I'd heard the grumbling as I'd taken photos and run errands. Fear and tempers were escalating and people who had lived peacefully together for years were becoming suspicious of one another, wondering where each other's sympathies lay.

Mr. Byrd sighed. "Illegal or not, many of those people are just following their dreams, like my own grandfather did. And because of the actions of some, people who are crossing that border legally are being treated poorly."

While I understood, I still couldn't see how my taking photographs would reconcile the issue. But when I voiced that concern, Mr. Byrd refused to give in.

"You have a rare talent for capturing emotions, Sorrel. Your photos tell a story. I'd like you to let your photos portray what our nation is all about—mostly good people taking pride in their families and working and living side by side."

It would certainly be challenging and fun and . . . time consuming. If it weren't for that, it would be just what I needed to take my mind off the vandalism. He sensed my hesitation to commit.

"Don't give me an answer this minute, Sorrel. Really think about it. I'd want several photos for a feature page—and I'd need them around the twenty-second. I'll call you in a couple of days."

Mr. Byrd was right. I did need to think about it. The project sounded fascinating, the kind of assignment any photojournalist ached to get. But how could I do it and get the store ready to open?

I dialed Teri's number.

"Sorrel!" she squealed. "I was afraid you were off somewhere taking pictures!"

"No, I've been here framing them instead."

"Good! Then you need a break and I have this terrific idea." Teri always had ideas, although most of the ones she'd brought to me were pretty good.

"As long as it doesn't involve going somewhere, I'm listening. I still have to clear up the mess and then clean myself up."

"Not over the phone. Some ideas just have to be . . . presented! Come over for dinner. I'll tell you all about it then."

I glanced at the clock. It was already three and I still had work to do besides cleaning up my work area and getting myself ready. But there was no way out.

"All the better not to have to cook dinner. Just be at the house around six or six-thirty—earlier if you want."

CHAPTER THIRTY-TWO

While Jose and the twins cleared up after dinner, Teri shared her idea, a craft room at the back of the shop.

"It will get people out there," she explained, "and if they are there, they'll see something and want to buy."

It was a wonderful idea, but one that I couldn't implement just yet. "I use that back porch for framing at the moment," I told her. "And I just don't have the funds for building on just now."

She was crestfallen but, as we talked, finally conceded that a craft room, while a good idea, might need to wait until I started to make a profit. We then discussed the plans for the Grand Opening until Jose joined us.

"I tried to get Reed to join us," he told me, "but those two murders are keeping him busy."

"Two? Neither of them has been wrapped up?"

He shook his head. "I don't think so. I think they just thought they'd wrapped one up . . . the guy. But now it seems they may have made a rush to judgment."

"I wonder how they're doing with Stephanie." For some reason, I just couldn't let go of her murder. It was just so senseless—at least, no one had figured out any real motive.

Teri shivered. "You two are giving me the creeps, mentioning those murders." And in typical Teri fashion, she changed the subject with food. "Soda anyone?"

When I got home, I dug the pepper spray out of my purse before getting out of the car and, gripping the canister tightly, walked to my door. Thankfully, the security light provided adequate light, and it was still early, only a little after eight. Teri had wanted me to stay longer, but I had pleaded exhaustion—closer to the truth than I had realized at the time. I licked my lips, the honey from the homemade sopaipillas sweetening them. The meal had been delicious, as usual.

As I prepared to unlock the door, I reminded myself of the rules I'd learned in self-defense classes, especially to be aware of things around me. I slid the key into the lock, slipped inside, and punched in the code. The door relocked on its own, but I also turned the bolt lock to be sure, then leaned against it, and finally exhaled.

Flash wove around my ankles, and I bent to pat her on the head. "Your mama is turning into a 'fraidy cat," I crooned. She sat on an envelope and looked up at me. "What? Where did you get that?" I stooped to pull the large brown envelope from under her.

There was nothing written on the outside of it and the flap had been tucked inside. As I pulled it out, several news articles began to slide out with it. They were copies, probably from microfiche, with the dates and newspapers printed at the bottom in a block-style print. As I quickly leafed through them, one thing was apparent. They were all articles about Kevin's murder.

I dropped them on the floor, along with my purse, and ran through the house checking windows, turning on lights, and scanning each room carefully for anything that looked out of place. I double checked the lock on the door into the shop and pulled open drawers on my desk. I opened closet doors and looked under the bed. Nothing seemed to have been touched.

Back in the kitchen, I took a bottle of cold water out of the fridge and opened it with shaky hands. Then I sank into a chair and took a long drink, letting the cool water calm me so I could think.

I gathered up the nasty pages and set them, along with my purse, on the table. Then I pulled out my cell and called a familiar number.

It rang three times before he answered. "It's over," I said.

"Sorrel?"

"My party is cancelled."

"How? Are you okay? What's happened?" John took a breath, giving me the opportunity to respond.

I described the envelop and its contents and heard him suck in his breath. "You sure you're alone?" he asked, his voice quiet and furtive as if he were the one possibly being overheard.

I assured him that I had checked everything. The envelope had just been shoved under the door. I reminded him that this was an old building. Although the door was sturdy, there was more space between it and the frame than usual—something I needed to fix for a numbers of reasons.

"This changes a lot of things, Sorrel. Let me call the . . . other guests and I'll let you know the next move."

"John," I said, "no changes. This is my party now."

Silence. Then a sigh. "Let me talk to them."

"Just give me their number and—"

"No!" His voice sterner than usual. He paused and then continued more reasonably. "Look, honey, we've been careful so far because . . . we don't want uninvited guests. Even though it appears that party crashers are threatening us, let's not throw all caution to the wind and assume the worst. Let's just proceed like we've always done."

I felt numb. "Okay," I said, but my voice seemed to be coming from some place far away. "But I'm not throwing in my plans. You tell them that." I could feel my anger at the whole situation smoldering, keeping me from giving up and running again. "I'm tired of moving around and looking over my shoulder. I've made plans. And I'm not giving up."

John acknowledged my feelings. Before he disconnected, he promised to be back in touch as soon as he could. I knew he didn't agree with me, but it was my life. I'd tried it their way, and all the cover-up had obviously failed. If I tried it my way and it failed as well, then I'd deal with it.

"Meow?" I looked down at Flash and realized I still had not fed her. "Poor girl," I crooned, walking quickly to the pantry. I opened a can of food and dished out her meal, continuing our nonsensical conversation. When she settled before her food, I made a cup of hot tea. This night was not going to be early or easy. Maybe the tea would help keep me focused.

I spooned sugar into my tea, Mom's remedy for "shaky" times, and stirred while I reviewed events that had brought me to Saddle Gap. Having reached the top rung in Houston, I had set my sights on the network spots in New York. Unfortunately, Kevin had hated the thought. He'd loved Houston and his job. We'd argued the night before his death when he accused me of putting our lives in jeopardy as I chased fame. We'd sat there as usual that morning, pretending that things were normal but realizing that our marriage had a serious fracture. Our goodbyes had been polite, an awkward peck on the cheek replacing the previous passionate kisses.

That argument—those accusations—had plagued me the first weeks after his murder. The therapist John insisted I see had led me through the guilt and horror to acceptance of the facts: I had a job that attracted dangerous people. I did not want that danger to descend on my home. I did not invite my husband's murder, and I certainly had no proof that the murder traced back to anything I had done. My job was honorable, one that provided a service to people. And my job was not the problem in our marriage. That had been the most shocking revelation!

As I talked and she occasionally questioned, I had begun to look closely at our short marriage. We had fallen in love with our images—not the people we were—and we hadn't been honest with each other about our expectations of the relationship. Kevin had seemed to be proud of my job but had actually been excusing me and my job to his family and friends. What once was exciting and showy had become scary and difficult for him, especially when my investigative reports involved the seamier part of society. He had frequently mentioned that I would want to stay home when we had children, but I had heard that as something not only unlikely but also far in the future, after I was an anchor. Kevin would then be happy because I would no longer be out on the streets.

Worse, I had had difficulty socializing with the wives of his friends. With their chatter about nursery school problems, debates about which foods were unhealthy for children, their endless descriptions of shopping trips or spas, I'd wished we could golf with the husbands instead. Soon I'd simply found myself too busy for their wifely chats, not caring that Kevin made excuses for my absences. Those absences had been, in fact, what instigated our last big argument.

We'd argued about my hours at work and about my attitude toward his friends and their wives—as well as his family. He'd finally complained that he wondered if I was planning my next story during sex. I would forever regret my reply: "It might be more exciting!" Even if it were true, I should never have said something so hurtful. I didn't usually try to hurt people, especially someone I . . . I cared about. Now I could never take it back.

CHAPTER THIRTY-THREE

My cell phone rang. "Ms. Janes?" The man's voice was unfamiliar, and I hesitated for a second before replying. "I'm calling about the cancellation of your party plans," he continued.

"And your company would be?"

A silence. Then a deep sigh. "Red Hot."

I shivered. That was our code word for danger. "Well, sir, the party has only been postponed, not cancelled." Either John hadn't relayed my message correctly, or they weren't accepting my refusal to run. The detective wasn't happy with my answer.

"In that case, ma'am, I need you to call our toll free number and speak with management." I was supposed to find a secure phone line immediately and call the number I'd memorized for such a situation.

"It's late. I can call in the morning."

"We're open twenty-four hours, ma'am, but—"

My response was interrupted by someone banging on my kitchen door. I froze. I glanced at the clock on the wall. Eleven o'clock. Had I been home that long?

"Sir, I have someone at my door, and—"

"I'll hold while you look through your—"

"Sorrel! Open up! Now! It's Reed!"

Reed? At this time of night? "Just a minute—"

"Sorrel, open now or I'm coming in!"

"It's the local police demanding to be let in," I told the detective." I'll have to call you later."

Just before I clicked off the phone, I heard him say, "Wait—!"

Reed pushed the door open as soon as he heard the locks click and rushed into the room. He quickly shut the door behind him and locked it, his eyes inventorying me and the kitchen behind me, pausing infinitesimally on the sheaf of papers. "Are you alone?"

"Of course!"

"No 'of course' about it!" He pushed past me and quickly searched through the living room and bedroom. He even peeked into the bathroom. "I need the key to the store."

"Reed, this is crazy! What's going on?"

But he wasn't listening, his eyes continuing to dart around the room expectantly. He held his hand out. I dug the key out of my purse and dropped it into his palm. He moved swiftly to the door leading from my living room into the office and unlocked it then flooded the room with light. "Do I need to deactivate any alarms?" he asked.

"I'll do it."

He waited impatiently, his eyes never still, while I entered the numbers. When the light on the alarm box turned green, he stepped into the store. "Lock the door behind me. And if you hear anything, call the station."

"What?" But he'd already pushed the solid privacy door closed, and I couldn't see what he was doing. I stood there quietly, hardly breathing, trying to hear whatever it was he thought I might hear. My eye caught the copies of the newspaper articles, lying in plain sight on the kitchen table. I scooped them up and hurried to the bedroom closet, stuffing them into a box of winter clothes.

When my cell phone rang, I jumped and then slipped back into the kitchen. "Hello?"

"Honey, are you alone?" John's voice sounded tight enough to break.

"A friend from the police department is in the store checking inventory."

"Honey," his voice echoing a father's concern, "that fox is in your henhouse."

Fox? Reed? I shivered. Then I heard a tap on door into the store. "So what do I do?"

"Be careful. Foxes are tricky creatures," he said. "You can't let a fox know you recognize him. You might be able to spook him, though, or fool him into thinking the chickens are gone. Either way, let me know when you get rid of him."

The knocking on the door grew louder. I put the cell phone in my jeans pocket, walked as calmly as I could to the door, and put my hand on the knob.

"Sorrel, open this damn door!"

"I'm not sure I like this new habit of yours, Reed," I called through the door.

"What?"

"Banging on my door. Demanding to be let in!"

Silence.

"Sorrel, are you all right?" His voice was a bit calmer, concern— maybe worry—seeming to override his irritation.

As soon as I turned the lock, Reed pushed through quickly then took a step back and reached around to turn out the lights. He strode into the kitchen, his rigid back to me. I reset the alarm, took a deep breath, and carefully walked toward the fox.

"Now," I began as coolly as I could, "please explain all this drama tonight?"

He didn't turn to face me, so I walked around the table until I was facing him. His face, except for his eyes, seemed frozen into a blank mask. His eyes bored into me. I must have imagined any feeling of concern he might have had.

"When were you planning to tell me?" he finally asked. I looked at him blankly. His eyes never leaving mine, he reached behind him and pulled a brown envelope out of his back pocket. "About this."

I had rehearsed this moment in my mind a dozen times. With practiced confusion in my voice and demeanor, I continued to focus on his eyes for several seconds.

He broke first. Waving the envelope in front of him, he spit out the words, fury lacing each syllable. "Were you planning to just ignore this? Aren't you at least concerned about your safety?"

My feigned confusion was now real.

Reed slapped the envelope on the table and I jumped. "See? You're as jumpy as a cat!" We both looked toward Flash, sprawled on her back on the rug in front of the stove. I started to giggle. He glared. "Even she doesn't care that—according to this report I didn't see until tonight—she came very close to dying in a desk drawer!"

"What report?"

"What report? This police report! Did you think I wouldn't see it? Are you totally fearless?" He threw his hands up. "Look, I'm trying to help you here. Maybe this is nothing more than someone looking for money, but you add it to the vandalism to your Jeep and it just doesn't feel random! Damn it, Sorrel, you have to—"

"—to what!" My irritation fueled by his attitude brought color rushing to my face. "Why in the world would I contact a detective—one with a murder investigation on his hands—over a break in? Worse yet, this is the sheriff's jurisdiction. Why are you here at all?"

Reed continued to stare, but I could sense his fury cooling. "According to our interfering friends, I'm supposed to be dating you! So, naturally, when a report like this one comes in, it finds its way to my desk."

"Dating? You have some nerve—"

"Teri—"

"—just because we danced—"

"Teri," he repeated patiently.

"Teri? How—"

"Her niece works dispatch." A smile twitched at the corner of his mouth. "And since the rumor cooled the niece's chase after me, I didn't think it would hurt to just ignore it."

"Is Teri related to this whole town?"

"No, just half of it. And most of the single ones have been after me until she decided we should be matched up. I've actually been able to stop running long enough to catch my breath."

The giggles erupted in spite of myself. I'd seen some of Teri's relatives, and they'd looked both sturdy enough and determined enough to give Reed a healthy chase.

He picked up the envelope. "Okay, I've made sure that the place is secure. How about we go over this in the morning when we're not so tired?"

"Again, no need for you—a city detective—to worry, Reed. You've put in an appearance for the niece. Go home and get some rest."

He picked the report up, walked over to Flash, and rubbed her belly. "You're in charge," he told her. At the back door, he looked back. "Set the alarm. I'd really like to get a good night's sleep without being called out."

He didn't glance back to see me stick out my tongue.

But after he left, the desolation of reality hovered above me. I'd run once and it obviously hadn't worked. I no longer desired to return to the bloody nightmare of my Houston home. And if my job caused it, I no longer wanted that job. Maybe I'd kept this dream of my own little shop and photography in my heart all along.

Now, to keep that dream, I had to find answers. How had I been found? Had I been followed all along? What should I do next? More important, who could I trust?

CHAPTER THIRTY-FOUR

"Are you going to accept the assignment?" Once again I was awakened by Randall Byrd's phone call and brusque get-down-to-business manner.

I fumbled for a response, my brain not having made the adjustment from dream state to consciousness. "Uh . . . "

He chuckled. "I woke you. Have a cup of coffee, a shower, breakfast. Then call me and I'll give you some contacts and a starter plan."

I was halfway through my toasted cheese before I realized I'd not turned down the assignment.

When I returned his call, Randall quickly sketched out a schedule for the photos and told me Jason was on his way to my place. Jason would help me navigate the area and note any details we might need as I shot the pictures.

By the time he arrived, I'd packed an ice chest with bottled water and sandwiches. He grinned as I handed him a bacon sandwich to eat on the way. "You'll make some lucky guy a wife," he said, grimacing at the word.

"Confirmed bachelor?" I asked.

"Divorced."

"Ah."

"Ah what? You've got a sister, cousin, friend you want to introduce me to?"

"No." I grinned. "But it might be smart for you to keep that information from Teri."

Jason rolled his eyes as he started the car. "You don't have to tell me that. I've watched her parade half the town before any eligible guy here. She has no concept of being happily single." He glanced at me. "Hasn't she been after you yet?"

I looked out the window. "A little."

"Right." He chuckled. "That concept is not in Teri's vocabulary."

I smiled and nodded. "So what's the plan for today?"

"Great subject change." He chuckled. "Actually, I thought we'd head out to that ranch where the owner was murdered a few months ago."

"I thought we were working on an immigration piece."

"This rancher was actually a sympathizer of the illegal immigrants. He was murdered in his own pasture, his cell on. From what he said, the murderer was one of them. He was offering them help when he was shot."

"How terrible! Why would a person shoot someone who was trying to help him?"

Jason concentrated on a tricky curve before replying. "Exactly. That's why some of us don't think it was an illegal at all but someone posing as one of them."

"Why? What motivation would someone have? Did this rancher have lots of enemies?"

"No, and that's been the most difficult part. He was well liked, from an old established family."

"So you think it may have been some sort of personal thing? Not a stranger who murdered him?"

"There are some of us who follow that opinion."

I waited, but Jason didn't elaborate. We rode in silence for a bit. "How far is this ranch?" I finally asked.

"About thirty-five, forty miles. Then we have to walk a bit to get to the spot . . . if the directions are right." He popped in a CD. End of conversation.

I couldn't ignore the comparison of this rancher to Kevin. Two men, well liked and respected, murdered at home. Was it impossible to solve a murder anymore?

And then there was Stephanie. She'd just been walking home after dancing, only to be murdered and thrown in a dumpster. I must have shivered because the music stopped abruptly,

"Scared?" Jason asked.

"No." And then I realized that I really wasn't scared any more. After the past months of death, threats, hiding, and always looking over my shoulder, I had finally set the fear aside. Life was too short. "You can either look evil in the face and take your best chances or spend your whole life looking over your shoulder at it."

Jason slowed the car and pulled over. He turned toward me, his brow furrowed, his lips pursed into a tight line. "We don't have to do this, you know," he said. "If the people who murdered Mr. Strand were really with the Mexican drug cartels, this might be putting you in danger."

"Mexican drug cartels? I thought you said it was probably personal?"

"The personal thing is one theory. The cartels are another. Lots of money changing hands. Great motivation for keeping the road along the border clear."

"Let's just do this."

He eased the car forward and made a sharp right turn onto a caliche road. "See that windmill about a quarter of a mile down there? That's where it happened." As he continued to drive, Jason gave me a brief biography of Strand. He had been a good man, well-educated and respected, the third generation of his family to live here. He left behind his wife and four sons, all still in school. After his murder, people were outraged. And most were afraid of retaliation. But, for a while, the traffic of illegal aliens slowed down.

Jason drove slowly and pointed out the window to my right, where a trail of trash—everything from plastic bags and cans to diapers—marked the route the illegals were taking. When Strand was alive, he had kept it cleaned up as best he could. Now it was just too much for his widow to keep up, as it was for most of the ranchers in the area.

"Sometimes they find cattle that have been slaughtered and partly cooked," he continued. "The rest is left behind for the coyotes to finish off. Still, when anyone spoke against the people crossing his land, Strand was compassionate."

Jason pulled over to the left and turned off the ignition. We had to walk the rest of the way to the windmill. As I gathered my equipment, he recounted the murder. Strand had driven over to check the water. This windmill had just been repaired and he was making sure it was working right. He must have come upon the murderer, who was either hurt or pretending to be, although no one was quite sure of exactly what happened. Strand had called 911 to get an ambulance and had just connected when he was shot twice, once in the abdomen and once in his chest. The dispatcher had heard the shots over the phone, and they'd been recorded as all calls coming into 911 were. By the time the ambulance and sheriff arrived, there had been no sign of the murderer. Strand had managed to live a couple of days after surgery but had never regained consciousness.

Jason pointed to the spot near the windmill where Strand had fallen. One would never know now that evil had been here. Cows were drinking from the edge of the metal tank and lying under its shade to chew their cud. I began snapping photos before the cattle decided to bolt, but they took little interest in us after a cursory glance.

We walked the area and I shot several photos of the debris scattered over the land. I wondered if we would encounter anyone; but Jason assured me that if anyone had been in the area, our vehicle would have warned them off.

"Why would the drug cartels bother Mr. Strand?" I asked when we stopped for water.

"He'd found some drugs a few weeks earlier hidden somewhere out here. Apparently, he called the Border Patrol and turned them in."

Déjà vu. I'd also been on assignment tracking drugs and gang involvement in the local high schools, but my face had been too familiar due to earlier stories on child pornography. When the opportunity came for the anchor job, I'd accepted it. A few months after I started, Kevin had been murdered. Were drugs, gangs, or some other story I'd chased the reason Kevin had been murdered?

We were back home by midafternoon. As I gathered my equipment from the back of his car, Jason suggested we meet at the border crossing the next day. Midmorning was the busiest time and should suit our needs perfectly. I agreed and waved distractedly as he left, hurrying inside to discover what I had captured on film. The challenge of telling a story through photos fed my spirit like crime reporting never had.

CHAPTER THIRTY-FIVE

I'd just finished editing and printing some of the photos and was getting ready to take them to newspaper office when John called.

"I almost wish I hadn't fixed you up with that job," he said. "Puts you in the open a bit too much. Speaking of which, have you reconsidered?"

"I love the job and what I'm doing here, John. And no, I have not reconsidered. I remember someone telling me that sometimes you just have to draw a line in the dirt and face things."

I grinned at his muffled swearing. "Me and my big mouth . . . and I think I was talking about an entirely different topic. So have you discovered the fox?"

I shivered. "I . . . "

"You need to do that before you find your hens injured or dead."

"You're right. I'm just not sure how to go about it."

"With a trap, of course. That's how you usually catch wild critters."

I only half listened as John told me about some photos he'd taken of waterfowl. He'd been a professor of mine before leaving the university to pursue his photography and was a good friend. I hoped I wasn't causing him trouble or putting him in danger, even though I knew he wouldn't listen to any arguments if I were.

I gathered the photos and headed to town, especially proud of the work. The pictures seemed to capture the emotions I'd felt today: the desperate race to a new life, the tragic struggle while losing one.

But during most of the drive, I thought about John's warning and about who the fox could be. Reed seemed the most logical choice. Teri and Jose weren't even on the list. Who else? Jason? That mysterious deputy sheriff I'd met when I'd first arrived? Mrs. Sanchez? Mr. Byrd?

I pulled into the parking lot, hoping the fox didn't exist.

"Sorrel!"

I stepped out of the Jeep and turned toward Jose.

"Teri's been trying to get in touch with you. We're all going to Bart's tonight. Join us?"

"Well—"

"Please. One of my friends in the Guard will be there, but he's single and Teri would love to have someone to talk to."

I hesitated just a minute. "Okay. See you about eight?"

CHAPTER THIRTY-SIX

Dave, the same performer I'd seen the first time I'd come to Bart's, was back, his popularity undiminished. "Hello, New Mexico!" he called amid cheers and whistles. I glanced around the bar, noting several vaguely familiar faces.

"What can I get you?" My waitress was older this time, her extra weight squeezed into tight jeans and a low-cut top.

"Diet Coke."

"Gotcha."

She moved to the next table, and I turned my attention to the dancers. The floor was crowded with couples two-stepping to a popular country song, some singing along in their partner's ear, others trying not to miss steps. Laughter erupted from a nearby table piled with gifts and festooned with balloons. Happy birthday to someone!

My waitress returned as the dancers filed off the floor. "I'll check back with you," she promised, wedging payment and tip into her jeans pocket.

"I look forward to New Mexico," Dave commented as he prepared for the next song. "People here will dance to anything I play, even if it's off key." Another round of laughter, clapping, and whistles answered him. "This little number," he said, punctuating each phrase with chords softly strummed on his guitar, "is for old friends . . . and lovers . . . and for those who may become sweethearts."

"Sounds like our dance."

I jumped. "Reed!"

He chuckled, pulling me to my feet. "Let's not make a scene."

"We're joining you!" Teri gave me a quick hug and then drug Jose out onto the floor.

Reed waited, his hand lightly at the back of my waist. "Well?"

Every table around us seemed to hush, listening and waiting. I moved toward the floor. Scenes were not my forte. We moved close to Teri and Jose just as the strains of a waltz began.

Reed pulled me close. I breathed in his woodsy cologne, moving a little stiffly away from his embrace. "Relax," he whispered, drawing me back, though not quite so close. "We have to look like we're enjoying this."

He guided us effortlessly around the crowded floor. In spite of myself, I was caught up in the twirling, the music, and the beauty of the dance. When the music stopped, I was breathless.

Reed hugged me briefly, his eyes serious. Then he smiled. "You're a good dancer."

"You two staying for the next one?" Jose asked, as he and Teri passed by.

I pulled away and began walking to the table, my cheeks warm. I was glad that the place was as dark as it was. The other three followed me, followed by our waitress. "What can I get you guys?" she asked. While they ordered, I gulped my drink.

Teri gave me another quick hug. "I'm so glad you came," she said. "I'd been trying to reach you, but you didn't return my messages, so I told Jose you were out on that story. I hoped he'd see you before he left the paper and he did!"

"I'm sorry. I don't even think I checked my messages. I only had time to eat a sandwich and shower before rushing the photos to the paper. Where's the friend?"

At Teri's blank look, I added, "From the Guard? "

"Change of plan." Teri raised her brows in that "you know men and their last-minute changes" way she often did. "Back to the photos—"

"Good stuff, as always," Jose interrupted.

"New story?" Reed asked.

"Just—"

"About the people crossing the ranchland from Mexico," Teri interrupted.

"That's not news." Reed cracked a peanut from the bowl in the center of the table. "Want one?" I declined. "I'm surprised Randy would be revisiting that topic. Especially with the unsolved murders."

"I thought you didn't have murders here," I said. "Now it seems you have three."

"No, Mr. Strand isn't in my jurisdiction. That murder happened in the county.

Border Patrol and the Sheriff's Department have it. Besides, they have more experience with the illegals than we do here."

The waitress returned with drinks just as Dave announced the Macarena. Teri and Jose jumped up. "You coming?" Jose asked.

"Not I!" Reed and I chorused. Then we laughed.

"At least we agree on that," he said.

As the music began, Reed leaned closer and lowered his voice. "Actually, I wanted to come tonight to look at the crowd. I really appreciate your acting like you're with me to dispel the idea that I may be doing just that—work."

"But I—"

"I know. You didn't realize that's what you were doing. When Jose and Teri invited me to come as a sort of partner for you, I grabbed at the opportunity. Besides," he grinned, causing my stomach to flutter, "Teri is darn hard to tell no."

I was surprised at the disappointment I felt. Did I want him to come because he wanted to be with me? Was he the fox? Why wasn't I angry at Teri's deception to get me here? I needed to think. "I'm going to slip out to the ladies' room," I said.

"Wait," he said, moving even closer. "When you go, try to notice any faces that you think were here that night."

Again, I felt a wave of disappointment wash over me. I didn't know what he expected me to remember that I hadn't already remembered, but I nodded.

His eyes held mine. "I know you've been over this before, but this case will go cold if I can't find something to move us forward. It's already been too long. I just want to see what it is that we are seeing but don't realize we're seeing." I understood, but besides the dance floor, the room was dark. I couldn't really see much as I threaded around tables.

The ladies' room was at the end of the brightly lit back hallway. Inside, none of the three stalls was occupied. I looked at myself in the mirror and took a deep breath before combing my hair and reapplying lip gloss. When I'd calmed myself, I put on my most confident face and headed back to the table.

As I stepped back into the hall, I collided with a broad shoulder and fell to the floor, dropping my purse and dumping coins and makeup all over the floor. Large hands gripped my shoulders and helped me stand up. "Are you okay? I wasn't looking."

I smoothed my clothing. "I'm okay," I said and found myself looking into a young face, the eyes shadowed by the brim of a cowboy hat.

As I reached down for my purse and started to gather its spilled contents, he apologized again. "I'm sorry for not looking. Need any help?" he asked, but he kept glancing around, obviously needing to be somewhere else or with someone else.

"No, but thanks." I smiled and scooped the coins up quickly from the floor as he hurried toward the outside door.

Walking back to our table, I was bothered by something niggling in my brain.

"You okay?" Teri asked. "Looked like you were almost mowed down by that cowboy. Was he drunk?" I assured her it was just an accident, as much my fault as his.

The guys had drifted over to talk with a buddy of theirs, leaving Teri and me to sip our sodas and chat. With Teri, I never had to fear about keeping up my end of a conversation. I just sat, sipped my soda, and listened to her idle chatter. It felt good. I'd actually begun a friendship with another woman who didn't envy me or was interested only in my connections.

After Dave played the last dance of the night, Reed walked me to my car. "Well, I had a fun evening," he said, holding my door open. "Didn't make any progress on the case, but I enjoyed the dancing and the company."

"I'm sorry I couldn't be of more help Reed."

"Well, as I said, it was nice anyway." He closed my door, waited until I started the engine, and waved as I pulled out.

The cowboy! Snuggled in bed with Flash cuddled against me, I remembered what had been niggling in my brain. The cowboy who I'd collided with was the cowboy who had waltzed with Stephanie—the one who had twirled her like a limp doll.

It had seemed odd to me then that he asked her to dance. She was at least ten years older than he was and not a very good dancer. But he hadn't really treated her like a partner, more like a mannequin.

I stroked Flash as I mentally watched that evening replay in mind, again seeing nothing that could help Reed with his case.

Reed. Another enigma. "I hope Reed's not the fox," I whispered to Flash, who licked my hand, yawned, and went back to sleep.

CHAPTER THIRTY-SEVEN

"So tell all!"

"Teri, I can't talk just now. I'm on my way to the garden show for the paper"— someday I would learn not to answer the phone—"and there's nothing to tell." But Teri was determined. After I'd turned down her invitation for coffee and lunch, she decided to meet at the show. I couldn't even use the monsters to keep her away. Her sister was taking care of them for the day.

"She's a pain!" I told Flash, as I listened to the dial tone after she disconnected—again without waiting for me to agree to her plans. But I smiled. I really enjoyed Teri's company. I couldn't remember the last time I'd had a real friend other than Sandy. High school maybe? Earlier? In such a competitive job, one didn't easily make friends. Before that, in college, I'd taken huge class loads and worked. Even dating had been casual. Until Kevin, I'd not dated anyone more than a couple of times— and then the dates had been because I needed a partner for some event.

I stepped into the shower, thinking more objectively about Kevin than I ever had. Maybe loneliness had pushed me into dating him. Where I was a loner, he'd been the center of a wide group of close friends with whom he socialized often. His attention had been flattering. But where I was comfortable in the public eye, he'd felt stressed. I'd loved him—of course, I had—but had I been in love with him?

When I turned off the shower, I heard my phone blasting from the bedside table, dashed toward it, grabbed it, and checked the caller ID before answering. "Hi, John."

"Just checking in. Any more surprises from your fox?"

"No. At least, not that I know about."

"Wish you'd stay focused on flowers."

I didn't miss the warning note in his voice. "I am. I'm on my way to the local garden show."

"Seriously?" He chuckled. "Only person I know who sticks her head up when told to duck."

I wrapped my towel tighter. "Can I call you later?"

"I'm going on a shoot. Be gone a few days, maybe a week. But I've been chatting with some friends. Seems like our fox checked out the henhouse then left."

"Maybe he lost interest?" I asked, hoping I was right.

"More likely he knows where his chicken is and is just waiting to catch her off guard."

"Silly man," I chided, forcing a light laugh. "You and your fairy tales."

"Fables, actually. Just practicing up for my grandkids," he laughed. "Take care."

Teri met me just as I'd finished taking several shots of a particularly gorgeous arrangement of tulips. "Oh!" she breathed.

"I know. Aren't they gorgeous? I think hot pink tulips are my favorite." I showed her my last shot. "Think this would look good on a notecard for the store?"

"Great! You know, you could have some postcards made up too."

"Come on. The judges should be starting in a few minutes."

While I followed the judges around and took shots of the winning arrangements, Teri wrote down names and other information to use in the captions. We finished just as the doors opened to the public, mostly Garden Club members and their friends—and a cowboy!

"Who are you looking for?" Teri asked, noticing my attention had wandered from the flowers to the people making their way through the entrance.

"Oh, I just thought I recognized that cowboy. Do you know him?"

"I know at least a dozen of them," Teri answered, grinning. "What's up?"

I glanced around and realized several men wearing cowboy hats had entered the show. I must be losing my grip, thinking I'd seen my mysterious cowboy again.

"Nothing," I said. "I just thought I'd seen him before." But before she could ask any more questions, another of her dozens of cousins came by, turning the conversation elsewhere.

Sitting outside at a local deli, I listened to Teri chatter on about the gossip from the paper, enjoying the chicken salad and the sun on my back. Inevitably, Teri turned the conversation to Reed. "I've been dying to ask about you and Reed," she said. "Did he ask you out? Anyone watching the two of you dance could see that there's a connection."

"Look, Teri. I don't want to hurt your feelings, but I'm just not interested in romance right now."

"You can't turn your back on chances that come your way, Sorrel. I know you're busy getting the store ready—do you realize that we open soon—but sometimes those chances don't come around again. You're so gorgeous . . . I can't believe you haven't been caught already. Don't you want a husband and kids?"

I took a deep breath, hoping if I gave her a small bit of information about my past, she'd be diverted from her matchmaking for a while. I just had to be careful not to reveal too much because whatever Teri knew, Jose and Reed would also soon know.

"I was married, Teri. I'm a widow. And I'm just not ready for any kind of attachment. And I doubt Reed will ever be ready for anything more than a casual friendship."

She gasped. "Oh, Sorrel, I'm so sorry. How awful!" I could see the questions ready to pop out of her mouth, but she graciously swallowed them. After a few seconds, she launched into a different topic.

By the time we finished lunch, we'd discussed several different issues, most important of which was the newspaper ad for the store. Knowing she had a better idea of what would appeal to the locals, I left the final design up to her.

With the boys due home shortly, Teri went home. I went to the newspaper to drop off the photos I'd taken that morning.

CHAPTER THIRTY-EIGHT

By dinner that evening, I was exhausted. When I returned from the newspaper, I'd blown up some of my flower photos and framed them. Then I'd printed three or four dozen note cards. As Flash and I ate, I discussed my plans with her, describing the cute baskets of notecards tied with ribbons and a variety of small, less expensive items I was offering in the store so no one would leave empty handed. Flash glanced from her bowl occasionally as if to agree with my ideas.

I continued discussing my plans, telling Flash about the other shots I planned to use—the birds, landscapes, and the windmill—when I realized I had no cat photos. There had to be other people owned by cats, and I certainly had the perfect model living with me.

"How would you like your picture framed for the whole world to see?" Flash glanced up from her bowl and meowed softly. As I was trying to determine whether she was flattered or amused at the prospect of being merchandised, I jumped at the sudden peal of the doorbell. I'd installed it a couple of days earlier but hadn't expected to hear it tonight.

After a quick look through the peephole, I unbolted the door. "Hello, Reed. What do you want now?"

"A pleasant evening to you too, Sorrel." He glanced over my shoulder. "Company? Can we talk inside?"

I scowled. "Just finishing dinner and chatting with Flash."

I walked back to the kitchen, leaving him to follow me. I heard him bolt the door behind him. Flash abandoned her precious food dish when she saw him and raced over to weave around his boots. He scooped her up in his arms. "Always nice to get a warm welcome. Law enforcement battles such suspicion and prejudice, but this young lady knows I'm just trying to protect and serve."

"I'm pulling up my jeans to wade through this garbage," I said.

"I'm hurt!" He gave Flash a squeeze and set her down. "And hungry. Something smells good."

"Chicken. I put it in the crock pot this morning."

"I've never met a chicken I didn't like." He sniffed and looked longingly at the table.

I giggled in spite of myself. "Oh, all right, I'll get you a dish."

After two servings of chicken, two glasses of iced tea, and helping me clean up, we walked into the living room. I could see the fatigue in his face. I turned on a lamp and pointed to an easy chair. He sat down, propped his feet on the ottoman, and sighed. "This place is cozy," he commented, looking around. "You've done a lot in a short time."

I settled on the sofa, tucking my feet under me. Flash strolled in and curled close to me.

"Sorrel, I've been uneasy with you all the way out here on your own."

"I'm okay on my own."

"I know but with the things that are happening around town, I'm just—well, usually I wouldn't even worry. These murders and pranks—I know they aren't related—but, Sorrel, you just always seem to be in the middle of them!" He stared into my eyes. "You move to Saddle Gap from—who knows where—and start turning this old place into a shop. I don't have to tell you that you don't look like a shop owner! You look more like a model or a television star or something! You're secretive about your past and jumpy as hell! And then you always seem to be around when people are murdered or—"

I sat upright and leaned toward Reed, my cheeks flushed. "Are you trying to blame me for—"

"Now don't get your underwear in a wad, Sorrel." He grinned at my outrage. "I'm just saying you add to my worries."

Flash strolled over to Reed, upset by my abrupt change in position, and butted her head against his hand. "Even this beast agrees." His eyes danced and seemed bluer tonight, like the ocean when you gaze at it in the distance. "I'm just stressed about your safety—and this girl's." He patted Flash, who had settled on his lap.

"Why are you here, Reed?" I sat back into the sofa, creating more distance between us, trying to keep my annoyance in check.

He sobered. "Look, I'm sorry for teasing you a bit tonight. I'm really exhausted and you're so easy to tease. It's sort of relaxing to do it."

His apology sounded sincere—if you didn't look at his dancing eyes. I waited for him to continue.

He sighed. "All right. I wanted to know if last night's experiment brought any more details to your mind."

I thought a bit, not sure if I wanted to continue this dance.

"Well?" he asked, leaning forward

"The cowboy she waltzed with was there last night."

He sat upright so quickly Flash meowed her displeasure and jumped to the floor. "Why didn't you tell me?"

"I didn't realize it until after I was home. Something had been niggling at me, but it wasn't clear until I'd gone to bed. And then I thought that if he was a regular, you'd already talked to him."

He looked at me deeply for a second or two. Finally, he sighed. "You're right. I have probably interviewed him . . . it was just a last attempt . . ." He stood up. "She deserves justice and I'm frustrated about not being able to solve the murder." He started toward the front door. "I'm truly sorry I teased you so much, Sorrel, especially after filling up on that delicious meal."

I followed him to the door, ashamed at my short fuse. "I'm not usually so grumpy," I said. "It's just been a long day."

As I reached for the bolt, he put his hand on mine and I looked into his face. "Don't you trust me yet, Sorrel?"

"I . . ."

"Okay. That wasn't fair. You have your secrets and they're yours to keep. But the next time something happens out here—or to you—I'd like to think you'll call me."

I nodded. "Guess for Flash's sake we ought to declare a truce."

His kiss was warm and moist and breathtaking. When I finally pulled back, he held up both hands innocently. "You said we ought to kiss and make up! At least, that's how it sounded to me!"

CHAPTER THIRTY-NINE

"You'd think I'd never been kissed before!" I told Flash, as I pulled the covers down on the bed and slipped between them. She yawned and stretched, clearly tired of the topic. I turned out the light, curled on my side, and willed myself to stop thinking about Reed's kiss. But sometimes your mind just doesn't do what you tell it to do! I could still smell him, sort of woodsy, and feel his soft lips. At the memory, my stomach flipped.

Sorrel, you'll get in trouble someday listening to some man's sweet talk! One of those mama lectures interrupted the sweetness. I remembered lots of mama lectures, even the ones Kevin gave me.

If you don't watch out, you'll find yourself lying dead in some alley the way you wander around scary places on your own and never let people know where you are. That one, spoken in anger, lingered from our last argument the night before Kevin died.

Both lectures were logical, but I'd never really listened to caution. Mama had blamed it on my red hair. Kevin had felt it was willful choice. Neither was really true.

I wondered if I'd have married Kevin—even dated him seriously— had he not been an easy choice. No, that wasn't fair, either to Kevin or to me. Every marriage has moments when one has doubts, doesn't it?

I sighed. Hormones. That's what it was. I'd enjoyed the physical side of my marriage, but that had been months ago. Reed was a handsome, sexy guy. No wonder his kiss had been unsettling. But we certainly weren't attracted to each other—at least, not on any level other than a casual basis. We didn't even get along very well. I had no clue if Reed was the fox I was looking for, but he certainly didn't trust me! Besides, it was just a kiss.

A kiss is never just a kiss.

CHAPTER FORTY

I'm not sure if I heard the phone ring when it began or if it just sort of filtered into my consciousness. I answered, only to be met with silence. I started to punch the off button when I realized I wasn't hearing a dial tone. "Hello?" I asked again. This time I heard the soft click of disconnection. Annoyed and tired from the mental and emotional games of the evening, I drifted off to sleep.

A motor starting up at the end of my drive woke me. I squinted at the clock. Two fifteen. My first reaction was just to ignore it and go back to sleep. Then I noticed Flash sitting up, her ears perked forward, staring at the window and sending the first shivers of alarm up my spine.

I threw back the covers but stopped myself from standing up. The windows were low, and I'd not closed the blinds completely—something else I could blame on Reed and his kiss. Anyone out there would see me if I stood.

I crept to the window and peeked over the sill. Taillights—higher, so likely on a pickup—were turning left, away from town. Who was on my driveway and why? Was it the person who had called and hung up? But that call had been two hours earlier. Surely they weren't related.

Continuing to kneel on the floor, I glanced toward Flash when she moved. Her fur was standing on end and she was headed toward the door. I crawled after her.

When she meowed at the door, I took a deep breath. Smoke! I jumped up, grabbed the phone, and called 911. Next I grabbed Flash and gripped her to my chest. I'd left her carrier on the enclosed back porch, so I grabbed a cloth backpack.

As I answered questions for the 911 operator, I stuffed Flash into the backpack. I looked at the pair of jeans thrown across the arm of the rocker next to my bed but knew I shouldn't take the time. Instead, I thrust my arms through the backpack and started crawling into the kitchen.

"Don't stand up!" the operator instructed me.

"I'm crawling."

"Good. Fire trucks are on their way. Can you hear flames?"

"No, I can't." I couldn't hear much over Flash's growling and hissing. By this time, I'd crawled down the short hallway and into the kitchen. My progress was slowed as I tried to hold the phone to my ear and absorb the pummeling of Flash's small body against my back. The smoke smell hadn't grown any stronger. Maybe the store was safe!

Sirens wailing in the distance gave some comfort. "I hear the sirens," I told the voice on the phone. I crawled to the door and put my hand cautiously against it. Smoke was stronger, but the door was cool. Maybe it would be safe to open the door and go out onto the enclosed porch. Just as I was about to try, the operator spoke, seeming to read my mind. "If the smoke isn't strong inside, the fire could be outside," she told me. "Wait for the firefighters."

Almost immediately, the fire trucks turned into my driveway and parked in the lot. Someone beat on the back door. "I need to go unlock the porch door," I told the operator. "Thanks for all you've done."

The smoke and heat almost knocked me backward when I opened the door. Flash became even more frantic, howling and fighting to get out of the backpack. Big hands grabbed me and half carried me toward an ambulance. "I'm okay. I'm okay. I . . . I need to see if the store is okay."

An oxygen mask was clamped over my mouth and nose, silencing me for the moment.

"Nice kitty," a deep voice crooned.

Several minutes later, the mask was removed. "You're okay," the deep voice continued.

"I've been telling you that!" But my voice seemed far away. I noticed that my blood pressure was being taken. I could hear water and unfamiliar voices. I felt Flash still pressed into the middle of my back. "I'm okay," I repeated, my voice sounding as if I were talking under water. Someone slipped some baggy pajama-like pants on me.

"Sorrel?" I turned toward the voice, trying to focus. "Sorrel."

A familiar hand touched my hand. "Sorrel, there's no damage to the store. Can you hear me?"

I looked up into gray-blue eyes. "What . . . what happened? Why are you here?"

Reed chuckled. "Now you're coming back to us. I'm here because of Teri. She's related to everyone in town, you know, and someone called her. And what happened is that a fire was set in that old building in back. Must have been a chicken house or something."

"My uncle's storage hut. I'd planned to have it torn down."

"Well, now you won't have to. It burned to the ground."

As a young paramedic began gathering his things, I realized I was sitting on the back of the truck. "How are you feeling?" he asked.

"A little disoriented but okay."

"Good. You're still a bit pale. The disorientation is likely due to shock. I'll transport you to the emergency room."

"No, I didn't inhale much smoke. I'll be all right."

When I stood up, Reed grabbed my elbow and guided me toward his pickup. He gently removed the backpack, crooning to Flash, who was trying to claw her way through its mesh sides, and put it in my lap. "Sit in here a bit while I talk to the firefighters," he said. I nodded, still shaky, and sank into the seat.

There seemed to be dozens of firefighters and several vehicles besides the big red fire engine. They had extinguished the fire but had yet to turn off the hoses. Smoke rose from what was left of the old, dilapidated shed.

I'd been petting Flash almost unconsciously through the mesh and could hear a very soft, breathy purr. "You and I are survivors, Flash."

She licked my finger through one of the mesh holes, just as she'd done all those years ago when I'd peeked under that old, rotting porch in the drug district, camera crew ready to shoot. Her tiny face had appeared and I'd scooped her up, not even thinking that she might hurt me. The tiny scrap of dirty fur had snuggled to my throat. When I turned around, a newspaper photographer had snapped the photo. The flash had made her dig her tiny claws into my neck, but I'd held on and we'd become best friends.

"Everything will be all right," I whispered again, hoping that was the truth.

"Looks like everything is finished except for the investigators," Reed said, as he walked back to his truck. He poked his head in the passenger-side window, wrinkling his nose at the smell. "You can get back in the house because it isn't damaged, although I imagine the paint outside will have to be redone. Anyway, let's go pack you a bag."

"Why? You said I can get inside."

He looked at me a moment and then pointed to the crews in back of him. "They'll be here for a while, and it's really late. You need some rest." His voice had changed to that tone a parent uses with a stubborn child.

"We'll be okay."

"I know you will. But why don't I take you to Mrs. Sanchez's just for tonight."

"That's—"

"Sorrel!" His tone was sharper yet.

I looked at him closer, not needing to be patronized. "What?"

"I'm tired too. If you stay out here, I'm going to be outside in my pickup all night to make sure the idiots who started this fire don't return. And I have a full day of work tomorrow. Can't you at least swallow some of that stubborn pride and think of the rest of us?"

He had a point, even if I didn't like it. "All right."

"Put Flash's backpack on the floorboard and I'll help you carry stuff."

"I won't need much." I gave Flash a pat and slid out of the truck. My legs felt rubbery, and although I'd never admit it, I welcomed Reed's hand on my elbow. "You can carry the litter box." I smiled sweetly, ignoring his quiet chuckle.

CHAPTER FORTY-ONE

The soft hum of a motor pulled me away from the fire-filled dream. I felt the sunlight on my legs where I'd kicked the bedclothes off during the night. My stomach growled and my tongue stuck to the roof of my mouth. I struggled to open eyelids that were almost glued together. Finally, they pulled apart and I gazed into big yellow eyes. "Meow?" I reached up, touched her head, and the soft motor raced. "Meow?" she repeated.

"Yes, I did pack the cat food. But let me get up first." My voice sounded rough, unfamiliar.

My first steps toward the bathroom were tentative. But aside from feeling a little lightheaded, I hadn't suffered any damage from the night before—or so I thought.

On the floor of the bathroom were the pajamas I'd stepped out of the night before. The smoke still hung in the air. When I looked up, I gasped at my reflection in the mirror. My hair was nearly standing up, dry tangles framing a pale face, puffy red eyes, and cracked lips. I'd taken a shower and fallen asleep without drying or braiding my hair. What a mess!

I needed to eat something, but repair work came first. "Meow?" No, feed kitty first.

It was almost noon by the time I'd showered, washed my hair, dressed, and packed our meager belongings—my overnight case and Flash's backpack, carrier, and litter box. I hadn't even brought my camera or computer!

Mrs. Sanchez must have been watching for us because she appeared immediately when I opened our door. "Oh, Miss, I'm so sorry about what happened to your place! But you can't leave without eating!" She held up her hand. " And here are your keys. Jose said to give them to you when you wake up. Your car is outside."

"I slept too long," I told her. "Flash and I will stop by the taco place—"

"That place! It is a disgrace to call that stuff Mexican food! You don't need food poisoning too!" As she spoke, she took Flash's backpack and started toward the kitchen. "I hope you won't mind eating in the kitchen. I don't want people thinking I now provide lunch as well as breakfast and dinner."

I had no choice except to follow after her.

"I'll just give this poor kitty a little something," she continued, "but I'll have to let her stay in her little house. Inspectors would be upset with a cat in the kitchen."

She motioned toward a table under a big window, and I settled Flash's carrier so that she could look out. In an instant, I was sipping a cup of hot coffee while Mrs. Sanchez bustled around the professional stove on the other side. Eggs scrambled with sausage and wrapped in flour tortillas topped with diced tomatoes and shredded cheese appeared just as quickly as Mrs. Sanchez chattered on about the dangers of young ladies living on their own. She sounded like my aunt and my spirits lifted. I felt thoroughly coddled and ready to face the trip home.

I tried to pay for my night, but Mrs. Sanchez refused. "Mr. Reed paid," she said.

I nodded. "Then I'll just pay him. Thank you so much for looking after Flash and me. I'm sorry that we inconvenienced you—"

"I was happy that nothing bad happened to you. A young woman needs a family to look after her."

I was touched that she would be so kind to someone she'd known only for a few weeks. In fact, I thought, as I loaded us up and started the engine, this was a good town with good people.

Thinking about caring people, I stopped at a convenience store and bought a throw-away cell phone to contact John. Before leaving the parking lot, I sent him a very short message: FIERY HOT BUT DIDN'T GET BURNED. It wasn't much, but I didn't want him hearing about the fire from someone else.

Before I could put the burner away, the *Peter Gun* theme blared from my regular cell phone. I checked the ID. "Hello, Reed."

"I thought I told you last night to wait at the B&B until you heard from me."

"Good . . . noon to you too!"

"Where are you?"

"On my way home."

"I'll meet you there. Don't take too long."

Perversely, I stopped at the market to buy apples, milk, and fresh bread. I even browsed the magazine section, reading the titles. Kevin had known better than to order me around. In fact, he'd usually allowed me to make the decisions. This country detective—well, that wasn't totally fair, I conceded. I really didn't know that much about Reed's background to categorize him with those TV country detectives. But I did know that his highhanded way of treating me was more than irritating.

"Did you find everything you wanted?" I looked up in surprise. I was standing in the checkout lane, although I didn't remember getting in it.

Back in the Jeep, I briefly considered running some other errands the naughty imp inside my brain suggested. But in deference to Flash, I drove on out to the shop

CHAPTER FORTY-TWO

Reed's pickup was parked in the shop lot, but he wasn't inside it. I didn't see him as I drove onto the gravel drive by the back door. I got out and carefully loaded up with my overnight bag, purse, and Flash. The groceries would require a second trip.

I backed away from the Jeep and squealed, losing my grip on everything in my hands. As I retightened my grip on the bag and purse, a hand grabbed Flash and then reached inside the Jeep for the market bags on the floorboard.

"You shouldn't creep up on somebody like that," I sputtered.

"And how did I do that? You saw my pickup out front."

I stepped on the porch, punched the code into the security system, and unlocked the door. "Just leave the groceries on the table in the kitchen," I muttered on my way to the bedroom. But Flash was yowling so loudly I doubted he heard me.

When I returned to the kitchen, the groceries were sitting on the counter and Reed was already coming back in the door carrying Flash's litter box. "The porch," I answered to his raised eyebrow. "Coffee?"

"I've had more than I need. But iced tea would taste good."

By the time he returned from the porch, I had placed two glasses of iced tea on the coffee table in the living room. I handed him a glass and sat on the couch, my feet tucked up under me. "Okay. What's up?"

"I'm not sure yet." Reed drank half the glass in one gulp then set it on the side table before sitting in the overstuffed chair. "And aren't we in a grouchy mood today!"

"You are? I knew I was . . . can't figure why though. After all, getting one's property—even if it was a shack—burned down in the middle of the night, not to mention vehicles cruising around your house after midnight and bossy detectives chasing you out of your house—"

"What vehicles?"

I glared at him. "Do you ever let me finish a sentence?"

"I don't have time! Your sentences stretch into infinity!"

A knock at the door, followed by the doorbell, distracted us. I walked to the door, peeked out, and saw another badge. When I opened it, I recognized a face from last night. "Hello?"

"Ms. Janes?" He put out his right hand, a badge in the other. "I'm Richard Padilla. Fire inspector. May I speak with you for a few minutes?"

I shook his hand and nodded. When he stepped inside, he grinned. "Hi, Reed. Guess you're here with questions of your own as well. I'll have a report to you shortly."

"Thanks, Ric."

"Would you like a glass of iced tea?" I asked, motioning for him to take the other chair across from Reed.

"Thanks but no. I just wanted to check up on you and take down the tape outside. This is a straightforward fire, I think. Kerosene seems to be the accelerant. I expect it was a high school prank. Seniors tend to do this sort of thing. I doubt they meant to burn the building down." His eyes stayed on my face, penetrating but not accusing. "How long have you lived here?"

"Not long. My aunt and uncle left it to me a couple of years or so ago, and I decided to come out and try to reopen their store."

He looked around. "Nice place. You've been busy. Are you already open?"

"No, but the Grand Opening is soon"

"Well, it's a good thing nothing was damaged."

"I'll say, especially since most of the merchandise is on consignment."

"Yes, I'd heard that."

I raised my eyebrows and then looked over at Reed. "Teri!" we chorused.

Inspector Padilla laughed and stood up. "Everyone knows Teri—or is related to her." He started toward the door.

"I'd like a word with you," Reed said and stood to follow him. Then he looked over his shoulder. "We'll finish our conversation later."

The inspector quirked his eyebrow, his mouth skewing into the briefest hint of a grin. "I'll keep you posted about what we discover," he said. "It will take a little time for tests to be done and returned. You have a security system?" he asked, turning toward me. "Fire alarms?"

"Yes. I had the fire department come out and inspect the store."

"Good." He waved his hand casually and left. Reed followed closely.

I walked through the store, eyeing each display for anything that would indicate someone had meddled with it. Everything looked the same. I sniffed an embroidered tea towel for smoke but found not a trace. Thank goodness! Nothing seemed out of place.

I couldn't say that for the living quarters. The smoke lingered faintly. I opened the windows in each room and turned on the ceiling fans Teri had suggested I let Jose install. I'd also bought bigger ones for the shop and, as an afterthought, stepped back into the shop to start those as well—just in case—and I opened the windows.

Flash had been following me closely. This latest incident must have frightened her more than I'd thought. I didn't want to dwell on the thought that we both might have died, but had I become some kind of beacon for death?

I remembered a television show I'd watched as a child where this lady mystery writer found dead bodies wherever she went. I wasn't superstitious, but just maybe a case could be made about some people being jinxes.

CHAPTER FORTY-THREE

I expected Reed to return after Inspector Padilla left, so I busied myself with household chores and listened for his return. Flash settled happily into a furry circle in the sunlight that spilled onto the foot of my bed while I scrubbed the bathroom and straightened the bedroom. As I leaned over to pet her, I heard both vehicles starting up.

"Guess he got called away," I told her. "It's just as well because I want to look at the shed and I don't need him there. Sometimes a person just needs solitude to reflect on what has happened."

Being raised alone since I was seven when my half-brother left home had given me plenty of solitude. Or maybe I was just born a private person. Kevin had complained I would be happier living on my own. I'd tried to share more with him but had guarded my work closely. Informants needed to trust that I'd never reveal their identities and other secrets. Kevin had also loved to entertain his family and friends with work stories, which usually ended in everyone laughing—often at someone else's expense. His stories had made me even more private.

As I stepped out onto the back steps, I instinctively wrinkled my nose and squinted. The acrid smell was still strong enough to irritate sensitive membranes. I walked toward what remained of the old ramshackle building, now a black scar on the red sand. I remembered hunting hen eggs in this building the summer I stayed here.

The roof had fallen in and burned. The last vestiges of the adobe walls that had blackened and crumbled with the fire and water rose in varying heights from the rubble. As I stared at what remained, tears suddenly ran down my cheeks, surprising me. My therapist in Branson would be pleased. She had urged me to cry. Silly of me, I thought, to stand here crying for an old building when I couldn't cry for my murdered husband.

But it wasn't the building that prompted my tears. It was the loss of the love and security and happiness I'd enjoyed here. Whenever my life fell apart and filled with horror, this had been where I'd returned mentally. Now even this place had been hurt.

CHAPTER FORTY-FOUR

"Sorrel?"

I wiped my eyes quickly at Teri's voice, but she saw the tears and wrapped me in a hug, instructing Jose over her shoulder to pull out his hankie. "Now," she said after a moment, "we have lots to do."

I wiped my face again and blew my nose as I became aware of movement—and voices. Several cars had arrived. People spilled out of them, each carrying something. Many of them were Teri's relatives, carrying shovels and other similar equipment. Others—people from the Senior Center—held dishes and boxes.

"We're all neighbors here," Teri said when I tried to speak. "Since the store opens in a few days, we need to get this cleaned up quickly. You don't want an eyesore around such a gorgeous store! And we don't want to have our BBQ on opening day with this in the background. People would be afraid we might burn the rest of the place down! So," she said, gesturing toward the group gathering at the shed, "everyone wanted to help."

"I don't know," an all-too-familiar voice called out, "you could always change the name of the store to Charred Collectibles. That has a catchy ring to it."

"Reed!" Teri exclaimed. "Why are you creeping up here and scaring us? Don't you have work to do?"

"And what are you doing? Did Padilla clear it for you to haul everything away?"

"Yes. He's designated a place for us to put the refuse in case he needs anything else. He said he'd already taken all the samples, photos, etc."

"I . . . I'll just step inside for my camera," I interrupted and started toward the house.

"Don't you scurry away, Sorrel! I need to talk to you."

I didn't slow down. "When I get time," I called back over my shoulder.

As usual, Reed ignored what I said and followed me inside the house. "I don't have time to play games," he said. "I need to ask you a few questions."

"But there are people everywhere—"

"—and Teri has them well organized." He reached in his pocket and pulled out a small pad. After studying it for a moment, he gestured toward the couch. "Want to sit down? I won't take long."

I didn't want to answer any more questions. I just wanted to wash my face and compose myself. But this man was obstinate enough to follow me around until I agreed to talk. So I chose a seat at the end of the couch, the farthest from the easy chair, sat down, crossed my legs, and folded my hands in my lap. Then I looked at him and nodded.

He didn't immediately move or speak. Instead, he looked at me, his eyes searching. I forced myself to hold his gaze. I'd learned long ago to think of something simple or innocent, like a baby animal or a beautiful sunset, to make my own gaze guileless. It had served well in my former career, making people tell me all sorts of secrets they might never have otherwise.

Reed broke the gaze first and sat on the edge of the chair. "Can you think of anyone who might want to hurt you?"

"No. I don't know that many people around here."

"No enemies?"

"Like I said, I only moved here recently. I hardly know anyone. I don't think Mr. Byrd or Jason or—"

"Jason?"

"The reporter from the paper. The one Mr. Byrd has had me working with."

Reed studied the pad in his hand. "When did you come here, Sorrel?"

"A week or two before Stephanie was murdered."

"When was the last time you were here?"

"Years ago. At least twenty."

"And you came here because?"

I sighed. "I've told you over and over, Reed. I came here because my aunt left this place to me. I like the wide open spaces. Why are you asking anyway?"

He sighed. "I have an ongoing murder investigation. This incident may be related, so the sheriff is aware that I'm here. I'll be sharing information with him. Now, have you had contact with anyone you knew when you came here as a child?"

"Goodness, no! I was only here one summer and I almost never went into Saddle Gap. I loved being out here."

"Where did you move here from again?"

"Baltimore."

"And what were you doing there?"

Again, I sighed, this time more dramatically. "I was a photojournalist for a small paper in the area surrounding Baltimore. I had aspirations for forensic photography and started training in the area. My love, though, has always been wildlife photography."

"Curious . . ."

"What?"

"When I checked into Baltimore, I found no record of a photographer named Sorrel Janes."

I willed my heart to slow down and then forced a soft laugh. "Well, maybe photojournalist is a bit pretentious. Maybe I should say 'aspiring.' To pay the bills, I snapped photos at social events or a vandalized building. But every free day, I hurried to the Chesapeake area to shoot photos of the wildlife." I knew I sounded partially credible because my story was partially true. Between my sophomore and junior years in college I'd spent the summer doing just that. My roommate had lived in Baltimore and had invited me.

"Can anyone vouch for you? A former employer? Friend? Lover?"

I stood up, feeling the heat warming my cheeks. "Reed, I've answered your questions willingly, not only today but other times. I understand that you are trying to find an enemy in my background who is trying to burn me out—"

"—cut your phone lines, snoop around asking questions—"

"—which could either be coincidence or plain teenage mischief." Reed stood as I continued, "But I think we have covered this subject well enough, and there are a bunch of people out there who have come to help me. I'm not staying inside any longer. I'm going out to join them." I started to the door.

"Sorrel—"

"Enough already! I just told you. I have nothing new to tell you!"

"Don't you want your camera?" He picked it up from the small side table and held it out.

"Thanks." I snatched it and headed toward the door, the image of his satisfied smirk lingering.

CHAPTER FORTY-FIVE

As I stepped outside, Teri grabbed my hand and pulled me into a whirlwind of activity. "I want you to approve this before we do any more," she said, half dragging me toward the rubble.

Only it was no longer rubble. Charred boards had been loaded onto a trailer in the parking lot. The ground had been raked clean. And stacks of rocks, wood, and supplies waited, along with so many people.

"We can build you a nice storage building," Teri said, "but my uncle Ignacio insists you will like this better."

A smallish man stepped forward and handed me a sketch. As I looked it, I almost couldn't breathe it was so beautiful. It wasn't a gazebo exactly. It was rectangular, with open walls and a roof and a fountain—or was that a bird bath?—in the center. And plants. "This is the most beautiful thing!" I whispered. I swallowed hard.

He smiled. "Sometimes we need to make something beautiful, Señorita, to erase the ugly."

"I love it!" I turned to Teri and whispered, "But I can't afford it right now! Can we just keep the design and do it later?"

"You don't have to pay anything," she said. "People have donated what they had." She gestured toward the parking lot. "See all of those people? They're also buying enchiladas and tamales to help with the cost of things we didn't have."

Uncle Ignacio interrupted. "Señorita, can you come with me so I can show you where we want to build? We need to start."

The rest of the evening passed in a blur. After approving the plans, I stepped back to watch the garden taking shape. The seniors had organized coolers with bottled water and sodas. Teri's aunts had arrived with foil-wrapped pans filled with food. Music blared, kids raced after a soccer ball, and I just stood a moment, trying to take it all in.

My aunt and uncle would have loved seeing this. My mama would have been a bit embarrassed, thinking we shouldn't take charity. And   I . . . I hadn't felt so loved in a very long time. I walked through the parking lot, hugging people I didn't know and thanking everyone.

"Let me help!" I said, grabbing the pan from the latest of Teri's army to arrive as I reached the food table and smiled my thanks. All afternoon, I had struggled with the dichotomy I was experiencing. Happiness seemed out of place, given the fire, Kevin's murder, and all the rest that had been happening to me in Saddle Gap. Yet it wasn't! Here in the aftermath of destruction was happiness—how wonderfully strange—and I felt renewed!

I'd come to Saddle Gap with high hopes for the future. As I looked around amid the clatter of dishes and friendly voices to see so many people willing to help me, I resolved to hold onto this happiness and to continue to pursue my dreams—even if doing so ended in my death. A life of fear wasn't worth holding onto.

CHAPTER FORTY-SIX

A paw patted my cheek. I swatted it and received a swat in return. I peeked reluctantly, seeing my hungry cat perched on my pillow, blocking out most of the sunshine that filled the room.

I had overslept. Not surprising, actually. By the time everyone cleaned up and left, it had been well after midnight. The surprising part was that I'd slept dreamlessly, something uncommon in recent months.

"All right, all right. Bathroom first. Then food." Flash hopped down and led me first to the bathroom and then to the kitchen, meowing grumpily.

"Here's your breakfast, beast." I fussed, scooping food into her dish amid her constant complaints. "Now I'll make coffee and get my own."

But I wasn't very hungry after all the food I'd eaten the night before. A banana and yogurt were more than enough. I might not be in front of a camera any more, but there was no sense in spreading out. Of course, I'd never had to worry with dieting, thanks to what Mama called our lean genetics. As I ate, I was aware of a restlessness growing within. I couldn't just sit here.

I finished breakfast quickly, showered, then headed to my computer, a second mug of coffee in hand. In no time, the photos I'd taken last night were printed. I began to look through them, an idea for another marketable project playing around in my head. Besides, Mr. Byrd might want some shots.

I shivered at the face that stared back at me from one of the pictures. When had he arrived? Why hadn't I seen him?

I grabbed the camera, clicked through the photos until I found the one in my hand, and enlarged it. Even with only half his face showing over Jose's shoulder and the beard he now sported, I recognized him—the deputy sheriff who scared me when I was working here at the house the week after Stephanie's murder!

Did Jose know him? Did I? I carefully examined the face. Yes, I'd seen him that day and talked to him face to face. He'd worn his hat pulled down over his eyes, and he'd turned slightly away from me as he talked. But now, in a tee shirt and jeans, longer hair and a beard, his face prompted the faintest of memories. I looked at the other people in the shot. No one seemed uncomfortable around him. That vague feeling of recognition niggled at me, but I shook off my discomfort.

Packaging the photos, I checked the clock. I had just enough time to drop them by the paper before my appointment with the insurance agent.

Leaving the insurance agent, I tried not to fume, which wasn't easy. Somehow, no matter what I said, she was convinced I was trying to file a claim for the building, despite my repeated statements that I just wanted to make sure I now had adequate coverage.

I checked my cell phone as I walked toward my car. How could I have received so many calls in less than half an hour? Teri wanted me to come over for dinner. Randall Byrd liked the photos. The Senior Center wanted photos of their Hawaiian luau next week. Two hang up calls. A call for improved phone service. Another hang up. I sighed.

"I feel guilty always eating here," I told Teri, handing her the carton of ice cream I'd brought for dessert. "The next meal is on me."

"Well, it sorta was last time. Besides, you're always bringing something to the monsters."

"I didn't provide any of that stuff. In fact, I'm beginning to feel like a mooch."

Just then the monsters appeared and chorused, "Can you read this book you brought to us?"

I smiled as Teri shooed us all out of the kitchen.

The boys piled onto my lap, and we began the adventures of a moose that wanted to eat a muffin. One reading wasn't enough, of course, and I livened it up even more with my own suggestions. The boys quickly joined in.

"Hey!" Teri was nearly shouting to interrupt their giggles.

I looked up. Jose and Reed stood on either side of her.

"Daddeeeee! Uncle Reed!" the twins cried as they abandoned me and the moose. I tried to slip past them into the kitchen, but a hand snaked out and grabbed my elbow.

"Not so fast! I need to speak to you a minute—outside."

"Can't it wait? Teri has dinner—"

"—almost ready," she called. "Don't be too long, you two!" She wiggled her eyebrows and grinned naughtily.

Reed opened the door to the back yard. I shivered, whether from the cooling evening or nerves I wasn't sure. "I've been trying to call you. Don't you ever answer your phone?"

"Sure I do, Reed. Why don't you try leaving a message instead of hanging up?"

"You have hang ups from me?"

"Unknown caller." I'd been staring out at the sunset, but Reed's silence pulled my eyes to his face.

"I don't use the unknown caller label, Sorrel."

I knew that. I hadn't really thought about the calls until he'd mentioned trying to reach me. I'd just assumed they were his. I shrugged my shoulders. "I had my phone on silent while I met with the insurance agent. I didn't see any calls from you."

"Are you filing a claim?"

"Oh, no. The little building wasn't covered. I was just seeing if I had adequate coverage for the shop—and I do."

"Are you still planning to open Memorial Day?"

"Next week actually, but the Grand Opening is that weekend."

"So you're opening next week?"

Something in his tone made me turn completely around. "Yes."

"Hey, you guys! Dinner's ready and the monsters are already gnawing on the table legs!" Teri called from the patio door.

"Be right there!" Reed answered. Then he leaned close, his eyes on mine. "Sorrel, I don't know what's going on here, but trouble seems to follow you around. It can't all be coincidence! When are you going to take these things seriously?"

"Hey, you guys!" the monsters yelled. "We're starving!"

Reed reluctantly turned and smiled at the boys. "I figured you two had already eaten everything!" he said, as he escorted me back inside.

Both of us tried to joke as we ate, but neither Teri nor Jose were fooled. I had lost most of my appetite and spent more time pushing the food around my plate than eating it.

"You and Reed have an argument?" Teri whispered as we cleared the dishes.

"No. I'm just not very hungry tonight."

"Seems he wasn't either."

I gave her a quick hug. "How awful for us not to eat the wonderful food you made!"

She giggled. "Oh, it isn't that! Jose and the monsters ate everything except the dishes." She glanced toward the door and then lowered her voice. "I'm just afraid that all of this vandalism may scare you off—or Reed and his grouchiness will." She smiled. "He isn't always like this, you know."

"So you say."

"It's that unsolved murder. Reed studies a puzzle until he solves it, and I think that one is more complicated than he thought. He danced with her, you know."

"With Stephanie?"

"Yeah. He told me once that she just looked lonely sitting there at the bar. I reminded him that almost every guy in the bar danced with her, especially after they'd had too many drinks. But Reed said that by the time the last dance came, the drunks were too drunk and that she deserved to dance the last one."

I nodded then launched into what had been weighing on my mind all day. "I noticed someone standing next to Jose in one of my photos. He seems familiar, but I can't quite place him. Let me get it."

I dried my hands and drew the photo from my purse. "See, the guy right there looking over his shoulder."

She looked. "Not anyone I recognize. Let me ask Jose."

Jose showed the photo to Reed as well, but neither recognized the man. "Do you need the name?" Reed asked.

"Well, I want to use the photo and I'll need it for the caption." I lied. "But that's no biggie." I shrugged and steered the conversation to the store, a topic Teri never tired of discussing.

Reed walked me out to my car a bit later and opened my door. He was unusually quiet as I got in and started the engine. "Sorrel . . . call if you feel uncomfortable."

"Why, Reed, that must keep you busy if every damsel in distress is calling."

He smirked. "That's the reason I keep my steed gassed up!"

CHAPTER FORTY-SEVEN

While Teri took the Grand Opening ads to the paper midmorning, I met Jason for the last of the photo stories Mr. Byrd wanted—photos of the Mexican–U.S. border crossing.

Jason stepped out of his car when I pulled into the parking lot. "This shoot's going to be hard," he said, reaching for my backpack.

"Why? I'd think this one would be the easiest of all." I slipped my camera out while he held the pack and then zipped it and slipped it on my back.

"With the other shoots, we had some sort of . . . story to follow."

"But we make our own story this way." I pulled two small lollipops out of my pocket and offered him one. "Why are they crossing? What's life like on the other side? Are they afraid? Are they working here?"

"Hey, this is a photo shoot, remember? Not a novel." He retrieved his tablet-sized computer. "And a lot of people don't want to have their photo printed—or their name in the newspaper."

I sucked on the candy a minute as we walked to the spot I'd scouted out earlier as the perfect place to start. "Do we really need to identify them? When I see crowd shots in the paper, they're not usually named."

"I know. But I still need to get as many releases signed as possible. Lawsuits do not a successful reporting career make!" A grin tugged at his mouth. "I'm venting, Sorrel. Don't spread sunshine on my cloudy day!"

"No byline?" I prodded.

"Oh, there'll be a byline for the very small lines beneath the photos."

At the border, a paved pathway led from the entry point to the largest store. Our spot was only a few steps from where the store employees were greeting each arrival in Spanish and offering a sheet of coupons and a cart.

Whole families, women carrying babies, elderly couples—the variety and the flow of shoppers seemed endless.

Something brushed against me. I glanced down into huge brown eyes, but before I could raise my camera, his face had disappeared behind his mama's leg. I raised the camera, focused, and waited. Mama leaned back, words spraying in his direction while her fingers loosened his fingers from her leg. She turned back toward the cart—and me—her hands squeezing up under his arms to lift him. He swiveled his head toward me and—click. "Got it!" I murmured. That was a masterpiece—or at least a really cute photo. But there was no time to linger. A never-ending stream of models pushed forward.

Jason roamed, speaking Spanish fluently and tapping notes into his computer as I continued to snap shot after shot of people arriving. We then crossed the street to capture shoppers, their carts full, heading back across the border.

"Ready to pack it in?" he asked.

I snapped a couple of more shots of an elderly couple, arm in arm, before turning toward him. "Already?"

He laughed. "Look at your watch."

It was almost three. We'd been here over four hours! The knowledge focused me. My shoulders ached, my stomach growled, and my nose felt as if I hadn't slathered it repeatedly with sunscreen.

"Why don't we store your gear and go somewhere to eat?" he asked. "Besides, I'd like to run some thoughts by you."

"Sounds good. I'm starving!"

"I know just the place. It's a little Mexican café up on Calle del Sol. Easy to miss if you don't know it's there, so follow close to me."

He was right. I'd never have found it. Outside it looked like a small adobe house. Inside it still looked like a small adobe house, but the food was delicious. Instead of menus, the waitress simply told us what was being served that day and we chose what we wanted to eat. Dish followed dish until I couldn't eat another bite, not even the sopaipillas that had sounded so good earlier!

As I took a breath and leaned back in my chair, I noticed Jason had reverted to his normal method of eating, quietly shoveling bite after bite into his mouth as if he'd not eaten in weeks. I waited for him to lay down his fork. "So what did you discover in your interviews?" I asked.

Jason lifted his glass of iced tea and took a long drink. "Nothing too heavy. Mostly just names and where they were shopping."

"That's what I thought. I can't understand why Mr. Byrd wanted this feature."

Jason took another drink. As he set his glass down, he focused on a sombrero on the wall across the room. "There's a group here who have accused people from across the border of committing our recent murders. I think Mr. Byrd wants to show that if this is true, it isn't the ones crossing legally."

I thought of the huge brown eyes I'd captured in that first photo. "So our challenge is to prove his point."

"Yep."

"A noble cause, but I'm not sure that anything I photographed is going to make much of an impact."

Jason shrugged. "Yeah, well, I wasn't so sure about this assignment and his purpose either." He continued between sips of tea to reiterate some of what he'd told me when we were at the Strand ranch. A lot of old families in the area were angry about the destruction to their land and feared for their families. They'd really like to close the border completely but, as we'd seen on our field trip, the businesses here were making a healthy profit and opposed any regulations on crossings.

"It's sad, you know," I said. "I'm sure those people crossing illegally are terrified, but they still keep coming."

"Dreaming of a better life here in the United States." He couldn't resist a few more bites from his nearly empty plate and chewed silently for a moment. "It's what started this country, you know. People coming for a life of their dreams—whether it's better or not."

"You sound a bit jaded," I teased.

"Where do you think they came up with that term, jaded?" he countered. "Isn't jade a green stone? Maybe it's the green. Money. Everything's about money. That's why we're doing this story, you know, so they can sell more papers for more money. Although nothing sells better than murder, when one's not available, focus on human misery." He stabbed another morsel from his plate.

"Do you think they'll ever solve Stephanie's murder?"

"What?" He stopped mid bite and lowered his fork. I had his full attention. "That's a huge swing to a different topic!"

His reaction took me a bit by surprise. "Not really. We were talking about murder and fear."

"We were talking about the illegals crossing the border and the destruction some of those people cause . . . as well as murder. We were talking about dreams . . . and clichés . . . and . . . ," he waved his fork in the air, "life! Stephanie is a totally different matter. She was a poor soul who was murdered because she was in the wrong place at the wrong time."

"Maybe."

"A random act of violence."

"Maybe."

"Come on, Sorrel! You were there when we interviewed the people she worked beside, the lady in her apartment building, and all the others who didn't say much at all. That case will never be solved. We just don't want to admit that a lot of people really do get away with murder."

"Someone saw something or knows something," I said, leaning in a bit closer. "The right question just hasn't been asked."

"Do you want a sopaipilla?" Jason's question caused me to glance up. I hadn't noticed the waitress standing there, and her materializing so silently spooked me a bit.

I couldn't eat another bite, but Jason's voracious appetite still needed feeding. I smiled as he ordered one. "I don't know where you put that!" I teased.

He grinned but waited until the waitress moved away before continuing. He leaned in a bit, almost conspiratorially, his voice lowered. "The story that makes me nervous is that rancher's murder. That one has the feel of organized evil."

I nodded. "I thought this was a quiet town."

"It is . . . mostly. Stephanie's murder and the stranger's murder—those are the first real homicides here in a long time."

I paused as the waitress returned with Jason's dessert and our checks. The sopaipilla did look delicious, but I was glad I hadn't ordered one. It was the size of Texas!

"So all this mischief isn't unusual? Just the murders?" He looked at me quizzically, so I held up my hand and counted off on my fingers. "The vandalism to my car at Cinco de Mayo, the building burning the other night, tripping my alarm system—"

"Wait. I didn't hear about that." Jason stopped pouring honey on his sopaipilla and stared across the table at me. "Have you made someone mad?" Then he grinned. "Those are just random pranks. Kids have to do something around here. Didn't they have juvie pranks where you came from? Where was that again?"

I made a show of glancing at my watch. "Guess I'll leave you to your sopaipilla."

"Busy lady. Mysterious too." I hadn't fooled him. "There's just something too polished about you," he continued. I studied the ticket and reached into my purse for my wallet. "I don't buy the amateur photographer thing. What did you do before coming here?"

"Oh, so here comes the reporter now that his tummy's full? And who said I was an amateur photographer? Don't you like my shots?" I'd gathered my things together as I tried to move the conversation in a different direction and stood to leave. Jason stood with me, his sopaipilla barely touched.

"Sure, I like your shots." He picked up his check and followed me to the cash register.

We walked silently to our cars, the noise and busyness of the area making conversation difficult. As we approached my car, he broke the silence. "Just be careful, Sorrel."

"I'm always careful."

"I'm not teasing." He reached out awkwardly and patted my shoulder. "You're noticeable—that mane of hair and your attitude. We're a small place in comparison to where you must have lived before, but danger lurks everywhere."

"I'm waiting for the scary music to start!" I smiled, got into the Jeep, and started the engine. "What? No offer to follow me home?"

He grinned. "Okay, okay. See you later!"

I gave him a playful salute and pulled out of the parking lot, my mind already moving to the chores ahead.

CHAPTER FORTY-EIGHT

"Perfect!" Flash looked up from her pool of sunshine and blinked in agreement.

I'd walked in the front door to get the full effect my customers would have. Light, airy, and colorful. The Grand Opening would be soon, complete with food wagons, local radio station, and whatever else Terri had orchestrated. But first there was today with its to do list that had already stretched into several errands. I took one more panoramic view of the store, scooped up Flash, and relocated her to another sunshiny spot in the living quarters. Then I locked up the store and stepped into the already warm day.

I returned several hours later, hot and sticky. My last errand, photographing Little League teams, had exhausted me. Cajoling wiggly kids to stand still long enough for a group photo had been challenging. Worse, I'd had no lunch. I loaded my bulky camera bag on one shoulder, stuffed the bag of rolled coins I'd gotten for the cash drawer into my purse, and staggered toward the door. Once there, I slid the straps off my shoulders and reached for my door key.

That's when I smelled it. "Skunk!" I involuntarily stepped back and looked on either side of me. Skunks weren't common to the area, but occasionally I'd had to dodge a dead one in the road. Maybe one had just been nosing around. The smell tended to linger.

"Whew!"

I jumped and screamed, my purse and other bags sliding off my shoulder. Reed reached toward me, one hand steadying me before I fell off the step and the other breaking the fall of my bags. "I hope you don't have anything breakable in these," he said, still holding me upright.

"Why are you always creeping up on me?" I pulled myself out of his grasp.

"I wasn't creeping. You were just making like a statue, holding your nose, and yelling."

I felt my cheeks heating up. "I wasn't yelling!"

"Well, you are now." Reed pushed by me, looked around my door, and then headed toward the front of the store, sniffing as he walked.

"Where are you—"

"It's getting stronger," he said and continued walking.

I followed behind him, pretending I wasn't a little relieved to have someone else investigate the skunk. I wasn't afraid of the creatures, but tales about skunks and rabies had circulated for years. Besides, they were stinky creatures.

"Stay back." Reed's voice was stern enough that I followed just to the edge of the building and peeked around the corner. Reed was studying a garbage bag hanging from my front door.

He pulled a glove from his pocket, slipped it on his right hand, and carefully pulled open the top of the bag while holding his nose with his other hand. "Skunks. Dead ones, thankfully, but rank. They've been dead awhile."

I started forward. "Stay back, Sorrel," he repeated. "This may be just another kid's prank, but it doesn't feel right." He slipped the glove off and walked back to me then steered me toward the door to my living quarters. "Let's get your things inside. Then I'll call for someone to come gather evidence."

"Oh, for heaven's sake! That's all I need—my first customers arriving to yellow crime scene tape!" As we reached the steps, I saw that my keys had fallen on the step, but, as I reached for them the strap to my purse snapped with the weight and spilled its contents everywhere. "Great!" I yanked my arm out of his grasp. "See what you made me do?"

"Go on in with your other things and bring a bag out," he said. "I'll make my call and then I'll gather up all of this important stuff you had crammed into your purse, giving yourself permanent danger of walking lopsided in the near future, and I'll try to carry it inside."

"Smart—"

"Careful! You're talking to a peace officer." Reed pulled his cellphone from his pocket, a grin playing with the corners of his mouth. Had his eyes grown bluer?

I turned around, unlocked the door, gathered as many bags as I could, and started inside.

"And there'll be no crime tape," he called after me. Was that laughter I heard lurking in his voice?

I grabbed a trash bag from under the kitchen sink and tossed it on the step with as much dignity as I could muster and a sweet smile on my face. I wasn't a bad-tempered person! I was just unsettled. But Reed was on the phone, his back turned toward me, and missed my performance.

By the time he had gathered the contents in the bag and brought it to the door, I'd made a pitcher of iced tea and sliced the leftover pot roast for sandwiches.

"You making one of those for me?"

I only jumped a little. "Don't you ever eat at home?"

"Not much."

I sighed. "Mustard or mayo?"

"Mustard . . . and pickles."

I added chips and sliced apples to our plates and carried them to the table. Reed followed with glasses of iced tea. In silent accord, we postponed conversation and ate. By the time we finished, my ill temper had vanished.

Reed gathered up the plates and refilled our tea. "The least I can do," he said, seeming to be in better spirits as well. "You're a good cook."

I ignored the sarcasm and held his gaze, waiting for him to lecture, warn, or say whatever he planned to say. But before he could start, we heard a car pull up outside. He went to the door. "That's the deputy sheriff. Be right back."

I put the change I'd gotten from the bank into the change drawer, made sure the store was locked up, and settled on the couch to drink my second glass of tea. Reed joined me a few minutes later, his glass of tea in his hand.

"He'll take the critters to animal control for disposal," he said and walked over to the chair across from me. I waited as he seemed to be choosing his words. "Someone seems to not want you here."

I countered with what was becoming my standard refrain when he brought up the various incidents that had occurred since I'd moved here. "Kids just need something to do around here." I took a sip of my tea.

He continued to stand, staring at me. "Why the big mystery?"

"About ?"

"Who you really are."

The frustration of having to keep dealing with this caused me to flush. Why wouldn't he just leave it alone? "Who I am is someone who's tired of the local welcoming committee!"

"Listen, Sorrel—," but my phone rang, interrupting what was sure to be another lecture.

"Excuse me," I said, setting my tea down and picking up the phone.

A warm, familiar voice greeted me. "Thought I'd show up for your Grand Opening."

"John! I'd love to see you! But you're a bit early for the Grand Opening."

"I know, but when you described the state park nearby, I thought I'd make this a good visit—take some photos and spend some time with you. Didn't stop to think it might be an imposition."

"You know better than that! I'd love to have you around always!"

Reed made a noise, but by the time I glanced his way, he was out the door. Odd, but I had yet to figure him out. "Where are you?" I asked, leaving analysis of Reed's peculiarities for another time.

"In town. Just give me directions, and we can talk when I get your place."

CHAPTER FORTY-NINE

"This is just how I visualized it . . . but better! You've got a nice variety of pieces. How have the sales gone?"

I'd led John into the shop first, wanting him to get the full vision. He hadn't disappointed me, his eyes first sweeping over the room before focusing on each of the displays.

"It's been light, of course, because I haven't wanted to advertise until the Grand Opening. Mostly we've had tourists who have wandered by."

"How do you manage, what with being gone as much as you are?"

"Teri is a wonder, organizing the seniors into a schedule. She and her family are running with the Grand Opening also. They feel like a whirlwind." I smiled wistfully. " I like that."

"Any regrets about leaving your career? Friends?"

"Not at all. I didn't really have many friends. The job was too cutthroat. Every moment had to be focused on the career." I shook my head and then smiled. "I love the people here . . . the slower pace . . . the freedom to be myself without worrying about my looks, my weight!"

John laughed. He looked around once more. "How about a glass of iced tea?"

"My specialty!"

John had insisted on grilling steaks for dinner after we'd looked through his recent photos. Under his gentle probing, I'd filled him in on the events since moving to Saddle Gap. He'd not said much, but as we washed and dried dishes, John suggested that I could just be the victim of a string of coincidences.

Settling in the living room to enjoy a cup of coffee, I finally asked, "John, why are you really here?"

"To support you in your opening, of course."

"And?"

"I was asked to let you know that Kevin's case is now cold."

"After all the upheaval, my career, the hush-hush—"

"Kevin's murder is being considered a home invasion gone wrong."

"And unofficially?"

"Unofficially, the Gang Task Force continues to follow leads and keep their ears to the ground."

I swiped at the tears on my cheeks. "I'd like to think it was a home invasion . . . it would make me feel less . . . guilty, less responsible."

"Sorrel, we've talked many times about this. Your stories on the gangs do not make you responsible for Kevin's death. You were doing your job—"

"—and Kevin hated it." I sipped then frowned at the now cold coffee.

"And you?"

"I don't think I realized how tired I had become. Being a 'big star' is lonely. Everyone is after your spot. But I did love the job. If all of us are afraid to expose the ugly, then the beautiful is endangered."

"And as Kevin's wife?"

"That was lonely too," I admitted. "We both knew we'd made a mistake, although I didn't realize that until after he was dead. But we were . . . a golden couple." I got up to dump and refill my cup, offering to do the same for John. He smiled but shook his head. Too much caffeine would keep him awake.

"My life here feels so free," I continued when I returned to the living room. "Every day I wake up to this excitement."

"Sorrel, I've known you a long time. This is the happiest I've seen you—in spite of the things that have been happening here." He paused and I could see he was thinking of how to phrase whatever was coming next.

"I sent you warnings as news came to me," he said, "but you need to know that your detective here knows who you are."

"Reed? How?"

John chuckled. "Well, he is a detective, you know. With today's technology, it's difficult to hide out, especially when you're a beautiful woman who has been in the public eye."

"Why didn't he ever mention it?"

"Probably didn't want to tip his hand. You have to admit you've been in the middle of some strange circumstances. You're among the last people to see a woman before she is murdered, you show up at another of crime scene as a fill-in photographer, and then all sorts of things start happening to you. Mighty strange."

I sat for a moment, sipping my coffee, mulling over what he'd just said. I reflected on Stephanie, knowing her murder was probably cold now too. I sat my cup on the table and reached out for Flash, perched on the arm of my chair, and cuddled her close. "Remember how people use that old cliché *get away with murder*? I guess people do that."

John reached over and squeezed my hand. "Honey, there are always some who do."

We both turned at the crunch of tires outside. "You expecting someone?" John asked.

"No." I went to the door and peeked out the spy hole. "It's Reed."

"Guess it's about time we met." He rose and carried his cup to the kitchen.

I opened the door before Reed could ring the bell. "Hi."

He stood quietly on the step and just looked at me.

"Are you going to come in?"

"I don't want to interrupt anything."

I shook my head. "You're not. Besides, I want you to meet my old friend." I whirled around, bumping into John. "Oops, sorry. John, this is Reed, our local police detective. Reed, one of my former professors . . . and long-time friend."

The two men stared at each other for a long moment. Satisfied, each stuck out a hand and shook. I stepped back. "Iced tea? Coffee?"

Reed stepped inside. "I wouldn't mind a cup of coffee. Just had dinner with Jose and Teri. Only coffee can lessen the burn of those jalapenos."

By the time I returned with coffee, Reed and John were seated close, not whispering but clearly in an intense discussion that stopped when I neared. "Since I expect I'm the main topic, how about including me in the discussion."

John winked at Reed. "Just like a woman. Always thinks she's the center of every topic."

I handed Reed his coffee, settled into the shabby armchair, and tucked my feet up under me. "What gives, Reed?"

"Not much for small talk, is she?" Reed sipped his coffee while he seemed to decide what to say.

"Neither am I." John gave me one of his knowing looks. "You've been snooping, Detective Reed. Why?"

"My job."

The two men looked at each other for a minute, each seeming to reach a conclusion.

Reed spoke first. "She's told you about the odd incidents since she moved here. The murder was just a coincidence. She happened to be at a bar and saw a woman who was murdered later that night. But the series of incidents that have happened since may or may not be related."

"Like what?" John, who was a good poker player, held his cards close to his chest, never suggesting that I had told him about each and every incident.

"Vandalism to her car, an old shed torched, strangers warning her off, someone snooping in her house." Reed took a long drink of his coffee and set it on the side table. "Could be coincidence. Could be kids' pranks."

"But you don't think so."

"No." It was the first time he'd admitted that.

John leaned forward. "Sorrel, I think it's time."

"John—"

"We had him checked out, Sorrel."

"What? Me?" Reed turned toward me, but John interrupted.

"We had to. You were checking Sorrel out."

Whatever Reed had planned to hear, that wasn't it. The two men stared at each other again, continuing to take stock of each other. Once again they finally seemed to reach a mutual decision. But this time so had I.

"Okay, guys. We all know the same things . . . sort of, so why don't we work together once and for all." Silence.

I turned toward Reed, but he wasn't meeting my eye. "I can't share information on an ongoing investigation," he said, resorting to the standard police line, his face set in his typical mulish expression.

"Then deputize us," John said.

Reed and I both looked at him quizzically.

"I was just being facetious," he said, standing up. "But we seem to have reached an impasse here. I've had a long day on the road and I'm not a youngster. I vote we take this up another time."

Reed and I stood as well. John gathered me into a big hug. "You get some rest," he said. "I think the people in this community are going to love you as much as the rest of us do. " He turned to Reed. "You coming?"

"One word with Sorrel." John nodded and stepped out the door.

Reed turned to me. "He's protective." His eyes questioned.

"Like the father I no longer have."

"Sorrel—"

"Reed, I know we need to talk—really talk—but after the opening."

He nodded, turned toward the door, then came back. "Guess I might as well wish you luck," he said, sweeping me into a big hug that ended with a soft kiss. "Sleep well."

I didn't expect to.

CHAPTER FIFTY

"Not another burrito!" Teri snatched one from her each of her sons' hands. "Go to Tia," she told them. "It's time for you two to go home for a nap!"

I'd like a nap, I thought. Thanks to Teri's family, we'd had a steady line of cars stopping by to look at the shop and sample the homemade Mexican food. Each vendor had donated something for the door prizes we were giving away, one each hour. Best of all, most of the customers had left with items from the shop. Teri's products had caught many eyes, and I'd sold some of my photography as well.

"Have you eaten anything? No, I can tell you haven't! Here, have a burrito!" Teri pulled me over to one of the picnic tables and pushed me down. She then sent Jose off to get us something to drink while she helped Tia get the boys in the car. I bit into the burrito as I watched the two of them scurry in opposite directions.

"She's a real asset. Knows how to organize."

I jumped. "John! I didn't see you!" I moved over for him to sit next to me. "Have you eaten?"

"I couldn't take another bite! But I wouldn't say no to that water." I hadn't noticed Jose was back already, standing beside me with bottles of cold water. I thanked Jose, handed one to John, and took a long drink from the other. With everything that was going on, I couldn't remember if John had ever met Jose, so between bites, I made sure.

"Sorrel, thought you'd like to know that we're starting to shut down the food wagons."

"Already?" I glanced at my watch. It was after two! The day had just flown! I took another long drink and another bite of burrito and followed

Jose's gaze. Teri was eating her burrito as she stuffed the boys into their booster seats and talked nonstop. "I don't know how she does it."

"Neither do I." Jose smiled and then gulped his soda, his eyes moving over the thinning crowd. "I thought I saw Reed somewhere—oh, there he is." He turned to John and shook his hand. "Nice to have met you." Then he started walking in Reed's direction.

John and I sat quietly for a few moments, drinking and chewing. Finally, I asked, "What's going on, John?"

"Hmm?"

"John, look at me." He turned reluctantly. "You, Jose, and Reed are extraordinarily preoccupied with watching the customers—and me. It feels like Operation Sorrel."

"A bit dramatic, Sorrel!"

I leaned toward him. "I have always wanted to be kept informed." As he looked behind me, he put his finger to his lips to quiet me.

A second or two later, I began to cough. I turned to see Mr. Byrd holding a cigar in his hand. "Oh, sorry, Sorrel. I forgot I still had this thing. My wife makes me smoke them outdoors, and I took advantage of lighting up. I'll get rid of it. "

I stood up. "That's okay, The wind is moving it away. And I'm glad you're here. I'd like you to meet my old friend who taught me what I know about photography. Oops! Of course, you know each other!"

"Not personally," John said. "We met at a conference a few years ago, exchanged business cards. You still interested in photography?"

"Interested but never followed up on it." Mr. Byrd smiled at my surprise. " One of those things you think you'd like to do someday."

The two men shook hands. "She's a great photographer," Mr. Byrd told him. "Circulation has gone way up since she started sharing her photos. Thanks for pointing her this direction."

"A real natural," John agreed. "But she was already headed this way. When I heard the name of the town, it nudged a memory. Do you have any favorite photo spots?"

Happy they seemed to have found a mutual conversation topic, I excused myself to check on the store. As I tossed the burrito wrapper, I realized something was niggling at the back of my mind—irritating—and it didn't leave, even as I headed into the shop. Most of the seniors who'd helped through the morning had left, but Teri had beaten me inside and had just rung up a sale.

Something rubbed against my ankle. "Flash! What are you doing out?" I scooped her up and headed toward the door at the back of the shop marked Private.

Before I could reach the door, Teri caught a glimpse of me. "Sorrel, could you—what's Flash doing out?"

"That's what I'm wondering," I said, smiling at customers while hurrying on. Teri reached the door the same time I did and tried the knob.

"It's unlocked," she whispered, smiling to appear unconcerned. "Don't go in. Let's call Reed. He's just out there—"

"No, don't do that. I probably forgot to lock it with all of the excitement—"

"I saw you. You checked it." We both jumped. How had Reed gotten in so quickly? "Just go on taking care of people, Teri," he said quietly. "We don't want to upset any of your customers."

"Good idea," she said. Reed took the purring ball of fur from my arms and passed her over to Teri, who calmly started back to the office, stopping to check on some ladies clustered around the jewelry booth.

Reed casually moved me over a bit and slipped through the door. "Wait for me," he whispered.

But I followed anyway, bumping against him as he stopped just inside. He sighed but didn't seem surprised.

"Since you're here, do you see anything out of place?" I could hardly hear him, my heart was pounding so loudly. I carefully looked around the living room and as much of the small kitchen as I could without crossing the room. Nothing looked like it had been touched.

"No," I whispered.

Reed slipped quietly toward the partially open door to the right that led into my bedroom. He stopped just beside the door and, as he motioned for me to follow behind him, I realized he had drawn his gun! The weird feeling I'd had all day returned—the way he and John and Jose had acted so casually while their eyes were constantly darting around, the feeling of eyes following me, that niggling caused by the—smoke! Cigar smoke!

"Reed," I whispered, "I need—"

He motioned for me to shush with his free hand and stepped around the door. "Can I help you?"

I heard something fall just before I poked my head around the door frame and looked into familiar eyes. The man who'd pretended to be the sheriff's deputy! Only he wasn't in uniform this time, and his face was covered with a scraggly beard that couldn't have been more than a few days old. "I'd like an answer to that!" I said.

"No need to shoot," the man said, raising his hands, imitating someone in an old western. "I was just looking for the bathroom."

"This is the private living quarters. The shop has no public bathroom. Didn't you see the portables outside? They're well marked." I hadn't heard John, and neither had Reed, who glanced toward him for just a second.

As he did, the intruder leaped toward Reed. John shoved me aside, joining the struggle, even though he wasn't much of a challenge for the younger man, who shrugged John off as he kept a death grip on Reed's gun, his eyes never leaving Reed's.

Suddenly, the man kneed Reed in the groin. Reed turned loose then butted his head into the man's stomach. As the stranger doubled over, the gun skittered across the floor toward me. I grabbed it and backed off.

"Looks like I'm too late to help." Mr. Byrd stepped through the door from the guest bedroom, taking the scene in quickly. "I'll take the gun, Sorrel, so Reed can clap handcuffs on this guy. I'm sure you don't know how to use it. But you sure have quick reflexes."

I backed away another step and pointed the gun toward Mr. Byrd. "I don't think so."

Reed had already snapped cuffs on the intruder and was looking toward me. "Sorrel? It's okay. We've got it all under control." Reed's voice had assumed the calm, soothing sound police officers use when dealing with someone mentally unbalanced. He thought I was crazy.

When Mr. Byrd stepped toward me, I moved back again. "I do know how to use this, Mr. Byrd," taking another step back. But I bumped against the bed and started to fall backwards.

"I guess we need to figure out what is happening here." John slid between us, keeping Mr. Byrd from grabbing the gun, which wobbled crazily in my hand, and casually moved Mr. Byrd back from the bed.

Reed's hand enveloped mine, steadying the gun before he took it from me. He first eyed me and then Mr. Byrd.

Mr. Byrd started backing up toward the door, laughing. "This is the craziest thing I've ever seen. This woman is nuts, Reed, trying to shoot me. What does she think I've done? What is she drinking?"

"Sorrel?" I wasn't sure whether Reed was talking to me or agreeing with Randy Byrd.

"It was the cigar smoke." I knew I wasn't making much sense. I looked at John, at Reed, at the imposter, and back to Mr. Byrd. "I told you. It was the cigar. I've been trying to remember what it was that I missed the night Stephanie died. I remembered the cigar but not the smoker. It's weird, but when you're among a bunch of strangers, you see them but their faces don't always stay with you. But the smell of that cigar did! And now I remember. You were there, Mr. Byrd. I thought Stephanie was looking at me, but it was you all the time."

"And that's why you were holding a gun on me?" Mr. Byrd had dropped the patronizing laughter, his voice getting louder with each word until he was shouting. "This is the craziest thing I've ever heard of. There are dozens of cigar smokers everywhere, and that young lady probably smiled at every male in the place, someone like her."

"Like her?" Reed asked. "You said you'd never seen her, knew nothing about her." He looked behind Byrd toward the hall, where Jose was now standing. "I could use some help, Jose. We need to take everyone here to the station and clear up things."

CHAPTER FIFTY-ONE

John and I followed Reed and the police car with Mr. Byrd and the imposter to the station. Before we went in, John patted my shoulder. "No matter what else is going on, that guy had no business in your house. He'd gone through the drawers and closet and no telling what else. Who is he?"

I told John about my visit from the deputy sheriff and about seeing him at my house after the fire. "I've had this feeling—often—of being followed or watched. Now I wonder if it was this guy. But why? What would be the point? And what's craziest of all is he was there at the bar that night, at Mr. Byrd's table. But Mr. Byrd didn't even acknowledge him here. And he never spoke to Mr. Byrd."

"Curiouser and curiouser. Randy Byrd doesn't seem to fit in here, but I don't really know him well. It could be a mix-up—or he's not the person he seems."

Mr. Byrd! The enormity of the situation hit me. "What if I've—"

"Sorrel, I've known you a long time. You have a keen eye and a good mind. Don't doubt yourself. Just try to tell Reed what you know, whether it helps him or not. He can put it together and see if it fits."

"I hope he's good at puzzles."

John laughed. "I think that young man is good at a lot of things."

When we entered the police station, we could hear Mr. Byrd demanding to call his lawyer. "Are you sure?" Reed asked. "I'm not charging you with anything. I don't really know why you're so upset."

"I'll tell you why! My family has run the paper for generations. We have never had our name smeared or been hauled down to the police station like common criminals," He sputtered to a halt, waving his arms helplessly. "Where's the sheriff? Shouldn't this all be his problem?"

"He's tied up with another case of slaughtered cattle, way out at the Vargas ranch. We work together."

"I want the Chief! I'll have your job!" Then he glared at me. "You are fired!" he yelled. "And I hope you find a doctor who can help you before you try to ruin someone else's reputation and family!"

"Randy, do you know the young man I have handcuffed in my interrogation room?" Reed interrupted.

"Of course not!"

"Never seen him before?"

"Never!"

"Then answer this question for me. Why were you in Sorrel's bedroom with the rest of us?"

"No thanks from her but I wanted to help if I could."

"How did you know she needed help?"

"I saw you and Sorrel sneaking in. The newspaperman in me kicked in so I thought I'd see what was happening." He kept glancing at me, barely containing his anger, but I didn't look away.

"How?"

"What do you mean?"

"I mean I shut the door after Sorrel and I stepped in. How did you follow us in?"

The room was silent as Mr. Byrd and Reed just looked at each other.

Reed asked again, "How did you get in? Jose arrived shortly after we went in, according to Teri and a couple of ladies in the shop, and he waited by the door to keep people outside. When he heard you shouting, he and John came inside."

He turned to John and me. "I need you to talk to you two as well. You can wait in my office." Then he turned back to Mr. Byrd. "And, Randy, I think you need to call your lawyer after all."

CHAPTER FIFTY-TWO

I got up early the next day to clean the store and catch up on bookwork. With so many people attending the Grand Opening and the food wagon leaving its inevitable residue behind, I had a big job ahead.

I hoped closing early the day before for my personal emergency wouldn't ruin the great start my shop had made. I'd only planned to be open four days a week and Teri had already set up a schedule of booth owners and seniors to help in the store, so I was covered if I needed to be away for a few days. Still . . .

John had left—reluctantly—after we'd finished at the police station, heading to a photo contest he'd entered. "You've paid the fee," I'd argued. "And this thing isn't settled yet. It may never be." We'd hugged and I waved to him until he drove out of sight.

Taping the signs with the store's new hours on the front door, I sighed. How had things gone so wrong?

Aside from trespassing, Reed had nothing on the imposter, a drifter named Jake Black. He'd been sleeping in his truck out at the national park campground and earning money doing side jobs. We hadn't found anything that he'd stolen and he'd refused to admit who had hired him— if anyone—so Reed had turned him loose with dire warnings if he showed up at my place again.

Reed had also calmed Mr. Byrd after both he and Jake swore they didn't know each other. In fact, Mr. Byrd had been telling the truth. He'd noticed the stranger around and his suspicions had arisen. And, once he had his attorney there, he had stopped talking. I apologized, but he eyed me frostily and turned to go. "Sorrel, I wouldn't be expecting any more work with the paper if I were you," he spit out before leaving.

201

All in all, I guess I'd made some powerful mistakes. Even Reed was polite but distant, unlike his usual irritating self.

It was close to noon before I'd finished the chores, and the afternoon stretched emptily ahead. Teri and I had spoken briefly, but I knew that she valued her job at the paper and close association with me could jeopardize it. Even she had said carefully, "I can't believe Mr. Byrd would ever be involved in anything criminal."

"I think I jumped to conclusions," I replied. Teri and I had grown close in my short time here, and she was invaluable to the shop.

Something still niggled in the back of my mind, but sitting here in my kitchen wasn't helping. I needed to retrace a few steps. As I sipped my tea, one place kept beckoning me—the apartment where Stephanie had lived.

CHAPTER FIFTY-THREE

I knocked at the apartment door, but Mrs. Birton didn't answer. I had already turned to leave when I heard the door open.

"Yes?" She seemed a bit leery of anyone visiting, as she peaked through the narrow opening between the door and doorframe.

"Hi. I'm not sure if you remember me, Mrs. Birton. I'm the photographer from the newspaper. I just wanted to thank you again for talking to us," I said, holding out to her the small bouquet of flowers I'd picked up at the market on my way to the apartment.

She brightened and opened the door wider. "Of course I remember you. What beautiful flowers!" She took them from my hand before fully opening the door and nodding toward the living room. "Please come in and sit down while I look for a vase for these flowers . . . just overlook how I'm dressed. I don't have people drop in unexpectedly now that that dear girl next door is . . . gone. She would surprise me by appearing unexpectedly."

As she hurried into the tiny kitchenette, I looked around the small living room, overflowing with tiny reminders of a past life and a larger home. When she returned, she carried a tray with two glasses of iced tea and a plate of cookies. "I hope you like peanut butter cookies dear. I don't need to eat the whole batch, but I love to make them."

We chatted about my photography and the new store and the kinds of merchandise I was selling. "Oh, my daughter and I need to come by!" she said, looking around her living room and smiling. "Don't know where I'd put anything, but I'm sure I'd find a place."

As I was trying to figure out how to bring up Stephanie, she did it for me. "I miss not having Stephanie next door," she said. "I saw her apartment once. It was so bare so I gave her a few little things. She so appreciated them."

"Sad," I said, nodding my head slightly. "I didn't really know her, of course. I'd only seen her that last night at the bar. Still . . ."

"Yes, poor thing. She loved to dance. Told me she always loved the last one."

I murmured encouragingly. "Well, all alone, no friends or family or boyfriend."

"At least not a proper one." She took a sip and then shook her head. "She should have known that a married man . . ."

"Really? That's odd because I don't think I've ever heard that she had a boyfriend. Did you tell the police?"

She shifted uncomfortably. "No. I never saw him, and it really wasn't any of my business, you know." She lifted her glass, took another sip, and then put it down again. "But you can't just ignore some   things . . ."

"True. Walls are thin."

"Oh, he didn't come here! I think she saw him at work . . . at that motel!" She leaned forward and lowered her voice to a whisper. "It was the gifts. She had this necklace—diamond— that he gave her. Well, she said it was from a friend, but no friend would have just given her something that expensive . . . and she had this little smile. She said she couldn't wear it out, just tucked it inside her blouse." Her eyes bored into mine. "So I knew he was married."

I nodded. "Poor thing. No family to look after her . . ." I let the comment hang and took another sip of tea. "I'm glad she had you."

She opened her mouth then changed her mind. I couldn't tell if I saw fear in her eyes—or just guilt at being a gossip. She offered me a cookie and then smiled. "Enough about that sad topic. You'll have to tell me all about the store!"

She was clearly uncomfortable, so I chatted for a bit before rising to go. "I've enjoyed our visit! Thanks for the tea."

"I hope you'll come again," she said, as she opened the door for me to leave.

After she shut her door, I stood for a minute in the dim hall, looking from her door to Stephanie's. The apartment hadn't been rented yet, but I could smell paint through the partially open door. I wondered what they had done with her things. Of course, Reed wouldn't have mentioned if they'd found a diamond necklace.

I peeked through the crack. Stephanie's apartment was a sort of mirror image of Mrs. Birton's, and if the unpainted wall nearest the hall was any indication, it hadn't been painted in a long time. The room was empty, so I inched forward and stepped inside. Her tiny kitchen wall facing out was a warm orange.

"Whatcha want?"

I jumped and stepped back onto a large foot. "Excuse me." I smiled, adding a flirtatious twinkle at the big guy in overalls. "I was looking for a girl I work with—Veronica?"

"Wrong place." He returned my smile and came around me, brushing against me a bit. "This one is empty. Interested in renting? You new to town?"

"Maybe."

"Want me to show you around?" This was going better than I'd hoped.

"Sure."

"How about five? I'll have this cleared up by then."

"Is it empty? I could look now."

"Can't. Gotta lock it up and get over to another one. Lady stopped up her sink." Darn! "Well, maybe I—"

I darted out the apartment and trotted down the walk before he finished his sentence.

I wondered again about the motive for her murder. Maybe it wasn't personal. If she had nice jewelry from this boyfriend, it could have been robbery. I hopped in my car and headed to the police station.

CHAPTER FIFTY-FOUR

Reed looked up when I knocked on his door. He sighed. "Now what?" he asked, as he motioned me inside. His pursed lips and the set of his jaw told me he was more than a little irritated with my arrival.

"Did you know that Stephanie had a married boyfriend? One that she only saw at the motel?"

He just looked at me several seconds before speaking. "Have a seat." As I sat down, I noticed how tired he looked. "And your point is, Miss Super Sleuth?"

I let the sarcasm pass. "Surely that points to a motive for her murder? And maybe a new suspect?"

Reed sighed again. "I think I'll pass on any more of your clues."

"Reed, this is a viable clue—"

"Maybe. But why should I trust you? You haven't trusted any of us here who have befriended you."

"I—"

"And don't bother to make up more lies." His voice was hard, full of anger and—hurt. "You've pretended to be someone you're not. Our community opened their hearts to you—and you lied to them."

I met his gaze, realizing that I'd waited too long to talk to him about Kevin, Houston, and the reason I'd come to Saddle Gap. Everything had happened so quickly the day of the Grand Opening, and now . . .

"I knew early on that you weren't telling me the truth. I checked up on you, remember? If you wanted to remain anonymous, you sure did a poor job of it!" Reed took a drink of his coffee, grimaced, and put it down. "I was worried for my friends who believed you. Dammit, Sorrel—or whoever you call yourself today—this is a good place. Sure, we have crimes and, rarely, we even have murders. But people here depend on their neighbors. And a man's—or woman's—word is more important than anything. I kept hoping you'd finally tell the truth . . . at least to me."

"So what do you really need to know, Reed? Isn't it enough that I needed protection or, at the very least, privacy and came here because I'd inherited the shop and wasn't really known in the area?"

His eyes hardened even more. "You didn't explain that you needed protection."

"Why are you so angry?"

"Why are you so evasive?"

"I—"

Reed's radio squawked. I couldn't understand the codes, but I recognized the address.

"We'll have to take this up later," he said, grabbing his hat and heading out the door. "Don't follow me."

I didn't have to follow him. I'd just left that address.

CHAPTER FIFTY-FIVE

I parked down the block from the apartment building. An ambulance had already arrived and onlookers were continuing to gather. I couldn't see Reed.

"What are you doing here, Sorrel?"

I jumped. I hadn't seen the car pull up behind me. "Jason! You scared a year of my life away!"

"You have a police scanner? Or are you working for them?"

"Of course not. I was just in Reed's office when the call came in."

He nodded his head and stepped back from the car. "Guess I'd better see what's going on." He shifted his feet, clearly uncomfortable talking about work.

"Mind if I join you?" I hopped out of the Jeep before he could answer. "I can keep my eyes and ears open."

"Mr. Byrd—"

"—doesn't have to know. I'm not here for a story, Jason. I just left Mrs. Birton half an hour ago and need to find out what happened."

Jason headed across the street. "I can't help where you go, but officially you're not with the paper now."

I hurried after him. "I liked her," I told him.

Jason didn't answer. I didn't blame him. He liked his job, and I'd made a serious enemy in his boss.

The EMTs wheeled out a gurney as we approached. I was hopeful when I saw Mrs. Birton on the gurney, not in a body bag. She'd been badly beaten. The EMTs had already started two IVs and attached electrodes to monitor her heart, but she was deathly pale. My hope faded. I prayed she hadn't been hurt because of my snooping around earlier. Could that guy in the overalls have been . . . ? Now I was scared of everyone and everything! That wasn't like me, and I refused to let it continue.

I waited silently with an assortment of neighbors and curious bystanders as they loaded her into the ambulance and sped away.

A couple of uniformed officers had put up crime tape to keep people away from the apartment. I could see Jason speaking to an older lady—maybe a neighbor?—but those around me stood silently.

A few seconds later, Reed stepped out of the building and scanned the crowd. When his eyes lighted on me, he headed straight toward me, turning his head to give instructions to one of the uniforms nearby.

As he reached me, he took my arm and propelled me toward my Jeep, opened the door, and pushed me inside.

" Hey! What—" But he closed the door, ignoring my indignation, and leaned against it.

"Sorrel—or whoever you are—"

"Sorrel Rose Janes."

"Whatever! You were here earlier today?"

"Yes."

"Why? And don't tell me it was for the paper. I was there, remember, when you were fired."

"I wanted to invite her to help in the shop. I've been recruiting seniors."

"A personal invitation? As crazy as things have been for you, you take time to drive all the way over here to invite her to work in the shop?"

"She asked me to come back," I answered. One of the perks of my career had been learning to lie convincingly. "I'd promised her I'd stop by."

Reed sighed and pulled a small pad out of his shirt pocket. He jotted something down and then his voiced changed to a more official tone.

"Did you see anything unusual? Anyone hanging out that shouldn't be here?"

"No." I started to mention the guy next door, but then I realized he might mention my wandering through Stephanie's apartment.

"Did she seem nervous?" Reed asked.

"No. Well, maybe a little edgy."

"Where did you get the part about the boyfriend?"

"Stephanie's? It kind of slipped out. I said something like Stephanie had been alone and she said there were expensive gifts that had come from a boyfriend. Then she got scared, said he was married, and changed the subject."

Reed looked at me for a minute. "Sorrel, you need to take a trip. Go visit someone. Give us time to—"

"I can't just close down the shop when I've only just opened it!"

"Sorrel—"

"Detective!" one of the uniforms called to Reed from across the street.

He waved acknowledgment and then turned back to me. "I have never seen a more mule-headed person—"

"Sure you have, Reed. You look in the mirror to shave, don't you?"

His face skewed in frustration, Reed turned away for a second. When he turned toward me again, he was calmer. "This is serious, Sorrel. You attract attention and you show up at the wrong place regularly. Look, I don't have time to argue with you right now. Will you at least do one thing I ask? Will you drop by the police station in an hour or so and give a statement? I don't want people to get the idea that you know more than you do, and they'll think that if they see you giving one here."

Without waiting for an answer, Reed leaned inside the window and kissed me, a long, thorough kiss. "That will give them something else to gossip about," he whispered and turned to walk back to the crime scene, waving to me over his shoulder.

I hadn't been kissed like that in a long time—maybe never.

As I reached to start the Jeep, I heard my name. I looked up to see Jason lope across the street. "How's it going?" I asked.

"No one seems to have seen much," he said. "Hey, I'm sorry I was standoffish earlier. Can we grab a cup of coffee or a bite to eat?"

"I'd like to, but I need to—"

"I've got some information you might want to hear." He smiled.

I sighed. "You know I can't resist!"

"Can I ride with you so I can save my parking spot? I need to come back here later."

"Where do you want to go?" I asked, as I unlocked the passenger side door.

CHAPTER FIFTY-SIX

I made a U-turn in the nearest driveway to avoid the traffic in front of the crime scene and headed toward a café we had frequented before. Both of us were silent for a few seconds as I maneuvered out of the tangle of onlookers and police vehicles and turned onto the next side street.

"You know, Jason, this just doesn't add up. Why would someone hurt her? I mean, Stephanie lived just next door, but what harm could a little old lady do to anyone?"

"Who knows? Accidents happen."

"Accident? I didn't get the details, but she was clearly beaten! Didn't you see her face when the EMTs brought her out? Someone wanted to hurt her, but why? If I hadn't been there asking questions—"

"Did she tell you something new?"

I glanced at Jason, suddenly uncomfortable. Maybe it was something in his voice—that casual but not quite friendly tone—or the way he was leaning in toward me. Something just wasn't right.

"Not really," I finally answered. The café was just ahead. "You know, I'm not really hungry, Jason, and I've got so much still to do at the store. Can I have a rain check? I'll just turn around in the parking lot here."

Jason didn't answer, so I pulled into the café parking lot and stopped. But instead of getting out, he just sat there for a couple of seconds before turning toward me. That was when I saw the gun in his right hand.

"I'm not so hungry either," he said. "Why don't we head over to the highway?"

I swallowed and looked in the rearview mirror and all around. The lot was empty. "I don't have much gas," I said. "Why don't you just get out and I'll—"

"—call your detective boyfriend? Right. How dumb do you think I am?"

"You're smart, Jason, and . . . talented and . . . a friend," I said. "Let's just talk—"

"—although," he interrupted, "I could just shoot you and be out of here before anyone gets out of that little joint. Gunfire isn't unheard of in this neighborhood. And most of these people know to stay inside."

I put the Jeep in reverse and started backing up. "Slowly, Sorrel. I wouldn't want this thing to go off," he said, raising his gun toward me ever so slightly.

I calmed myself. Panicking wouldn't help, and I couldn't let him take me out of town. "Jason—"

"—why am I doing this? Isn't it obvious, Sorrel Janes—I mean, Stacy Lee Jamison.."

I gasped and he laughed. "I knew who you were the first time I saw you, the night Stephanie . . . died. You were clever to change the hair color, but you should have been less dramatic in your color choice. That red hair is a flame."

I started to turn back toward town, but Jason yanked the wheel to the right.

"Evening News anchor/crime reporter in Houston. On the fast track to New York," he continued. "You should have kept your nose out of . . . other people's business. Your husband would have preferred that for sure!"

I'd been deliberately driving under the speed limit, forcing us to stop at the next stoplight. "That wasn't my fault."

"Really?"

I glanced at Jason. "You know something about Kevin's death?"

"He tried to bargain, you know. He offered to tell us anything we wanted to know about you if we'd spare him."

I prayed for an opportunity. If I could just keep Jason talking, maybe I could figure something out. "I don't believe that," I said. "Kevin was honorable . . . and he loved me."

"He cursed you as he died." Jason laughed. "But he was happy to tell us some of your secrets, like your real name, in hopes of saving himself. He even gave us the location where you liked to run, but you didn't show.

"I had a headache, so I changed my mind about running. I went on to the station to finish a story since Kevin wouldn't be home." Keep him talking, I reminded myself.

"Oh, he was home all right. My friend stayed with him while I tried to find you. When you didn't show, we got rid of him. He screamed in spite of the gag. And you have a nosy neighbor. She called the cops."

"I wondered how they came so quickly. Were you the one who hit me? And you killed Kevin?" It sounded like my voice was talking from far away—in a tunnel or something. "How did you know she heard?"

"I saw her on the phone through a window. She was too scared for it to have been one of her old gossips. So I whacked you and we left out the back door. I meant to finish you off, but we couldn't risk it. We knew we'd find you someday."

The images he brought to my mind blurred my vision and I swerved.

"Watch it!" Jason shouted, poking the gun into my ribs.

"Why? You're going to kill me anyway! Just like you killed Stephanie!"

"She was just in the wrong place at the wrong time," he laughed. "She saw me in the parking lot—with my partner. Even as dumb as she was, she might have eventually put us all together."

He glanced over and laughed. "You still don't know do you? Stephanie didn't have a married lover. But she did have a dad—an influential one whose wife didn't know about an illegitimate daughter. The wild seeds of his youth."

"And he killed her?" I asked, hoping he would stay focused on the story and not on my driving. I had begun to wind back through the neighborhood, trying to avoid any direct route to the highway.

Jason, caught up in his tale, laughed. "Of course not. But she knew me because I work for him . . . and I didn't want her to tie me into your murder."

"Mr. Byrd? He was her father?" I asked, ignoring the statement about my impending death. Just then a dog darted in front of the Jeep and I slammed on the brakes.

Jason braced himself and then looked around. "You think you're too clever," he said. "You think I didn't notice you made a wrong turn and are trying to keep me occupied?" He laughed.

I almost did it too, I thought. I pulled over to the curb. "Let me get this straight. I was working on drug involvement through gangs in the high schools. How did that turn into all this—with my murder? And Stephanie's murder? And Mr. Byrd? And—"

Jason's fist smashed into the side of my face, slamming me into the door frame. I cried out, instinctively grabbing my head. Jason reached over and turned off the Jeep. I saw a window curtain twitch as I looked past Jason. Or was I imagining it? I tasted blood where I'd bitten my lip. My right eye was already starting to swell.

Jason leaned close to me and whispered into my neck. "Whoever made that curtain move will think we're lovers who have had a tiff. We're going to kiss and make up." He brushed his lips against my numb mouth.

"And now we're going to drive out of town. If you try anything else, I'll shoot you. By the time they find us, I'll have a convincing story about how you went crazy—have been crazy for a long time over your husband's murder—and tried to kidnap me."

"You'd never get away with that."

"That's an old cliché from black and white movies. We get away with it all the time."

"Then do it! I'm done!"

He hadn't expected that. Neither did he expect the knock on the passenger window.

"Drop it!" Reed's voice sounded muffled through the glass.

Jason turned toward him, his gun moving with him toward Reed.

I heard a gun discharge, deafening me, and felt blood and flesh as they erupted, covering everything.

"Sorrel? Sorrel!"

EPILOGUE

"I don't think I've seen so many flags, stars, or twinkling lights in my whole life. Teri has been here."

"It's July 4th weekend," I said, "and with the big festival downtown, we should have lots of tourists."

"Not to mention all the food Teri's family will be pushing in your parking lot."

Flash had jumped out of her bed and was weaving around Reed's legs. He reached down and scooped her up. "It's good to see you back in the shop," he said. "But since you're not open, can I beg a glass of iced tea?"

Neither of us spoke as we walked back to the kitchen and I poured the tea. "Let's get comfortable on the back porch," I said. "I've had a window unit installed."

Once settled, with Flash on his knee, I asked, "So why haven't I seen you?"

Reed took a long drink. "First, you were in the hospital." He looked down at Flash then up at me. "Dammit, Sorrel, you nearly gave me a heart attack. I thought I'd killed you!"

"And whose fault would that be?"

He ignored me. "I'd yanked open the door and was trying to start CPR before I realized I'd killed Jason, not you. You'd just fainted."

"Don't forget the concussion and the loss of hearing, temporary though it was, and—"

"All that too. And then John came back and took you and Flash off from the hospital to recuperate. I was left cleaning up the mess here."

"How did you know where to find me?"

Reed actually flushed. "I put a tracking device on your car."

"You what? Of all—that can't be legal!"

"John suggested it."

"And you accepted his suggestion? A college professor? Both of you trying to play—"

"I got especially worried after the fire. It couldn't just be childish pranks, so I looked into your background seriously. You'd covered yourself pretty well, but we knew who you were by then and why you were in danger."

"Not well enough I guess. Tell me all. I have a right to know."

"I guess you do." He took another drink. "None of us suspected that Jason had been recruited by a Mexican drug cartel. He was a local kid, so he had legitimate connections around here. But he got into a bit of trouble as a teenager and the court let him move to Houston to live with his grandparents. That's when he learned about big trouble. There, he became involved in gang activity, selling drugs at school. He became one of their enforcers but was able to keep his clean appearance. When he moved back here just a few months ago—not long before the Strand murder—we were all happy to see how he'd grown up. He was smart and he was a good reporter. He'd gone to college there in Houston and had actually worked as an intern at your television station. We know the cartel wanted you hushed, so they must have recruited him for the job."

"How would he have known I was here?"

"As best as we can tell, he'd moved here after Kevin's murder and your botched murder to participate in the border drug activities with his partner."

"The deputy sheriff?"

"Right. Randy Byrd is still shaken. He's not still upset with you, by the way."

I wondered if that was because of my photographic skills. "He said that Stephanie was Mr. Byrd's daughter."

"Yes, an unwise affair when he was younger. He never knew the girlfriend was pregnant when she moved away. He never heard from her again. Apparently, Stephanie traced him here a few years ago and got in contact with him. It wasn't blackmail or anything. She just wanted to know him. In fact, by that time he wanted to acknowledge her, but she wasn't ready for that. So they met secretly. He gave her gifts. They were discreet, but apparently Jason's partner—"

I gasped. "Was that the guy—"

"Yeah. The murder when we met."

His eyes had never been so intense, so sexy.

"Anyway, he and Jason had met that night in the bar parking lot, and Stephanie came along and recognized both of them. Both had danced with her and, of course, she knew that Jason—"

"—worked for Mr. Byrd." Finally, it was making sense. "Did Jason—"

"It was his partner who killed her, according to the DNA evidence we found, at Jason's request. Then Jason killed him so he wouldn't talk if caught. We think they worked together to kill the rancher. Apparently, this rancher had been working with the Border Patrol to try to catch the drugs being smuggled across the border among the illegal aliens."

"And Kevin?"

"We don't know yet for sure, but from what he said to you we know that Jason was involved. I'm so sorry, Sorrel."

"It is Sorrel Janes, you know," I said. "Stacy Lee Jamison was my professional name, along with the blonde hair and the thin body. And by the way—doesn't anyone ever call you Chris?"

"You're still thin. Too thin!"

I felt my face warming.

"The cowboy!"

"What? What cowboy?"

"The good looking one who danced with Stephanie. I've seen him around since, Reed, and I think he may be involved—"

"—in an undercover operation for the Border Patrol. They've pulled him since you noticed him, afraid his cover had been blown."

"I guess you're going to blame me for everything."

"I've been way out of line, Sorrel. I've never been that way with someone. I'm lucky I didn't get fired, pulling in favors from people so I could try to protect you. The Chief saw through it, but I think he was too entertained with my head-over-heels—his term—chase. Besides, he didn't want to lose his chances in the lottery."

"Lottery?"

"About how long it would take for me to admit that . . . " He grinned sheepishly. "Do you think we could just start over?"

"No," I said and stood. He stood as well, doing his best to mask his surprise and disappointment. He placed his glass on the table as I walked to the door. I opened the door and turned toward him as he came toward me.

"You could call me Chris."

"Too late."

"Sorrel—"

"No, Reed, I don't want to start over. I want to continue." I smiled. "Starting with that kiss you gave me just for show."

Reed stopped a few inches from me, his eyes searching my face, almost caressing my lips. "I can do much better than that," he said, drawing me into his arms. His eyes smoldered and locked with mine. Impatiently, I arched up toward him, and gasped when he drew back. He whispered, "No. Let me show you, Sorrel Janes."

Finally, he did.

TERI'S ENCHILADAS

Serves 4-6

Meat filling:

Put ¼ cup of water in a large skillet. Heat until the water is hot. Add 1 lb browned lean ground beef. Add 2 heaping tablespoons of flour to the meat and cook until the water is gone. Turn off flame. Stir to coat meat with flour.

Add 2 to 3 tablespoons chili powder, 1 hot and 1 or 2 mild. (I use the chili powder in the cellophane bags, not in cans.) Stir again until well-coated.

Add enough water to cover (6 cups). Stir as you mix and add water slowly to avoid clumps. Turn up heat; simmer. Let cook. Add salt and garlic powder to taste.

Assembling enchiladas:

In another skillet, heat olive oil or vegetable oil. Dip each corn tortilla to cover each side with oil. Cover the bottom of large casserole dish. Cover each tortilla with ½ cup meat mixture, shredded cheddar cheese, and chopped onions. Layer as many as mixture will make. Sprinkle cheese on top and keep warm.

When you serve, pour chili sauce on top and added chopped lettuce and tomatoes.

(Mama put lettuce and tomatoes between the layers.)

ACKNOWLEDGEMENTS

1. I thank my family and friends for their encouragement, their patience in listening to my ideas, and their faith that I'd finally get this book written. My children—Monica, Marissa, and Nathan—always "knew" we'd reach this stage. Their pride in me gave me courage and confidence.

2. A special thanks to Ron for all of the technical help and moral support. His computer savvy, problem solving techniques, and optimistic suggestions kept my computer going (in spite of me).

3. I thank Detective Steve Halvorsen for his help with police matters and procedures.

4. I thank Marissa Enox Hrisco for her photos that appear on the cover for the book.

5. I send special thanks for "Teri's Enchiladas" to my longtime friend, Lucinda Chavez Nials. My son still would walk 5 miles through snow for her cooking.

6. I thank Othello, Oliver, Emma Claire, and Elsa Grace—my "fur" family—who inspired the character of Flash.

7. Finally, Sandy Stogsdill. What would I have done without her patience, encouragement, frank honesty, and expertise as she edited my book? From the day we first began to the end, she has been my "rock". Thank you, friend.